Portrait of Deception

A Southwest Suspense Novel

Kathryn Dodson

Renegade Reads

Contents

Chapter 1

Margo McAllister had promised herself her photographs would change the world. That dream would come true in a mere fourteen hours. Just a few shutter clicks away.

Favored to win the Butler Prize, the world's most prestigious photography award, Margo surveyed the crowd gathered for the pre-announcement soiree. If her peers and mentors were right, she'd win not just tomorrow's prize but the fame and adulation that went with it. Just like her father had thirty years earlier.

She raised a brow at a passing waiter. He handed her a flute of champagne from a silver tray before sauntering away. "To me," she whispered. "And to you, Dad." Margo raised her glass to the starry sky.

A cool breeze fluttered the sleeves of her custom gown, a splurge but one that seemed worth it when you finally went from struggling for a life goal to attaining it. She wondered what her father had worn on this night so many years ago. Probably an elegant tux. Her mother had been at the party as well. They'd met there, the famous photographer and sophisticated fashion model. But the storybook romance had ended just three years later, in a war-torn valley in Afghanistan.

Margo had never even met him. She'd come into the world two months after he'd died. But he was still her hero. Still the person her mother had loved above any other. Of course Margo had followed in his footsteps. Although, she'd stayed far away from the battlefields where most photojournalists became famous.

"Drinking alone?"

The question came from behind her, and she turned to see the firm jaw and tanned skin of Kirk Jones, badass war photographer extraordinaire and fellow Butler prize nominee.

"So, they let you in." Margo smirked, then looked into his bold green eyes, entranced as always. She let her own eyes wander the length of him. He'd slicked back his usually spikey black hair and wore an actual suit with a tie instead of worn cargo pants and a ratty T-shirt. "You clean up well."

"So do you. You're gorgeous tonight." He stepped close and bent to kiss the tender spot between her cheek and lip.

All the feelings came swooning back. The week they'd spent in Zanzibar lying on sugar sand beaches under a hot African sun—when they weren't in the hotel room. The half-dozen other one-night stands when they happened to be in the same location.

She took a step back. "This is a big night. We have to be on our best behavior." The farthest thing from well-behaved, Kirk walked the line between brilliance and madness. Known for blowing up when things didn't go his way, he'd been tossed out of several countries and fired by half a dozen magazines. She didn't need that tonight. Green eyes stared back at her. She didn't need it, but boy did she want it.

"Come on, Margo. This is your big night. Everyone says you're a shoo-in for the prize. If this isn't a night for misbehaving, then I've been living my life wrong."

That made her laugh. "I think there may be a few people who would argue about how you're living your life."

"Tomorrow, you'll have fame and fortune. In this fickle business, the rewards of winning this prize last a lifetime. I'd say it's better than sex, better than love, lasts longer anyway." He turned and looked toward Lake Como.

He almost had it right. This kind of fame brought adulation and love. It had for her father. Admirers still talked about his brilliance and how much they loved him, loved his work. And he had found real love here, with her mother. A love so strong she'd never recovered. If it happened, if Margo won the prize, all that would come her way. She had a shot, but the outcome hinged on tomorrow.

"There are no guarantees," she said. "And your photos of the Russian military camps are extraordinary."

"They're just war photos, love. A dime a dozen these days. They don't compare to the shot of your Venezuelan refugee mother and her kids. Amazing." He shook his head.

"Thanks." Her heart squeezed at the thought of Maria Luisa and her four children. Margo had found them on a treacherous path through the Panamanian jungle. A constant stream of immigrants had passed Margo that day. When she saw Maria Luisa, she'd been afraid the child splayed across her chest was dead. When the woman asked her for help, Margo gave her a liter of water mixed with powdered sports drink.

The mother kissed the boy and put the bottle to his lips. He sputtered awake, then drank. Alive, though far from healthy. Margo held up her camera, silently asking for permission, and photographed the family. She'd taken over a hundred photographs as Maria Luisa tended to her children. Margo could almost see the tendrils of love holding the exhausted family together. She became invested in their journey, entwined in a mother's love stronger than any she'd ever known. Of course the photographs were good. They represented that love.

Margo brought herself back to the starry night and the handsome man in front of her. She craved love, had searched for it with him, with others. So far, she'd only found love in photography. When she fell in love with her subject, she could translate that emotion into an image that would last forever. It never failed. When she really fell in love with her subject, others fell in love with the photos.

Her photos of Maria Luisa had earned her a shot at the Butler Prize, but there had been many prizes before that. This one would change everything. Like with her father, people across the world would know her name and admire her work. She couldn't wait to feel that kind of love.

Until then, perhaps Kirk's would do. "So, what did you have in mind for tonight?" she asked.

"Well, champagne is lovely, but you should try this." He pulled a flask from the inside pocket of his blazer. "Hold your glass steady. This will make your drink even better."

Half a dram of amethyst liquid swirled into the champagne. Margo brought the glass to her lips, sipped, then coughed. "What is this? It tastes like herbs and dirt."

"Latin Quarter Absinthe. A specialty made here in Italy." A dimple appeared in his cheek as he smiled.

"Absinthe. Are you crazy? Isn't that like a drug? Besides, I thought absinthe was green." She should have known better than to trust him.

"It's a special kind, and it's totally fine. The taste will grow on you." He took a sip straight from the flask. "Let me know when you're ready for more, and I really hope to see you later." He put the flask away and stepped forward again, this time lifting her chin and kissing her gently on the lips. "I miss you."

She licked the trace of absinthe he'd left on her lips as she watched him fade into the crowd. This was her night. She should have fun. She took a long sip of the champagne. Time to stop being a wallflower and enjoy the party.

She spied the editor of *World Geography Magazine.* Dave Hirschhorn had published her refugee photos. Dapper in a tux and paisley bow tie, his six-foot-six-plus frame dwarfed the man beside him. Margo recognized the shorter man's face but couldn't place him. She approached the men.

"Dave, nice to see you." Margo stretched her hand to him in greeting.

"Ah, the star of the show. Margo, I'd like to introduce you to Andrei Andropov, president of Tiranistan."

So that's why he looked familiar. The newly minted dictator of a small Asian country tucked between Russia and Western Europe had spent his first year in office threatening the countries around him and building the republic's nuclear capability. At least according to what she'd read in the media.

"Nice to meet you, Mr., um, president." Her words flailed, but she offered him her hand.

"Please, call me Andrei." He took her hand and leaned toward her, placing a damp kiss on each cheek. He smelled of strong cologne, and arrogance filled his icy blue eyes.

Ugh. She pulled her hand from his grasp.

"I just told Dave how beautiful your photographs are," Andrei said in heavily accented English. "You are sure to win tomorrow."

"Here's hoping." Margo crossed her fingers behind her back. "Thanks for supporting my work." She nodded at Dave.

"We certainly have high hopes for her," Dave said. "The refugee photo series has some of the most traffic we've ever seen on the magazine's website. It's impossible to look at them without being pulled into that world, feeling the love of that mother for her children. That's Margo's secret, you know. Love."

"What do you mean?" Andrei asked.

Dave cocked his head and looked at Margo. "Is it a trade secret, or do you share it?"

"It's not a secret." She turned her attention to Andrei. "There's this moment. It only happens sometimes, but when it does, I feel myself falling in love with the subject. It can be a person, an animal, or a landscape. I know the photo's going to be good when I fall in love."

"Is this true?" Andrei asked.

Dave chimed in. "The white wolf you photographed in Canada, the first picture we bought from you, did you have that feeling then?"

"Head over heels. He was so beautiful. His coat captured the light against a backdrop of glowing snow, and intelligence filled his yellow eyes."

"I know this photo," said Andrei.

"You really are an amazing photographer. One of these days, we're going to have to put you on staff," Dave said.

"I'd love that." The magazine rarely took on new photographers, and Margo had only worked with them as a freelancer. Perhaps this prize would bring a steady paycheck as well as fame. She smiled at the possibility of a golden future opening before her.

"Give my office a call when you're back in the States, and we'll set up an interview."

"Thank you, I really appreciate that." She wanted to hug him but settled for drinking the rest of her champagne.

"Before you start working for this man, I have a job for you." Andrei reached out and grabbed her hand. "I need new state photographs of myself. I would like you to take them."

"Oh, thank you, but I don't do portrait photography."

"But your photos in the show are of that woman. If you can fall in love with her, then surely." He leaned back, arms wide. His perfectly cut suit stretched across a broad chest and thick biceps.

"Um. It doesn't work like that." Margo wanted to laugh at the audacity of this guy. She looked at Dave instead. He shrugged, no help at all.

"But you can try. You can come to my castle in the mountains, be my guest. I am sure that if you spend some time with me, see the beautiful ways of my people, you will find something to love."

"Thank you for the offer, really. I just don't do portrait photography. I tell a story with my work to make the beauty I see accessible to others. It's art."

"That is what I need. Other people, these big countries, they don't see the pride and power of Tiranistan. I need to tell the world this story. I lead a fine people, and I am their chosen son. Your photographs could make people believe."

"I'm sure your country is wonderful." Margo scanned the crowd for an escape. "Perhaps I can recommend someone who does this type of work. It's nice to meet you, but I need to circulate."

"Wait. I will pay you one hundred thousand US dollars to take photos of me. Spend two weeks in my country and take my portrait. No one else will pay you this much."

Holy shit. Was this guy real? That was crazy money. Even tomorrow's prize, extremely rich by photography standards, only paid forty thousand. Still, she couldn't imagine spending two weeks with this jerk, much less falling in love with him. Thank god for that prize money.

"Thank you. That's an amazingly generous offer, but I promise you, I am not the best person for this." She almost couldn't believe her own words. Most people would take the money and shoot the best photo they could. But her father had passed his talent to her. She couldn't abuse this gift by giving this guy credibility via her photos.

She slunk away from the two men, hoping to lose herself in the crowd.

"Think about it," she heard Andrei say. "I leave you with this offer for thirty days."

After she'd threaded her way through the throng of black suits and sparkling dresses, stopping only to swipe another glass of champagne from a tray, she reached the edge of the terrace and sat on a stone bench. The applique flowers and vines sewn into the layers of chiffon pressed gently into her skin where the dress met stone. What had she done?

Adrenaline coursed through her. Had this Andrei guy really just offered her a hundred thousand dollars to take his picture, and worse, had she just turned him down? What was wrong with her?

The profit from selling her grandparents' house and the money she'd inherited after her mother died had allowed her to purchase an extremely modest apartment in New York, and her work paid the bills, but she didn't have a retirement plan. At twenty-seven, she hadn't thought she needed one.

She shook her head. She'd had a negative reaction to Andrei from the second she'd met him. *Trust your gut.* There had to be a catch. No one would just offer a photographer that kind of money. More than once, her grandmother had said that if a deal looked too good to be true, it probably was. Her grandmother always directed the admonition at her mother, while Margo, a nearby shadow, watched the women argue.

She shook her head again. Thinking about her beautiful, foolish, dead mother only led to sadness and anger. This night was Margo's. She studied the posh surroundings: an Italian villa, twinkling lights, and sparkling people. She made her way to the balustrade overlooking the lake. The moon cut a shimmering path across the water. Her father's legacy had brought her here. She had earned this night.

Soft footsteps approached from behind. She turned to see Kirk, then his warm palm landed on her bare back. Just for a moment, she wanted to snuggle into him, to find that cocoon of love she forever sought. But Kirk was definitely the wrong person. Party boy, hotshot photographer, he'd slept his way around the world more than once.

"Hey, stranger," she said.

"Why are you out here all alone on your big night?"

"I just needed a break from the crowd. You know, there's no guarantee I'll win. You've got a shot too." A familiar doubt pushed its way in. Too many people had said she'd win the prize. It made her nervous. Life was rarely that easy.

"No, you'll get it. The woman in your photos was exactly the type of person these upper echelon, artsy types like to vote for. War is passé." Kirk removed his hand from her back and leaned his elbows on the balustrade.

What an ass. Trying to save face by making it about Maria Luisa instead of Margo's talent. She could have told him his photos would be more powerful if he'd focused a little less on blood and gore and a little more on the tragedy before him.

She turned, her back to the lake, and watched him. He stared at the water a long minute before straightening and facing her.

"Hey, would you like some more of my magical elixir?" He pulled the flask from his jacket. Then he grinned, seeming to return to himself, all dimples and smiling eyes.

"Sure." She offered him her half-full glass. Photographers drank, it was in the job description. Whatever that flask held, it didn't seem to have a negative effect on her.

She smiled at him. It had been a long time since she'd shared her bed. Way too long. And in Zanzibar, she'd learned photography was his second-best talent.

Her smile must have conveyed her thoughts, because he came in close and kissed her. Every synapse and nerve ending in her body lit up. She pressed herself against him. His kiss grew stronger, deeper. He wrapped an arm around her, grabbing her and pulling her hard against him.

Some of the champagne had spilled out of the glass and onto her finger. "Wait." She licked the liquid from her hand.

"That's hot," he said, watching her. "Let's pick this up after the party's over. I'd love to spend the night with you."

"I'd like that. And I've got a suite with a gorgeous view of the lake."

"That sounds magnificent. It's going to be a wonderful night." He kissed her again, resting his lips against hers for a moment, then backing away. "You need to get out there and work the crowd. This is your party."

She nodded, warmed by his touch and the thought that she didn't have to go to bed alone tonight. She took a deep breath and a sip of her drink and stepped toward the crowd. Tonight, she'd snagged an interview and a night with Kirk. Who knew what else the evening held?

This time, the amethyst addition to her champagne had a wonderful effect. Margo approached people she didn't know, and words flowed from her tongue. Normally, she preferred engaging with her eyes, preferably behind a camera where people couldn't see through to her heart. But tonight, everything spun loose and free. She transformed into the person she'd always envied, the woman who could speak with anyone, charming and full of intelligent conversation. Her mother had been like that. The light of every party. Margo could picture her in this crowd, her father spying her, perhaps on this same patio. Falling in love in an instant.

Margo used that energy as she moved from one person to the next. Would she fall in love tonight? Doubtful. But at least she had plans for later. She spied Kirk a few people away, deep in conversation with Andrei Andropov.

She inhaled sharply, turning her attention from whomever she'd last spoken with. Was Andrei offering Kirk a hundred thousand dollars to take his portrait? Kirk would take that deal in a second and wouldn't even think about it. Why had she let morals get in the way of money? It wasn't even morals, just some deep-seated aversion, some message from her father begging her to turn down the offer. If it had even been that.

She kept them in sight, using other people as shields so they couldn't see her watching them. Not that they would have noticed. They leaned slightly toward each other, buried in a conversation that seemed to cancel the noise around them.

Finally, Andrei reached his hand out. Kirk looked at the gesture for a moment, then nodded his head once and palmed the other man in a firm handshake. Just after that, Andrei looked off to the side and raised a finger. Soon, a large man in a black suit and shirt approached Andrei and Kirk. He pulled something out of his breast pocket. A small envelope? A business card? Margo couldn't tell for sure. Andrei took it and offered it to Kirk. Whatever it was, Kirk slipped it into his back pocket, shook Andrei's hand again, then looked around the crowd.

Margo ducked to the side and found herself standing in front of a tall woman. She introduced herself automatically, still wondering what had happened between Kirk and Andrei.

"It's nice to meet you," said the woman. "I'm Sonja Brava with Nikon."

"Oh, very nice to meet you. You make wonderful cameras." They did, but her dad shot with a Canon, so Margo had always done the same.

"We do make excellent cameras. By the way, your photos for this contest are extraordinary. Have you ever considered changing cameras?"

Had this woman crawled inside her head? "I've always used a Canon. It's what my father had."

"Ah, yes. Mike McAllister. I knew your father."

"You did?" Many of the older people in the industry worked with her father, and she always loved hearing about it.

"Yes, we were on assignment in Iran together and then again in Afghanistan. Although not the last time he went."

The time he died.

"I'm sorry," Sonja said. "The world lost a brilliant photographer that day, but I'm sure it was nothing compared to losing your dad."

"I guess," Margo said. "I never knew him. He died a couple of months before I was born."

"I'm sorry to hear that. He was a wonderful man, not just a great photographer. When he knew what shot he wanted, he'd stop at nothing to get it. He was the rare combat photographer who saw the story behind the war. How everyone loses in war. But he was also kind. That's not something you see in the field."

"What do you mean?"

"Well, he always had something in his pocket for the kids. He hated the hazing that comes with the industry and tried to stop it when he saw it. He helped me out a few times."

"Thank you for telling me. I hadn't heard that about him before."

"You know, you're at least as talented as he was. Your images show something beyond what's on the paper. There's such emotion in your work, it's like you've layered something extra between the gloss and the pixels."

"Thank you. That's a really nice thing to say." The compliment resonated in Margo. She didn't want to admit love provided that extra ingredient in her photos. That sounded crazy. But Margo knew it was true. Those special photos, when Margo fell in love, they did have something extra. It was a bit of herself that she left in the image. And tomorrow, when she won that award, the adulation she expected would refuel all she'd given. She'd waited so long for this.

"Margo, I have a proposition for you. Would you be willing to try a Nikon? I'll give you our top of the line, free. Just test it out. If you like it, I'd love to talk to you about a sponsorship deal."

Oh, my god. The future fell into her lap with each person she talked to. "Of course, I'd be happy to test the camera."

"Wonderful. Here's my card. Contact me at your convenience, and I'll get you that camera. Thank you. I think this could be the start of a wonderful partnership for both of us."

"Absolutely."

The woman smiled, then drifted away. Margo stood amongst the glittering people under the starlit Italian sky. Perhaps she'd slipped into a fairytale. Who knows what offer would come in next with midnight still an hour away? Speaking of offers, Kirk walked into her vision.

If Andrei had offered him the deal he'd offered her, she'd probably hear about it pretty quickly. "Hey there, having fun tonight?" she asked.

"It's a good party, but it's even better to be with you. I brought you another glass of champagne." He took her empty one and replaced it with a fresh glass filled with bubbling liquid the color of cornsilk with a touch of honey.

"No absinthe?" she asked.

"Um, not this time. I'm almost out, and you don't need any more. It's potent stuff."

"Or maybe since I've already agreed to spend the night with you, you don't need to waste any more of your magical elixir on me."

"Oh, it's not like that." He added a low growl to his voice and stepped in close. "I can't wait to get you on your own. We wouldn't want you to get too drunk to have a good time."

Margo laughed. How could one man be so arrogant and so achingly attractive? She took a long sip of the drink. "Well, thank you, I guess, for looking out for my best interests."

His playful gaze disappeared for a moment, and she watched worry cross his brow. His bad-boy veneer rarely dropped.

"Hey, what's going on?"

"Nothing. It's nothing. I, um, I just forgot to get myself a drink now that the flask is empty. I'll be right back."

Then he was gone. She wondered if something had happened with Andrei. Perhaps he'd told Kirk about what he'd offered her to take his portrait. That would not have made competitive Kirk happy. After all, if she won the award, then he'd lose. And if he thought she'd receive some big payout from a dictator, well, that wouldn't do much for his ego.

The night became more interesting still. She wondered what would happen back in her room. Hopefully, the drama only resided in her imagination.

"Miss Margo." The accented voice came from behind her.

She turned, and sure enough, Andrei stood before her. "Hello, again."

"How is your evening? This is a beautiful villa, yes?"

"It's lovely." She took a long sip of champagne to keep her mouth busy. She hated that her questionable decision had returned to haunt her.

"If you like this, you will love my castle. I believe you will see it someday. I want to give you my card." He handed her a black business card. "It has my private phone number and email in case you decide to take my offer."

"Well, you certainly are persistent." She reached for the card. She'd expected paper, but the black metal had sharp corners and heft. A gold seal embossed one side, a phone number and email the other. No name. Shady.

"Ah, Mr. Jones. Have you met Margo McAllister?"

Kirk's warm hand pressed firmly into the bare skin of her back as he came up beside her. Clearly, they'd met.

"Yes, Margo and I go way back."

"She is a very talented photographer," Andrei said. "I look forward to seeing more of her. Until tomorrow." He raised a glass of caramel colored liquid in a toast, then melded into the crowd.

"I've met some people who have an afterparty planned. Are you in?" Kirk asked.

She looked into his green eyes, a sudden happiness surging through her. The twinkle lights brightened, and the colors deepened, darkening the midnight sky while slips of gem-toned silk glided through the crowd. "I think the absinthe may be getting to me. Besides, I thought we were going back to my place."

"Oh, we'll definitely make it back to your place. Finish up your champagne and I'll take you to meet this crew. You'll love them. We could move the party to your place if it's more convenient. Come on, toss it back." He touched her glass with a finger.

Margo lifted the glass to her lips. Buoyant just a moment ago, she now felt the energy draining from her. She leaned into the hand on her back and imagined herself in her suite's king-sized bed with the unbelievably soft linens and Kirk touching her.

"Hey, you okay there?" he asked.

She must have closed her eyes a little too long. "I'm here. I'll meet your friends, but I'm really thinking about you."

"Come on, let's go. We've got a long night ahead of us." He wrapped an arm firmly around her shoulders and led her out of the party.

Tiredness pulled at her as they walked across the marble foyer and out the door. A group of six people, four large men and two beautiful women, looked up at them from street level, their faces lit from the villa's entry.

"Who are they?" she whispered. She hadn't noticed them at the party, and the men's ill-fitting blazers and gum-soled loafers didn't rise to gala standards. Both women had long straight brown hair, heavily lined eyes, and low-cut knit dresses. She understood why they would have drawn Kirk's eyes. They exuded his renegade charm.

"I told you, they're friends. Lots of fun." He pulled her toward the steps.

"I think I'm just going to go to my hotel." Sleepiness took over. She'd have sat right there, laid her head on the cool stone steps and slept, if he hadn't held her up. Instead, she missed the first step and tripped. Two of the men surged forward and caught her. She closed her eyes.

———

Margo woke to banging. Groggy, she lifted her head. The room swirled around her. People in black strode back and forth through her vision. She heard something shatter and looked right. Kirk sat on the bed beside her.

"Hey," she mumbled. "What's going on?"

"We came back to your place, just like you wanted." He leaned back and spread his body along hers.

"Why? No. What was that noise?" Her jumbled thoughts refused to assemble properly. She laid her head back as Kirk trailed a finger along her temple, then down to her chin. She let herself sink back into darkness.

Chapter 2

Stop the banging. Margo's head pounded as she forced her way to consciousness. Bright sunlight flooded the room, making it difficult to open her eyes.

"Ms. McAllister. Ms. McAllister," a male voice yelled from far away. More banging. Why wouldn't they go away? "If you don't open up, we're coming in."

"Fine." She dropped her head back into the plush pillow, unsure whether she'd thought or spoken the word. She closed her eyes as she heard the quiet click of the lock. She needed more sleep.

"*Che cosa!* What have you done?" The shock in the man's voice finally forced her eyes wide open.

Margo looked around the room. Except for the pristine bed on which she lay, it was a disaster. Furniture had been overturned and a painting hung askew, the art falling out of the frame as if it had been sliced.

"No! Il pavimenti." The man's voice slid from shocked to angry.

Margo leaned over, the room seeming to tilt with her. A layer of water covered the honey-colored wood floor and darkened a once vibrant oriental rug. What had happened here? She forced herself to sit up. She still wore the ivory party dress with applique flowers. Scenes from the soiree flitted through her mind. Didn't she have somewhere to be?

"Oh, my god!" she yelled. "What time is it?"

"It is half-past eleven. I need to get you out of this room," the man said, walking in from the bathroom. You left the water on in the bath. The floor is ruined, and there may be structural damage."

"Okay. I have to get ready for the announcement. I've got just over two hours." Her brain tried to focus on the one important thing, the photography prize. She couldn't comprehend the mess around her, didn't want to think about it.

"Madame, I will need you to come with me."

"God, I hope my stuff's not wet. Do you have a place I can change?"

"Ms. McAllister, you have destroyed this hotel room. You need to come to my office. The charges . . ." He looked around the room, shaking his head slowly. "I have no idea. We need to reach an agreement about this."

"But I didn't do this." She closed her eyes, the seriousness of the situation finally reaching her. What had happened last night? She didn't even remember leaving the party. But she did. She remembered Kirk's arm around her. Seeing the strange men and women on the street looking like the Russian mafia. Falling into them. She vaguely remembered waking up on the bed, those people in her room, Kirk beside her.

"There's been some mistake. There were people here, but I didn't know them. They must have done this."

"How did they get in? Did you invite them? The door was not broken."

"No. I don't know. I think I was drugged."

"Then we will call the polizia. You must come to my office." The man reached a hand toward her as if to help her off the bed.

"First, I need to go to the award ceremony." She would find a way to take care of this, all of it. But not until after the ceremony. She had to stay focused.

"Madame, you will not leave this hotel until we have a solution. Unless it is in the custody of the police."

"Wait. No. There's prize money. If I win the award, I can use some of the money for this, at least until the police figure out who those people were."

"Madame, this room is in your name. You are fully and solely responsible for it. Now come with me, or I will call the police right away to arrest you."

Oh, shit. This was serious. Truly serious. She'd never been in this kind of trouble before. She swung her legs off the bed and stepped into an inch of cool water. "May I please get clothes to change into?"

"No. We must get the experts in here right away to take care of the damage. They will bring your things to you when they can. Please follow me."

Margo expected things to take a long time in Italy, but once Francesco De Luca started working the phone, the situation got worse in a hurry. He called the police, remediators, housekeeping staff, and the Butler Award director.

Activity swirled around her while she sat at a small table in a corner of his office. Barefoot and in a party dress, she felt remarkably over and underdressed. His assistant stood in the doorway like a sentry while Mr. De Luca took one person after another to see the room. At least the assistant brought her coffee, although the clarity that arrived with caffeine made her realize how much trouble she was in.

Two police officers interviewed her, but they seemed far more interested in her identity than in listening to her story about the gang who must have ruined the hotel suite. She couldn't believe the one time she'd done something nice for herself, spent a little money on a fancy hotel to celebrate her achievement, something like this had happened. She should have known. Her life had always been a shit show.

"Who is the man you were with last night, the one who knew the other people?" The young police officer brought her out of her thoughts with his question.

"Kirk. Kirk Jones. I'm sure he can help identify them. If I can get my phone, we can call him. I left my purse in the room."

Rapid Italian flew back and forth between Mr. De Luca and the officer. De Luca picked up the phone on his desk and called someone.

"There was no purse, no cell phone found in the room," De Luca said as he set down the receiver.

"That can't be. I had my phone. My wallet. It has to be there."

"Didn't you say you blacked out on the way back to the hotel?" the officer asked. "What drugs did you take?"

"No. No drugs. I had champagne at the party. That's it. Well, Kirk gave me some of his absinthe, but just a little. Please, we have to contact him. He'll be at the awards ceremony. You have to let me go."

"You told me you did drugs." De Luca's comment took her by surprise.

"No. I said I thought I was drugged. Like maybe someone put something in my drink."

"What drugs did they give you?" the police officer asked.

"Damn it. Please listen to me. We need to go to the ceremony and talk to Kirk. We can get this sorted out."

The police officer turned to his colleague and said something in Italian. "My partner will go to the ceremony and find Mr. Jones. You will stay here with me."

"Please." Margo tried to stop the tears, but they slipped out anyway. How could this day get any worse? "The ceremony starts in thirty minutes. Can we just go there?"

Just then, a man in black jeans, a black button-down, and heavy work boots walked into the room. He showed a clipboard to De Luca and spoke in rapid Italian. The police officer whistled under his breath.

"What is it?" Margo asked.

De Luca pressed a few keys on a desktop calculator. "He says it will cost $46,000 to repair the damage to the room."

"What? That can't be true." Her voice came out in a ragged whisper.

"It is true." De Luca's angry voice slammed into her. It seemed her day could, indeed, get worse.

"The hotel will add this fee to your bill, and you must arrange payment before you leave."

"But I can't pay that."

"You have damaged the hotel. If you refuse to pay, I will have to arrest you." The officer's voice had grown cold. "Plus, there is the matter of the drugs."

Margo wanted to protest but had nothing to say. The room had been damaged, trashed really. And she'd been alone in the room when she'd woken up. While she hadn't directly caused the damage, she had known about Kirk's terrible reputation. She left with him when he said he wanted to meet up with friends. And, she'd willingly agreed to drink the absinthe, twice, even though she'd heard vague stories about its danger. Heck, if it had even been absinthe. She'd willingly accepted something he'd poured from a flask. The blame adjusted itself onto her shoulders.

"I don't have that kind of money right now, but if I win the Butler Prize, I will. That's part of the reason I need to go to the ceremony." She addressed De Luca, hoping her eyes matched her pleading voice.

"Do you have to be there to win?" he asked.

She hesitated. One of the finalists hadn't even made the trip to Italy.

Margo had come. She'd desperately wanted the in-person adulation, social media boost, and general glamor of the situation. Thus, the fancy room. This whole trip had been a mistake. She didn't bother answering his question.

He departed his office with the contractor, leaving Margo and the police officer alone. Was he there to make sure she didn't try to run out on her bill? She'd already given them a credit card for incidentals, and they could easily track her down. As the minutes ticked by, she lost all hope of making it to the ceremony.

Finally, the police officer's partner returned. "I found Mr. Jones. He says he does not know what happened to the room. He says Ms. McAllister invited several people back to her room after the Butler party, but then she fell asleep on the bed, so they left."

"You should have brought him back here for an interview," the other officer said.

"I could not. He said he had a press conference to attend. Then he told me that unless I arrested him, he needed to leave. He is not a suspect, so I let him go."

"He had a press conference?" A chill ran through Margo.

"Yes. When I was there, they announced him the winner of the Butler Prize."

Margo sunk her head onto the table. Of course he won. Any hope for the future drained out of her, leaving her exhausted.

She ignored the Italian flowing around her until someone knocked on the door and a new face entered the room.

"Ms. McAllister, I apologize for not getting here earlier."

Margo looked into the face of the executive director of the Butler Prize. "Oh, my god, Mr. Moore. I'm so glad to see you."

"Well, I won't be here for long. Mr. De Luca called this morning and told me what happened."

"Yes," she said. "It was terrible."

She watched confusion cross his face, rapidly replaced by a stony gaze. "As soon as we heard, the board of directors had an emergency meeting and voted to remove you from the competition. I'm sure you read the terms and conditions when you applied for the award. We have a stringent morals clause. What has happened here is in strict violation of that."

"What? Would I have won the award?" His words had ripped her chest in two. The terrible unfairness filled her with rage at what Kirk had gotten away with and made her insides crumble in humiliation.

"I am not at liberty to say. However, I am here to warn you that you need to," he gestured around the room, "take care of whatever has happened here. And if you want to be eligible for the Butler Prize in the future, you need to ensure that the media does not pick up on this in any way. We are a reputable organization and refuse to be associated with this type of behavior. Do you understand?"

She stared at his sanctimonious expression, rage overcoming despair. "Do you understand that your morally superior prize winner drugged me and brought in a bunch of goons to destroy my room while I was passed out?"

"That is an extraordinary accusation. Do you have any proof of this?"

She looked down at her hands. Nothing, not one shred. Unless—"Can we fingerprint the room?" she asked the police officer.

"The remediation crew is already working. It is their fingerprints that will be there now." De Luca's factual delivery, without a trace of emotion, slammed the door on whatever hope remained.

"I promise you," Moore said. "Taking care of this quietly will save your reputation. Professional photography is a small field, especially at your level. Your father was a real hero to people in this business. You don't want to destroy his reputation or yours." With that, he turned and left the room.

Margo sat absolutely still and struggled to comprehend everything that had happened. Inside her, something trembled. Her gut? Her spine? She wasn't sure, but she had to wrap it with every steely emotion she possessed to keep it from imploding and completely shattering her. With every breath, she struggled to maintain her composure.

"Now, about the bill," De Luca said.

"And the drugs." This from the police officer.

A burst of rapid-fire Italian flew between the two men. Finally, De Luca almost shouted. "Abbastanza. Di cherto. Enough."

The police officer jerked to his feet, then nodded at De Luca.

"My colleague here," De Luca gestured to the officer. "He has agreed not to pursue any charges as long as you pay the hotel what it is owed."

A numbness had taken over Margo. "Forty-six thousand dollars?"

"Plus, of course, your room charges."

How would she ever pay that? She'd used most of her savings and inheritance to purchase the New York apartment. Perhaps she could get a second mortgage, but that would take time. She had less than ten thousand dollars in savings, most of that in an IRA her grandfather had set up. She'd always thought she'd have plenty of time to save for the future.

She could call her Aunt Joyce. The shame in that plunged a dagger through her gut. She'd been so mean to Joyce after her mother and then her grandparents had died. She'd been done with family, and Joyce wanted to act like a replacement mother. Given the mother she did have, the last thing Margo wanted was another one. But she knew Joyce loved her enough to bail her out.

A lone tear trickled down her cheek. Everything else she kept caged inside. "Okay, let's figure out how to do this."

Chapter 3

Margo lugged the giant green duffle up the last set of stairs and into Liliana's apartment.

"Christ, you have a lot of stuff. You know you're only staying until you're back on your feet, right?" Liliana asked. Fortunately, she delivered the line with a wink and smile.

"I know. I can't tell you how much I appreciate this." She shrugged out of the heavy backpack full of camera equipment and set it gently on the floor. "I was lucky to find someone to rent my apartment so quickly. And lucky that you agreed to take me in for a spell."

"No worries. You can honestly stay as long as you'd like. I could use some help with the rent, and the couch is mostly empty anyway."

"God knows I've spent enough time there." Margo looked at the forest green corduroy sofa. Liliana had purchased it in the heat of summer just a few days before both women had started their junior year at RISD, the Rhode Island School of Design. They'd seen it in the window of a used furniture shop, and it had looked surprisingly pristine. Almost a decade on, it still looked pretty good, especially since Margo needed a nap.

"So, give me the lowdown." Liliana sat on the couch and patted the cushion next to her.

Margo slumped beside her. "Life just sucks so much right now."

"Why? The last time we talked, you were headed to Italy to win some prize that was worth a ton of money. I've had one text from you since, asking for a place to stay, then you show up here in a cab. What's going on?"

Margo groaned. She barely remembered the optimism-filled woman who'd left the city less than two weeks ago. "I am in a world of hurt right now. I didn't win the prize. In fact, they disqualified me from the contest after some goons destroyed my hotel room. I blacked out. I think I was drugged. The damage to the room cost forty-six thousand dollars."

"You have to be kidding me. How did that happen? You've never blacked out before, and in college, we drank our share. Do you know who could have drugged you?"

"Kirk Jones. He gave me something he said was absinthe."

"Isn't he that cute photo guy you introduced me to at O'Brien's once? The one who looks like the Green Day lead singer?"

"Yeah, that's him. And I willingly drank what he gave me. I'm such an idiot."

"So now they want you to pay the hotel forty-six thousand dollars? That's crazy. You can probably still build a house in El Paso for that."

"I doubt it." Margo sighed. She'd met Liliana freshman year because they were the only two students at RISD from El Paso, Texas. Both were scholarship students, one photography, one fashion. They'd stayed friends, even though they spent less time together as their careers developed. Still, Margo trusted Liliana more than anyone else.

She steeled herself for the next part of the story. "They wouldn't let me leave Italy without paying. So, I borrowed forty-thousand dollars from my Aunt Joyce and wired the rest from my savings account."

"Oooh. You don't even like Aunt Joyce. Yikes." Liliana's eyes had grown big.

"It's not that I don't like her. It's just that she always tried to mother me after everyone died, and that's not what I wanted. Anyway, I have to pay her back as soon as possible. She's like in her sixties and is retiring next year. I'm sure she'll need the money."

"You just called her up and asked her for forty-thousand dollars, and she said yes and got it to you? Nobody in my family could come up with that kind of cash so fast. I'm not sure she's hurting for money."

Margo had hated making that call. She'd last seen her aunt in person at college graduation. Aunt Joyce flew to Rhode Island, attended the ceremony, then took Margo to dinner. They'd planned to spend the next day together touring Providence, but at dinner, Joyce had brought up how much her mother loved her and how proud she would have been.

Margo had said some mean things. True, but mean. Her mother had spent Margo's childhood searching for a man who would love her the way her father had. A lot of bad men had come through her mother's life. Some who talked big, then stole her money. Others who yelled. One who hit. And finally, the last one. The one who drank. The one who drove his Corvette off Transmountain Highway, the pass through the knife-line of desert mountains separating East and West El Paso. Neither survived the crash.

Margo had moved in with her aunt for the summer before she returned to her Colorado boarding school. That summer, her aunt had tried to comfort her by telling her how much her mother loved her. What bullshit. Margo had been right there by her mom's side as she went through one man after another. The spotlight of her mom's attention illuminated every jerk in town. Margo would have given anything for her mother to shine that light on her just once. She'd always been right there by her side.

Aunt Joyce didn't see it. She had a good heart, she just thought her little sister was the same. Fourteen years older, Joyce couldn't see the truth through the years that separated them. But Aunt Joyce was Margo's only family, and definitely the only person who could have helped her out of the Italy fiasco.

She'd phoned her aunt from the Italian hotel and explained what had happened. After that, other than an "oh honey, that sounds horrible" and "let me talk to the man," she'd hardly spoken with her.

Margo had handed De Luca the phone and sat there for fifteen minutes while they spoke. When Margo had taken the phone back, her aunt told her she had taken care of it. Margo wanted to cry at her aunt's generosity. Hell, for a moment, she'd wanted to crawl through the phone line and into her aunt's lap to be taken care of like a little girl. But instead, she thanked Aunt Joyce and hung up the phone.

She'd learned from De Luca that her aunt wanted to pay the entire bill, but Margo refused to let that happen. She gave De Luca her banking information and paid a portion. Everything she could afford.

Now, she owed her aunt. She probably should have gone to El Paso to visit her and thank her in person, instead of staying with Liliana. Except New York had better job prospects, and she needed to rent out her apartment for income to pay the mortgage. And she'd promised herself she'd never go back to El Paso. Growing up there had been painful enough.

"Hey, come back to me." Liliana gently pulled on her shoulder. "Man, this has really done a number on you."

Tears threatened. Liliana had created the first safe space for Margo since everything went down. She brushed a finger across her cheek. She needed to stay tough, get herself out of this mess, get back on track.

"Why aren't you fighting this?" Liliana asked. "You are one of the feistiest, most independent people I know. What happened was totally unfair. What's your plan?"

"That's where you come in. I rented my apartment, so I'd have some sure cash coming in every month." She didn't tell her friend she'd talked to her realtor about selling the place. It had been a relief to hear that the softening real estate market meant she wouldn't make much, not enough, not after commissions and fees. When she'd asked about refinancing, the realtor just shook her head and explained that prices had dropped because interest rates had gone up. Her payments would increase if she refinanced.

"But don't you have a mortgage? Is your renter paying more than that?" Liliana asked.

"A little. Enough to cover the taxes and a couple hundred over that. I'll still need to work, obviously. But if I can save money by staying here when I'm not on assignment, it will help. And I have a job prospect." The one bright spot from the trip to Italy remained the conversation with Dave Hirschhorn.

"A job?" Liliana looked at her quizzically. "A real job, not an assignment?"

Margo told her about the conversation about becoming a staff photographer at *World Geography Magazine*. The thought of a steady paycheck glowed like a lifeline in her thoughts. It would definitely be a step forward in her career.

"When's your interview?" Liliana asked.

"I haven't had a chance to contact him yet. With the apartment and all, it's been crazy busy. I didn't expect it to rent so quickly."

"Margo, get to it. Contact this guy right now and get that job. And as soon as you do that, you need to call Kirk and chew him a new one. He did you wrong."

Margo dropped her head to her hand. So many emotions swirled through her when she thought about Kirk. She hated him for getting her wasted, and especially for inviting those goons into her hotel room. But she'd willingly imbibed. That he'd left without a word, hadn't tried to fix anything, was terrible. She didn't even want to think about the award. Maybe he would have won anyway.

"I don't know. I'm not really sure what happened that night. I wish I hadn't passed out." Telling Liliana he'd won the award would be one humiliation too far. She sealed her lips.

"Didn't you just tell me he brought people you didn't know into your hotel room, let them destroy it, and then left? That's some bad stuff, and you need to call him on it. He should pay that hotel bill."

"There's no way that's ever going to happen."

"Not if you don't call him." Liliana crossed her arms, her eyes boring into Margo with a furious stare. "Give me your phone."

"No. It's really complicated."

Liliana grabbed the phone sitting on the coffee table. "What's your passcode?"

"Lili, don't."

"Margo, sometimes you have to do hard things. You've had it bad for this guy for a while, but it's not like you guys are in a relationship. Heck, even if you were, you'd have to talk to him about what happened. What he did to you—that's not okay."

"Fine. I'll call him."

"Now." Liliana handed her the phone.

Oh god, she didn't want to do this. What had happened in Italy, her behavior, she had disgraced herself. Despite Kirk's role in what had happened, she knew better. He liked to party, had a reputation for getting in trouble, and this time, he got in with the wrong crowd. Surely, he couldn't have known how bad it would be. If so, she'd stunningly misjudged him. She'd been responsible for herself for a very long time and had always kept herself out of vulnerable situations. Until now. She glanced at Liliana's stony gaze, then punched the numbers.

Voicemail. She was about to end the call, but Liliana waved her finger back and forth in front of her. "Hello, Kirk. This is Margo. We need to talk about what happened in Italy. Call me back."

"There, doesn't that feel better?" Liliana grinned.

"Not really."

"Too bad. Now contact that magazine guy."

Liliana was right. She had to get her life back on track. She pulled her laptop out of her backpack and emailed Dave.

The next morning, the phone rang. Margo, ensconced on the green couch editing photos, glanced at it. Dave Hirschhorn's name and photo lit the screen.

"Good morning, Dave. Thanks for getting back to me so quickly."

"Hi, Margo. Let me get right to the point. We are not going to be able to bring you on as a staff photographer. Certainly not at this time."

"But I thought . . . You just mentioned it to me a week ago, at the Butler Prize gala."

"Yes, and I certainly wish things had turned out differently, but after what happened at your hotel . . . Well, we, the magazine, have a certain reputation to uphold."

The shame started at the tip of her head and turned her body red hot as it flowed down through her shoulders, her gut, and even into her toes. "How did you . . ." She couldn't finish the sentence.

"I've got colleagues on the Butler Prize board. Margo, everyone in the industry knows what happened."

She was going to be sick. Everything she'd worked so hard for, gone. She'd spent her whole life on photography. She'd won her first prizes and been published in *Time* in high school. Then, she'd earned the scholarship to RISD. Won more prizes. She'd been on the verge of achieving everything. The fame and adulation her father had enjoyed, and all the love that shone on him because of that, had been in her grasp.

"If you don't have anything else, I need to get to a meeting." Dave's voice brought her back from her thoughts.

"You said everyone knows what happened. Dave, no one knows what happened. Not even me. I was drugged. I passed out. People I'd never met before came to my hotel room and destroyed it. This is completely unfair." The words tumbled out, her voice high and scratchy.

"Those are serious accusations. If you can prove that happened, well, that might change things."

She let the silence fill the distance between them. Finally, she spoke. "I can't prove anything. I wasn't conscious."

"I'm sorry. I don't know what to tell you. Perhaps Andrei Andropov will still hire you. I've got to go."

The line went dead. She hadn't thought of Andrei since before everything happened.

Shaken by one more piece of bad news, Margo had to move. If she spent one more minute on the green couch, she'd self-destruct. She grabbed a canvas bag with her best camera and a couple of lenses and left the apartment.

Liliana lived near gorgeous Morningside Park. The late afternoon sun filtered through the trees and onto a gravel path that could have been laid last year or two hundred years earlier. A thick wall of gray stones and an iron lamp equally ignored time.

She pulled out her camera and started shooting, trying to capture the timeless feeling. She willed herself to create a story from the images, a place lost in time, a story from another era. It reminded her of the Italian villa. The building, the lake. But for the electrified twinkle lights, the party could have taken place in another era. She lost focus.

Angry at her inability to stay in the moment, she searched for something grittier. New York City had much to offer. She wandered, not caring where, constantly searching for interesting colors or angles, something to draw her eye. Once, she stopped to capture the glow of the setting sun on red bricks with crumbling edges. She needed more, something bigger, something where she could get lost in the world of the lens. Sometimes, she stepped through that doorway. The real world faded away, and she entered a universe that consisted only of her eyes, her camera, and the subject.

She almost passed the alley without stopping. The lights flashed on as she strode by, causing her to turn her head. It couldn't have been more than twenty feet wide, a cement path lined with tall buildings. Graffiti covered the walls, occasionally interrupted by oversized and rusting roll-up doors.

The fading light of evening brought out the grime of the city, while the mass of graffiti screamed color and creativity. Toward the end of the short alley, someone had put out potted plants. Beyond the plants, Christmas lights framed a powder blue door. She could see a menu in the doorway. This alley was everything New York. Old and new, commerce and decay, beauty and concrete. She lifted her camera.

When she finally stopped, the sky had turned sapphire. She briefly considered going into the restaurant, dragging out the time before she had to return to Liliana's green sofa and the rest of her life. Her ramen budget would not allow a restaurant splurge.

She stared at the menu a moment longer. Her mind drifted from the soups and salads to an approaching conversation. Two men speaking some Slavic language passed by and entered the restaurant. Their voices reminded her of Andrei. Perhaps it was a sign.

———

When Margo opened the door to the apartment, Liliana stood in the kitchen, a glass of wine in her hand. Margo smiled, grateful she wouldn't have to spend the evening alone.

"I picked up Chen's on the way home. Mapo tofu, your favorite. And a bottle of wine." Liliana raised her glass toward Margo.

"That sounds amazing. Why the celebration?"

"It's called dinner. Besides, you've seemed a little down, for good reason. I thought this might cheer you up."

"You've got that right." The day had started out beyond crappy, but between the photo session and a night with a good friend, it was looking up.

"So, how did your day go? Did you hear back from Romeo?" Liliana asked.

"Nope. I even sent Kirk a text. Nothing. He's officially ghosting me." Perhaps an assignment had taken him deep into territory beyond the reach of cell towers. Wishful thinking. He didn't want to talk to her.

"Smells like fish to me. That boy's hiding something."

"It's possible. He's probably off on some tropical beach with the model of the hour." Margo poured herself a glass of wine. She took a long sip of the hearty red. Kirk's betrayal ached. Beyond the casual sex, she'd thought they'd been friends. Why had he done that? A niggling fear in the back of her mind suggested he did it to win the prize, but listening to that would make her crazy. Her mom had taken misjudging people to an artform. Margo used to pride herself on having better taste. Perhaps the flaw was genetic.

"Okay," Liliana said. "We'll figure out how to get to lover boy. Hey, I told you I was going back to El Paso for my abuelita's birthday. You should come with me. You need to thank your aunt."

"I can't. But tell your grandmother happy birthday for me."

"You can't go, or you don't want to?"

"Both, actually. I have no desire to return to El Paso, like ever. But mostly, I can't spend money right now. Plane tickets aren't cheap."

"Did the magazine call you back about the job? Regular income would be good for you right now."

Margo squeezed her eyes shut. She'd tried to forget about the call with Dave. Tried shoving it beneath pretty photos and a glass of wine. It came roaring back to demolish her.

"They heard about the incident in Italy, and they don't want me. Everyone knows what happened, and everyone thinks it's my fault. It's like they think I suddenly turned into some drugged-out rock star. No one even wants to hear my side of the story unless I have proof. The magazine won't even consider a permanent position. I can only hope they'll keep using me for freelance work, although I was afraid to ask."

"Oh, babe. That totally sucks. I'm so sorry." Liliana wrapped her arms around Margo and squeezed tight. "Don't you worry about finding your own space. You can stay here as long as you want."

"Thanks. I may have another option."

"Spill it."

"At the gala in Italy, Dave introduced me to this horrendously arrogant dictator named Andrei who happens to run a small country in either far eastern Europe or far western Asia."

"You mean Tiranistan? It's in Asia."

"How do you know that? You're in the fashion industry."

"Babe, fashion is global. So, you actually met Andrei Andropov? He's kind of an old school, I want to rule the world type of leader."

"Well, that makes sense. He certainly doesn't like taking no for an answer."

Liliana tipped her chin and stared at her. Margo recognized the look. Liliana wanted answers. If Margo told her what had happened, it would make it real, and she'd have to act. Some small part of her resisted. She couldn't explain why she hoped she'd never see Andrei again, much less work for him. Something in her gut told her to stay away. In the end, her gut needed to eat. She couldn't rely on friends and family forever.

"He wanted me to take his portrait. This was before all the bad stuff happened. He may be like Dave and decide I'm untouchable now. But he offered me one hundred thousand dollars to take his picture."

"What! How could you keep this from me? This solves all your problems."

"Maybe, but it feels like I'm selling my morals for money. I can't explain it. I'm sure my dad wouldn't have sold out."

"Oh, honey. Your father is gone. You can't put thoughts into his head. You have no idea what he might have done. But I know you. You are an artist. If this one job will help you get back to where you need to be, then do it."

"I guess there's no art without money. No film, no plane tickets, no camera." Liliana was right. Take a few great photos of a vile man and get your life back.

"That's right. Take the rich man's money. It's just a few pictures."

"Well, I'd have to go stay at his castle." Margo raised her fingers in air quotes, realizing it didn't sound that bad. "And I'm sure I'd have to take a series of portraits. We didn't exactly talk specifics. He seemed more intrigued by the fact that Dave told him I had to fall in love with my subjects to take a great photo. I think he saw it as a challenge."

"Okay. Well, that's a little creepy. But honey, take the money."

"I guess that's the easiest way to repay my aunt and get my life back on track." Now she just had to figure out how to take a great photo of a man she could never love. If the deal still existed.

Chapter 4

Five minutes into the phone call, Margo knew she'd made a mistake. She'd emailed the address on the top-secret metal card, and they'd set up the call. The second she picked up the phone, he'd told her how happy he was she'd changed her mind. As if she had already decided to take the job. Since then, he'd droned on about the types of shots he wanted.

"We must go beyond the typical photo of a leader in military uniform. I need those as well, of course. I must look dignified. You said you told stories with your art. The world does not take my country seriously. That story must change."

"What other ideas did you have in mind?" she asked, imagining him fighting a bear or riding a horse bare-chested.

"I am sure you have ideas. I rose through the military. It made me great and strong. We have a long history of war in my country. War begets bravery, and pride. We are a small country with big dreams. You will tell that story."

Margo shook her head at the thoughts spewing through the phone. The job was impossible. She wasn't that kind of photographer. Was she supposed to showcase every facet of his inner ego?

"I'll try my best." She interjected the words when he paused to take a breath. "As I told you in Italy, I am not a portrait photographer."

"You are the right photographer for this job. The best photographer. You only need to fall in love with your subject. That is what Mr. Hirschhorn said."

Impossible. Falling in love with this man, even for the second needed to press the shutter release, would never happen. "It's not really a require-ment. It's just something that happens with some of my better photos."

"You will fall in love with me, this I guarantee. Come to my castle, and you will see. I would like you to stay here for two weeks. When can you come? I assume your schedule is open."

A flash of anger surged through her at the assumption, quickly followed by the greasy quease of shame. He knew. Everyone knew. "Why would you assume that?"

"Well, I think what happened the night of the gala, it might not be good for your career. Everyone important in the industry was there. When you did not come to the ceremony, there was a lot of chatter."

"Great," she whispered, hoping he wouldn't hear.

"Do not worry. You will restore your reputation with your photos of me. You have not photographed a world leader before. You can win the prize next year with these photos. I will put in a good word for you."

Would the word vomit ever end? Having Andrei Andropov vouch for her in the photography community would hurt more than help. And if she ever became known for a portrait of him, she'd shoot herself.

"You must believe in your talent. You are an excellent photographer. Mr. Jones is not as good. Your photos capture the heart and soul of a person, just like your father's did."

A moment of shock jerked her head back. "You knew my father?"

"No, no. I am too young. But I have seen his photos from war. They stir pride in my heart. People give their lives for a country they believe in. Your father understood honor."

This guy got so much wrong. Her father's photos depicted the horrors of war. They were a plea to those in power to open their eyes and see the devastation they wrought.

What would her father think of her working for some third-rate, want-to-be dictator? He wouldn't be proud, but he hadn't had to worry about owing people. His life had been charmed. Everyone she talked to said so.

She closed her eyes. She wanted that life so badly it made her belly ache with hunger. But while her father had worked hard for his fame, he'd paid for it with his life on a Taliban battlefield.

Photographing Andrei was just a detour, a sidestep she needed to take to get back on the right path. She'd follow in her father's footsteps, minus the wars, become famous, and earn adulation. His light shone so brightly people couldn't help falling in love with him.

She took a long, deep breath. This was the way forward. "I'm available. When would you like me to come?"

"I will have my assistant make the travel arrangements."

"I require a fifty percent deposit." Margo didn't trust this guy for a second.

"We can negotiate that," Andrei said after a pause.

"Have you worked with world-class photographers before? They all require half up front. This is a deal-breaker, so if you need some time to think about it—"

"No. Of course not. My country has money, dollars. My assistant will handle that as well. Come as soon as you are ready. Bring clothes for riding horses, formal evenings, a bathing suit."

"Andrei, I'm going there to work." She really hoped he didn't have the wrong idea. It disappointed her enough to sell her ideals. Nothing else was on offer.

"Yes, but you cannot work twenty-four hours. And you must see me in my element. When you truly understand who I am, you will be able to photograph me the right way."

As long as that money hits the bank. "I'll do my best. I have a limited clothes budget."

"Margo, with what I am paying you, you can buy clothes."

Three days later, her stomach flipped as the airplane began a steep descent. She placed her elbows on the armrests, stretching to reach them in the roomy first-class seat. She'd never flown first class before. On the first leg of the flight, she'd felt like a princess crossing the ocean. She accepted a cheery glass of champagne, then slept soundly in her lay-flat seat.

This flight, on a much smaller and older plane, had been a four-hour bumpfest. At least it would end soon. She glanced out the window. Mountains rose in the distance. Below, green fields of varying shades flowed beneath the plane. A city approached, buildings rising beige and gray in a sea of green next to a steely lake.

The airport terminal looked new, all concrete, marble, and soaring glass. It could have been any airport anywhere built after 2000. There seemed to be one model, with the variations no more than icing on a cake. At least this one had a view of gorgeous green mountains, with the shadow of a snowcapped peak further on.

She found a man holding a sign with her name on it. He looked disturbingly familiar. Big. Broad face. Shoulders wide enough to block light. At five-four, she must appear like a child beside him. He reached for her backpack, but she pulled it away. She never let others hold her cameras, and she didn't want any help.

After visiting baggage claim, they exited the terminal to a waiting Range Rover. Margo acquiesced to the man putting her bag in the back, then opening the rear door for her. He got in the front passenger seat next to a driver of the same size. She felt like a child, small in the giant vehicle and ensconced in the back seat with everyone else in front.

Margo shook her head to dispel the thought. The long flight and uncertain future had given her a bad attitude. She should be happy about this lucrative adventure. After all, fifty-thousand dollars had already hit her bank account. Of course, most of it she immediately transferred to Aunt Joyce.

She'd had to call her aunt to get her bank account and wire transfer information. Joyce began, as usual, telling Margo she could keep the money a little longer. When Margo told her she didn't need to, her aunt asked her flat out what she'd done to raise fifty thousand dollars. Joyce had never surprised her before.

Aunt Joyce had always treated her mother like she'd break if anyone questioned her or said a harsh word. She'd treated Margo the same way, especially after her grandparents and then her mother died. Other people, she bossed around like nobody's business.

Joyce ran the El Paso YWCA, and she worked people hard. During summer breaks, Margo volunteered at the organization, which helped families with job training, housing assistance, and Margo's favorite, childcare centers. Several photos in her portfolio featured YWCA children.

Once, she made friends with a daycare worker who struggled to get to work on time. Aunt Joyce met with the woman, and ten minutes later, she came out crying. She'd told Margo Joyce had fired her, then she gathered her purse and lunch container and left.

The tone Aunt Joyce had used to call the woman into the office had crept into her voice when she asked Margo where the money had come from. Margo told the truth. She'd been paid for an assignment, and she'd be leaving the country in a few days. Her aunt asked if she'd come to El Paso for a visit. Margo skirted the issue, too guilt-ridden to say no but having no desire to return to a place no longer her home.

So, instead of viewing a desert, she looked out onto green mountains as the Land Rover climbed into the foothills. The road curved ever upward, sometimes along a rushing river, other times through green forest or alongside black cliffs. Finally, the mountains parted to form a wide valley.

As the vehicle slid around a curve, Margo saw a line of snowcapped peaks beyond a forested ridge. The river had returned, as had civilization. They passed houses, a waterwheel, and large barns set amid fields of cattle and sheep. The countryside gradually transformed into a town. They passed a beautiful domed church, Soviet-era concrete apartment blocks, and shops secreted down alleys. In just a few breaths, the town disappeared behind them.

A few miles later, the vehicle turned off the main road and began climbing again. They twisted up the road, sometimes unnervingly close to the edge, then the car slowed and entered a gated drive.

Two sentries in olive green, military-styled uniforms stood in front of a gate fabricated from crosshatched iron panels. The gate hinged into an ancient-looking wall, seemingly held together with moss instead of mortar. It had to be twelve feet high and six feet thick.

Stories began forming in Margo's mind. Knights on horseback, women with long skirts trailing through the pine-needle undergrowth, illicit affairs, desperate attempts to escape by scaling the walls, bloody knuckles. She shook her head free of the thoughts, but part of her held on, wanting to tell the stories with her camera.

The gates swung wide, and the vehicle proceeded. Soon, the forested drive opened onto a meadow framed by rocky cliffs. She caught her first glimpse of the castle, which looked nothing like the edifices of princess dreams. This castle echoed the Tibetan architecture of the University of Texas at El Paso with layers of square roofs covering a building of stone and stucco. Made of reds and grays, promenades and archways, the building hummed with movement. Her eyes hardly had a chance to rest. She had to keep herself from climbing over the back seat to grab her Canon.

The building rested against a black cliff, with a sweeping flat plateau to one side. As Margo surveyed the area. she saw outcroppings of rock capped with crumbling stone buildings. Someone had plunked a castle into an ancient fortress.

The vehicle stopped at the apex of a circular drive. Margo opened the door and slid to the ground before her giant caretaker had gotten out of his seat. She grabbed her duffel and camera case and trudged up a massive staircase. The entire way, the man asked to carry her gear. He finally placed his hand over hers and carried the larger bag with her. Finally, at the top of the stairs, she relinquished the duffel. Just because he gave her the creeps didn't mean she had to act like a jerk.

Despite the bright sun, a pinch of cold hit the air. She smelled nothing but clean pine. And herself. After the long plane rides, she needed a shower.

They crossed a stone patio and trotted up shallow steps to a covered entry-way. Alcoves with statues framed a massive wood and stained-glass door that opened as they approached.

A tuxedoed butler and two maids in black dresses and white starched aprons straight out of Mary Poppins stood at attention. Margo almost didn't want to step into the strange scene, except her eyes drew her forward, caught by a stunning chandelier shining onto a floor patterned with rose and emerald marble.

"Welcome," the man said in accented English, performing a little half-bow. "The president is not here at the moment, however, we are at your service. The ladies will show you to your room."

"When do you expect him back?" Margo asked.

"We are unsure. He has business in the capitol. Perhaps in two days."

Relieved that she wouldn't have to deal with Andrei yet, she followed the two women past a sweeping staircase and then down a corridor with arched windows looking over the valley. She couldn't wait to wander through the buildings and grounds, ostensibly looking for photo shoot locations, but mostly to satisfy her curiosity.

She trailed the ladies into a stunning room that could have held her entire New York apartment. Lustrous parquet floors matched identically colored molding and paneled ceilings. Teal damask walls, an amethyst velvet settee, and a four-poster bed completed the room. Margo imagined a princess from long ago lounging on the settee.

Then she remembered the persecution this country had suffered so the elite could live in luxury. That was a story worth telling.

"Dinner will be served in three hours. Would you like something before then?" the younger woman asked. Margo guessed she was in her mid-twenties.

Perhaps she could find time to talk to her and learn about life here in the country and on this estate. Maybe she could even pick up a few tips about how to deal with Andrei.

"No, thank you. I think I'll have a shower and then walk around the grounds. Am I free to roam about the building?"

The girl conferred with the older woman in a language Margo didn't recognize.

"On the first and second floor, it is fine. Please do not go to the third floor. That is the president's private residence."

Soon Margo trotted back down the grand staircase. She noticed the butler standing on the third-floor landing, not even trying to look busy. The ladies probably warned him she'd asked about touring the palace.

Not today. After too many hours on airplanes, she needed exercise and fresh air. She headed out the front door and took a few photos from the balcony. Grander than she'd realized, the grounds swept across the plateau. A formal garden with fountains and sculptures abutted the palace. That gave way to a more natural area with a pool and an obelisk along a path that led to a metal bridge spanning a gully. Beyond the pool lay a meadow, and just before grass turned to forest, a large canvas tent sat out of place in the luxurious space. A man near the tent moved among a semi-circle of easels. Curious.

Margo threaded her way toward the tent. The castle, as Andrei had called it, seemed more a mishmash of aspirational styles. The architecture of the building, with its echoes of a Tibetan monastery, may have originated in Tiranistan, but now she walked through a Western European garden that would have gone unnoticed at Blenheim Palace or in Versailles.

As she approached the pool, she noticed the tiny multi-hued tiles that coated it and made it glow like a fairyland. Just beyond, the obelisk mirrored a mini-Washington monument, while the bridge in the distance resembled a railroad trestle or a length of the Eiffel Tower laid on its side. She could barely take her eye from the viewfinder with so many fascinating things to shoot.

She closed in on the man near the tent. He seemed not to notice her approach. Could he be an artist? He held no palette, wore no smock. Instead, he had on faded blue jeans and a white tee shirt. She paused, not wanting to invade his space, but dying to know the who and why of him.

The moment she stopped, he looked at her. He was gorgeous. Brown skin and an untamed shock of black hair highlighted knife-sharp cheekbones and full lips. Black-framed glasses rimmed eyes so dark they stole light while emitting intelligence in exchange. The most physically alluring person she'd ever seen, she longed to photograph him from every angle.

"Hello," he said, an undercurrent of British English tinging his Indian accent.

"You're gorgeous. I mean, your face, it's striking. I'd love to photograph you." What the hell was wrong with her? She'd never spoken so boldly.

"I think we should get to know each other first." A left-side dimple emerged with his smile.

Embarrassment burned deep in her breast. She looked down. Sure enough, her chest glowed red, probably her cheeks as well. "I'm sorry. My name's Margo. I'm a photographer."

"Darpan." He closed the distance between them and offered his hand. "How did you make it all the way out here?"

"Andrei Andropov hired me to take his portrait." A new humiliation burned through her at the thought of how far her career had fallen. "What are you doing out here with those easels?"

"Mr. Andropov hired me as well. I'm a communications technology expert."

"And you're working in a field with a tent and easels?"

"I convinced him that my work was more secure out here, away from prying eyes. Most of what I'm doing is ideation, which can happen anywhere, and I much prefer the outdoors to that drafty building."

Margo glanced back at the beguiling castle. It looked solid, not drafty. Each word from Darpan intrigued her more. "So, tell me about this ideation."

"Oh, it's nothing," He waved his hand, as if dismissing his work. "Andropov just wants to build a communication network. It's hard out here without the infrastructure of more modern societies."

"Fascinating. Can I look?" She stepped toward the tent.

"I'm sorry, but my work is confidential. You have a camera. That could be a problem."

"Oh. Okay."

"We still have an hour or so of daylight left. Would you like a tour of the grounds? I'm sorry about the no photos rule."

"Sure, I'd like that."

She waited while he put everything inside the tent, then zipped it and turned on a device she hadn't noticed above the door.

"Camera?" she asked, nodding at the device.

"Motion detector with video."

"Couldn't someone just go around back and slit the tent to steal your stuff?"

"The sensors are everywhere, and they automatically stream to several locations, including my phone and my watch. Come on, let's go."

He led her toward the bridge. As they neared, she saw it cut across a steep ravine. Leaning over the edge and seeing the murky blue water cascading below them made her stomach drop.

"I had no idea this gash cut through the landscape. It's amazing." She removed the lens cap from her camera and lifted it to her eye.

"Between this and the cliffs, the area is extremely secure. That's why they've built here over the centuries."

Despite the amazing landscape, she could barely control the urge to turn her camera toward Darpan. "Tell me about yourself."

"Well, I'm from Madhya Pradesh in central India. I went to graduate school in San Diego, worked for companies in Bangalore and London, and now I consult."

"How old are you?" she asked.

"Bold." He gave her a sharp look, as if surprised by her audacity.

She'd been surprised as well. He unleashed something in her. She wanted to explore his mind and photograph his angles. But she needed to dial it back. "I'm so sorry. I don't know if it's the long flight, the fresh air, or what, but I'm not acting like myself."

"It's fine. I'm thirty-five. You? Or is that question still off limits with women?"

"I'm twenty-seven."

"And what made you travel halfway across the globe to take photos of Andrei Andropov?"

She looked at him, his elbows resting on the bridge railing, just like hers. She needed to gauge his reaction. "Money."

He stared directly into her eyes. "I think that's why most people work for the president. Have you met him?"

"Oh, yes. I met him a couple of weeks ago. He's, um, persistent."

"He definitely has a plan, and he'll do anything to make that happen."

"Plan?"

"Yes. He wants to build a dynasty."

Margo rubbed her forehead. This was news. She probably should have read up on him, but in her haste to leave, she hadn't done her usual research. Normally she would have, but the last few weeks had been so—much. "What, exactly, do you mean?"

"I suggest you google him. He gave a speech at the United Nations earlier this year where he unnerved his neighbors by threatening to restore his country's ancient borders. In a land of constant battles, no one really knows what those are."

"Perhaps I should have thought this through a little more." Of course, she had agonized over the decision, but money won out.

"I'm surprised he brought you here now. It's not a safe place to be. He's building military encampments along the borders of Tiranistan. His neighbors are responding in kind. Europe, even the United States, have their eyes on this dictatorship. This entire region is a tinderbox."

Shit. She needed to finish this job and get back to New York. "Why do you work for him?"

"Well, like you said, the money is good. And I'm used to working in dangerous places."

Margo hated dangerous places. She didn't want to end up dead on a battlefield. She turned toward the river, wondering about the man beside her. Motivation and money. Tricky subjects. Kirk would have taken any job for money. Before she really needed money, Margo had higher standards. Where did Darpan fall on that spectrum? Did need or want drive his decision? She hoped she had time to find out.

"We should get back. I'm sure you met Humphries, the butler. He doesn't like it when people are late for dinner," Darpan said.

She turned to face him just as he did the same. Just inches away, she caught his scent, pine forest, mint, and sage.

"Your eyes are so blue," he said. "They're the exact color of the sky right now. With the reflection, it's almost like looking in a mirror."

Yours are like drowning in the night sky. At least she didn't say it out loud.

Chapter 5

They dined outside, overlooking the valley. The staff had prepared the dining room for them, but Darpan let her know he usually ate on the patio.

"It seems strange that we're the only people besides the staff in this huge place," Margo said, picking at her salad.

"Sometimes there are a dozen or more guests here, other times, it's just me. You never can tell. The president spends most of his time in the capital. There are always more people here when the president visits."

"I hope he returns soon. I'd like to finish this job so I can get back to the real world."

"Why do you think he chose you for this assignment? I mean, I'm sure you're a wonderful photographer, but I always wonder what his angle is."

"Angle?" The night she met Andrei, she'd shone bright before blowing up her life like an oversized star.

"Yes, there had to be a reason he chose you in particular. Andropov always does things for a reason. You said you met him a couple of weeks ago?"

"Yes, in Italy. Bellagio." The embarrassing words stuck in her throat, but she pushed them through. "I was in line for a big award, and we met at the pre-party. That's when he first asked to hire me."

"Oh, so you're kind of a big deal in photography. I'm sorry, it's not something I follow."

"Well, I was supposed to be."

The butler cum sommelier approached with a bottle of red wine. "For dinner tonight, you have your choice of rack of lamb or pasta arrabbiata. May I serve you a glass of chianti to enjoy with your meal?"

"Yes, please, and the lamb." Margot sat back as Humphries poured garnet liquid into a crystal vessel.

"Pasta, and no wine for me." As soon as the butler retreated, Darpan picked up their conversation. "You were supposed to be a big deal? I don't understand."

The glass she held glinted in the darkening light. On another night, she'd drunk champagne with abandon. The grogginess of waking on the hotel bed with people in her room came back to her. She'd closed her eyes then and woke later to a nightmare. She set the wine on the table.

"I've been fortunate in my career so far. I've won prizes, had photos published in famous magazines, but the Butler Prize is the pinnacle in photography. Many people thought I would win. Instead, I had a horrific night I hardly remember, and then the head of the prize committee disqualified me." Somehow the story didn't hurt quite so much when told to a stranger on a dark night. He'd learn about her failure, then reject her like Dave had, like the unreturned phone calls to Kirk.

Darpan leaned forward, projecting focus and concern. "I still don't understand. What happened that night? Why don't you remember?"

"Can we please talk about anything else? It wasn't my finest moment."

"I apologize. I did not mean to pry."

"That's okay." She waved a hand, as if to bat the words away. "I need to take a series of photos of Andrei when he arrives. He's one of the few people who still has faith in me. He thinks my photo of him could be a contender for next year's Butler Prize, but I can promise you that's not what they're looking for. Anyway, he wants to look dignified. I think he's tired of the leaders of other countries looking down on Tiranistan. If you know of any locations that might be good backdrops for that sort of thing, I'd appreciate the input."

"I'm sure he does want to look dignified." Something dark crossed Darpan's face. "He's on a thin edge, balancing between legitimacy and bullying. But sure, I can think of a few places. Have you been up to the tower yet?"

"No, is that the highest level of the castle?" she asked.

"He called this a castle?"

A queasiness rippled through her stomach. The same instinct she'd had when she met Andrei re-emerged. Something here wasn't right.

Darpan rubbed his chin. "I think you need to be careful with Andropov. He's searching for legitimacy. At the same time, he's undermining that by threatening his neighbors. He thinks there aren't consequences to his actions, but the world is watching. I don't think the world will tolerate his fantasy of growing his empire."

"You work for him." She wasn't an idiot or some girl that needed to be taken care of. She'd made her decision based on her need, not Andrei's. Darpan had likely done the same.

"I do." He leaned back, his eyes on her, but his thoughts seemingly somewhere else. "I shouldn't have said anything. It's just a photograph. It's not like it's going to change the world."

Margo relaxed into her chair and looked into the night sky and the million stars of the Milky Way. Her heart ached as she thought of her father. Photos could change the world. His had. Citizens became enraged, new political conversations started, all because of the way her father portrayed war.

She wanted her photos to mean that much. She couldn't photograph wars the way he had. She'd tried. The one time she'd embedded with the military, she'd been terrified the entire time. She didn't want to be captured, held prisoner, murdered. That video had played in her head every day of her youth.

So, she made her own way, taking photos of things she loved, falling in love with the things she photographed. She could get back to that. She had to get back to that. This was merely a detour. A very lucrative detour. Legitimizing him wouldn't delegitimize her. It couldn't.

The conversation faltered. Fortunately, the arrival of the main course made the absence of words less noticeable. She savored each morsel of lamb.

Darpan had ordered the pasta. Was he Hindu? He didn't drink, or at least hadn't had a glass of wine. The vegetarian pasta would fit with the religious dogma. She hoped her plate of meat didn't bother him and suddenly felt inordinately full.

"Do you mind if I ask if you're Hindu?"

"Lapsed. But please don't tell my mother."

"Not a chance," Margo said. "If drinking and well," she gestured toward her plate, "bothers you, just let me know."

"It's not a bother, seriously. I learned in university that I can be a stupid drunk, and I generally feel better when I don't eat meat. It's all just self-preservation, really."

"I should learn a little of that. Seems I've been more focused on self-annihilation."

"I thought it was just a bad night."

"Yeah. A bad night with some long-tail repercussions." She looked into the warmth of his liquid eyes. She wanted to open up and tell him all the things that bothered her, the dashing of her aspirations, the desperation to follow her father's footsteps to fame and adulation. The need for love. She gazed at Darpan.

Stop. She needed to refocus and take advantage of this opportunity. She'd dropped into a fairytale. A castle. A tower. Perhaps an ogre for a ruler. Caught up in that, she'd chosen the first handsome man as a prince.

Margo had never dressed as Ariel or Elsa. She'd learned early that fairytales did not come with happy endings. Her parent's marriage, her mother's string of men, and her own handful of disastrous relationships had taught her well. Perhaps the chaos of her recent life had her searching for the easy way out. She'd resist the pull of a handsome man.

She had a job to do. Take photos. It was the one thing she was good at, and it had the power to make her exquisitely happy. That moment when she fell for her subject seared itself into her. No permanence came with this love, but in her bones, she knew it would lead her where she wanted to go.

She looked at Darpan twirling pasta onto a fork. "Do you love what you do?"

"Love?" He set the fork down and steepled his fingers, seeming to study her question with the seriousness it deserved. "I've never thought of it like that. I have fun with my work. Most of the time, it's like solving a puzzle. I love to stretch my brain like that. At times, I feel honored to have this job, especially when my work makes a difference. I've improved communications networks in Africa and India to enable the people there to fully connect with the world. That work is meaningful to me. I don't know if I would call it love."

"Do you have a family?" She'd meant to ask if he had a wife, despite the lack of a ring, but the question changed itself on the way from brain to lips.

"I have family back in India. Mother, father, siblings. One brother is in California, a sister in England. Grandparents and aunts and uncles and cousins. I guess I have a lot of family, actually. You?"

Now she remembered why she wished she'd asked the question a different way. "No. Well, I have an aunt."

"Is this true? You are an orphan?"

"I'm twenty-seven. I don't exactly consider myself an orphan anymore." Although, she did.

"I wonder which is more difficult, being surrounded by family or having no one to disappoint?"

It was not the question she'd expected. Normally, people asked her what had happened. Why did people do that? Clearly, the answer would veer tragic. His answer exposed his own wounds. "In my case, family tended to disappoint me."

"Really? What do you mean?" He paused a moment, running a hand through his thick hair, leaving it in the same state of disarray. "Wait, I'm sorry. You don't have to talk about this if it's painful."

"It's fine. My mom was a complete disaster after my dad died. Unfortunately, that lasted all the years I knew her." The cruel conversation came easily. Years of practice. She'd loved her mom with every little girl dream she'd ever had, but the reality couldn't live up to the expectation.

"My dad died before I was born," she continued. "But I was mostly raised by my grandparents, and they were wonderful." Pancakes and fresh baked bread, hikes in the desert. Her mom mostly spun outside their orbit, an isolated planet in the same house.

"I'm sorry about your parents."

"It was all a long time ago. Besides, it sounds like you've got your own issues with family."

"Nothing like what you went through. I just haven't become the son my tight-knit parents hoped for. Family is everything where I come from. I travel, don't check in, haven't settled down. They have expectations, and I never meet them. I think they are just afraid that I've lost my way."

"Have you?"

"No. Not at all. What I do is important." He shifted in his chair, ran a hand through his hair again. "I have not looked for a traditional life. That is not what I want."

"What is a traditional life anyway?" She set her napkin on the table, while her mind and her heart spun tales of stable marriages and happy children. "Thank you for sharing your table with me. I think I'll go to my room now."

"Would you like to see the tower first?"

She followed him up the never ending stairs. "The staff told me not to go to the third floor. Are you sure it's okay to be up here?"

"Well, you probably won't get permission, which is why I tend to explore first and ask permission later. Besides, the tower is only accessible from the ground entrance and a locked door about halfway up, probably at the third floor level."

They reached the final floor. Covered by a roof and surrounded by a waist high parapet, the top floor opened to the elements. Margo walked toward the side that opened onto the valley.

"It is unbelievably dark here."

"No light pollution. And the moon's not up yet."

She could make out the mountains on the far side of the valley outlined in starlight. She turned, but the cliff behind them had turned invisible, more of an ominous presence than something her eyes detected. The fairytale darkened.

"Why do you work for Andrei if he's such a bad guy? Are you connecting people to the world here?"

"No, not exactly. I am building a communications network, but it's more government than community related."

"Military?" A yes would disappoint her.

He remained silent.

"But why?" Margo's voice barely rose above a whisper.

"Sometimes, we just have jobs to do."

He had spoken her truth. His words stripped her bare. "That's why I'm here also. This isn't what I do. This isn't art, and it definitely isn't love."

"Love?"

In the darkness, she could say anything. "That's how I shoot. It's how I tell stories. It comes from my heart."

A long silence passed between them. Finally, he laid his hand on hers where it rested atop the brick parapet. "We can love the world without loving everything in it."

His words almost broke her heart. As if it were a choice.

Chapter 6

The next morning, Margo explored the grounds, camera in hand. She'd fueled up in the dining room, at a sideboard laden with meats, cheeses, and hearty breads. Most importantly, she'd found a silver urn that dispensed thick, strong coffee. She hadn't seen a single person in the house and found no one outside.

She made her way toward the cliff and scrambled up to a rampart built near the base. Once atop the mound, she found decaying stones that stretched farther along the cliff than she'd seen from below. She guessed the series of low walls made of lichen and moss-covered stone formed the foundation of an ancient building or trenches from a bygone war. She photographed them from various angles, finally getting down on her hands and knees, framing them like rows of manmade mountains marching into the distance. How old were they? What had happened here? The ruins made her want to bring the past to life.

She explored each rise and depression, and finally, close to the cliff face, she found a stairway leading down into the base of the cliff. The half-dozen stone steps ended in an iron door, rusted except for a padlocked crossbar and shiny silver hinges.

She photographed the door, then imagined photographing Andrei in front of it, an ancient tomb with new locks and hinges. No one could look at a photo like that and not ask what lay behind the door. She touched the metal. Deathly cold seeped into her fingers. She jerked her hand away, as if she'd touched fire instead of iron.

She picked her way down the mound of rubble and continued along the cliff face until it curved toward the river. A narrow paved road led into the woods, but the locked metal door had been creepy enough. To stay in the sunshine, she turned back toward the castle and formal garden. If she'd read Andrei right, he'd much prefer this European-looking backdrop to the ancient cliffside battleground.

She made her way through the garden and photographed potential sites, aware of her feet moving closer and closer to Darpan's tent. She stopped at the pool, its multicolored tile shimmering in the sunlight. Undeniably beautiful and incredibly out of place, she couldn't figure out how to use it in a shot. She needed a giant lily pad for a uniformed Andrei to lie on and then some kind of scaffolding so she could shoot him from above. It could have a trippy seventies vibe like the pool itself. He'd never go for it, but that shot would be art, not propaganda.

Finally, she crossed the meadow. She turned her camera back toward the castle, dwarfed by the imposing cliff. This shot, with Andrei dressed in full military regalia and aboard a white stallion, would be the perfect shot. If she could get some type of military equipment, perhaps a sleek missile or burly tank, it would bring the past, present, and perhaps future of his country into perfect focus. That would be a propaganda shot. Her fingers began to tingle. If what she'd learned about Andrei were true, it might be exactly the shot he wanted, and the one the world needed to see.

Finally, she put her camera away and moved on, her attention fully focused on Darpan's tent. No easels graced the field today, and the tent door was zipped closed. She waved at the motion detector. Nothing.

She continued beyond the tent and entered a widely spaced wood. Thick-trunked trees reached toward the sky, their branches intertwining and creating a canopy that darkened the ground before her.

Trails spun off in every direction. They looked well used, and she tramped down one and then another. They looped back on themselves. She ran across odd artifacts, a porcelain bathtub on taloned feet. Around another corner, an eye-level tap jutted out of a tree. She passed four brass cricket cages strung between branches.

At each curious object, she lifted her camera. She changed lens after lens, focusing closely on a crop of tiny transparent flowers growing from a decaying stump, wider on a statue of a headless Venus perfectly spaced between trees with slim trunks. It was like she'd entered some mushroom-crazed Alice in Wonderland dream state.

She wandered back in the direction of the field and tried to break the forest's tug, which seemed to want her to travel deeper into the lair of trees. When she caught a glimpse of green and sunlight, she trotted toward it, swinging around an especially massive trunk. She jerked to a halt when a dark figure stepped from behind a nearby tree. Her heart jumped to her throat.

Then she recognized him, and relief flooded through her like warm water. "For fuck's sake, Darpan, you scared me to death."

"Sorry. What are you doing here?"

"Scouting for shots. What is this bizarre place?"

"I wouldn't go into the forests alone if I were you. There's some weird stuff around here."

"That's for sure. Why is there a bathtub and cricket cages? What goes on here?"

"I can't explain the bathtub, but I bought the cricket cages at a market in the capital. It's so strange here that I thought I'd add my own flair to the cacophony. As to why these strange items are here, I have no idea."

"Well, it's bizarre. Thank god the light in here is horrible. I don't have to worry about this for a photoshoot. Besides, half-crazy probably isn't how Andrei wants the world to see him."

Darpan gave her a dimpled smile. She noticed how his thin T-shirt hugged his body. She smiled back, her heartbeat slowing from its early scare, the beats now heavy with desire. What was it about this guy? She wanted to kiss him. The heft of her camera pulled at her fingers, and she started to raise it to her face.

"No." Darpan's smile disappeared.

"Okay." She lowered the lens, fighting the hands and mind that wanted to capture his full lips and arched brows. "Why don't you want me to photograph you? Andrei's paying a ton of money for the privilege."

"That alone is reason enough. I am as far from Andrei as you can get."

"And yet, you do his bidding." She knew the comment cut, regretted it immediately. His look darkened, making him even more attractive.

"As do you. Do not photograph me, ever." A command, not conversation.

"I won't. I promise." Contrite. She was a professional, even if she couldn't manage to act like one around him. "You do have amazing bone structure and coloring."

The dimple returned, followed by a gleaming smile. "I should be mad at you, and yet you make me laugh. You are incorrigible."

"Incorrigible? Did you just step out of a Jane Austen novel?"

"Well, this landscape does seem like a remnant from a long ago tale."

"Totally. I'm not quite myself here. Let's get back in the sunshine."

As soon as she stepped from dark wood to blue sky, the danger faded. "I found an old metal door going into the cliff."

"There are several of those. I think there's a tunnel network in the cliffs. They're all locked, though."

"Don't you want to know what's behind them?"

"Not enough to pry the lock off."

"Perhaps I'll ask the staff." Surely someone knew, and the younger housekeeper seemed friendly.

"Good luck with that. Besides, I think they'll be busy. Andropov is supposed to arrive this afternoon."

"Really? I better get moving. I still need to scout the castle for photo locations." She stepped toward him. "Thanks."

"For what?" A fine line wrinkled his brow. She wanted to smooth it.

"I don't know. But I'm glad you're here." Why had her voice turned breathy?

He lifted a hand, paused near her face, then tucked a lock of hair that had escaped her ponytail behind her ear. "Be careful here. The woods are—creepy. And Andropov, he's not the world's nicest guy."

"I'll be careful. How long will you be here?" The trace of his hand on her cheek still burned. She wanted to step into that fire.

"At least a few more weeks. Let me know if you need anything."

She could think of a few things she needed. She was drawn to him like a paperclip to a magnet, completely overpowered. She'd felt this pull behind the lens, but never without it. At least never before. Had she not been holding her camera, she might have reached for his hand or wrapped her arms around him. The bulk of the device, and his aversion to it, kept her chaste. She smiled up at him one last time, then turned and walked toward the castle.

———

Margo opened the door to her room, Darpan still in her thoughts. She stopped in shock when she saw the younger housekeeper, Radmi, at the bureau, a camera lens in her hand. Radmi jerked in surprise, staring back through guilty eyes.

"Careful. That's a very expensive lens." Margo fought to keep her voice calm.

Radmi placed the lens back in its case and zipped it. "I am so sorry. Please, do not get me in trouble. I really need this job." She clasped her hands, as if in prayer.

"Why are you in my room, going through my stuff?"

"I am so sorry." She dropped to her knees, hands still clasped before her. "I looked at you on the internet. The photographs you take—they are beautiful. I was curious."

"I don't believe that for a hot second." As the shock leaked from her system, anger replaced it. Had Andrei sent down word to go through her stuff or was it the creepy butler?

"It is true. I just wanted to look."

Margo sighed. She didn't have many options. "Please, get up. Did you take anything?"

"No, nothing. I swear." Radmi clambered to her feet. She looked at Margo from under long lashes. "Sometimes I dream of going to America to become a model or movie star."

"I don't have any way to keep you out of my room, but I suggest you not take anything. I know what equipment I have, and I guarantee you'll be my first suspect should anything go missing."

"I promise I will never take anything from you. I just wanted to see how you took the photographs. My grandfather had a camera, but an old one. I know it is different now. I wanted to see what you had in all these cases." The young woman looked at her with pleading eyes. "Please do not tell anyone here. I can lose my job."

An idea bloomed. "Do you like working with Humphries and the president?" If Radmi hadn't taken anything and was just curious, maybe she'd provide Margo with information.

"I do. This is a very good job for my country."

"Are you from this region?"

"Yes, my family lives at the end of the valley."

"I'll make a trade with you. I'll teach you a little about photography if you'll teach me about your country and things here at the castle."

A blaze of excitement lit Radmi's face. "Really? You would teach me about photography?"

"Yes, but you have to answer my questions. And you can never look through my things without permission. Do we have a deal?" Margo swept her hand toward the young woman.

Radmi met her palm-to-palm, acknowledging the deal.

"Let me know when you have time."

"Maybe after people have gone to bed?" Radmi's voice softened.

Margo didn't know how that would work for photography, but she'd take what she could get. She hoped Radmi could answer questions about the metal door in the cliff, and she had plenty to ask about Andrei. "If I ever catch you going through my things again, our deal is off, and I will tell Andrei and Mr. Humphries."

"It will never happen again. I am sorry. And thank you. Thank you very much."

Chapter 7

"Margo." Andrei opened his arms wide, and the four other men in the sitting room turned their attention to her.

Fuck. What was she supposed to do? Hug him? Curtsey? She offered her hand. He pulled her forward and kissed her on each cheek, a seemingly genuine smile on his lips.

"You must meet my guests." He turned to the men in the room. "This is Margo McAllister. She is a world-renowned photographer here to take my portrait. We are honored to have her in our country."

With that, he introduced her to men with impossible names and high-level positions in the government.

"You must have a drink with us," Andrei said.

Margo noticed a tall, intricately decorated glass bottle on the sideboard. Small, multicolored shot glasses surrounded it. Alcohol had proven not to be her friend, but this would be a tough situation to wriggle out of. "I think I'll pass."

"But this is our national drink," Andrei said. "I promise, it will be better than the champagne you had in Italy."

She looked at him, pressing her lips together to keep from spewing what she really wanted to say. That night had ruined so many things. "Alcohol is not always my friend. And it definitely wasn't that night."

A look of surprise passed over his face, then it went completely still. The air hummed between them, their audience silent.

Finally, Andrei dipped his head. "I understand. I would still like to make a toast to you. I will give you a glass to hold only. Perhaps you can smell its aroma or dip your tongue in it to taste the rich flavor. I, however, will drink on your behalf."

Dip her tongue in it? Weird. Nonetheless, he poured the clear liquid into six of the colorful glasses. He handed her an emerald green shot glass after pouring a few drops of water into the glass from a crystal decanter.

"The water will release the bouquet." He distributed the remaining glasses, then raised his high. "To Margo, welcome to our country."

The men around her downed the alcohol in one sip, then slammed their glasses to the sideboard with cheers. Margo lifted hers to her nose and sniffed. It smelled of spicy licorice. Curious, she took the tiniest of sips. A mix of anise, cloves, and pure grain alcohol hit her tastebuds. While the flavor intrigued her, the force of the raw alcohol turned her gut. She and experimental drinks didn't mix.

Humphries entered the room and announced the meal would be served in the formal dining room. As they followed him out of the salon, Margo glimpsed Darpan on the patio.

Andrei must have seen him as well. He opened the closest door. "Darpan, you must join us for dinner."

With an ease that made it seem like he'd been waiting for an invitation, Darpan gave a quick smile and nod and then joined them.

An intricate lace tablecloth covered a large table set with silver, crystal, and china so fine Margo could almost see through it. The room had waist-high, polished wood wainscoting, with the upper wall a kind of antique mirror. Andrei sat at the head of the table, and oddly, she sat at the foot with the men on the sides between them. It brought back her magical kingdom and princess thoughts. Although given that she wore leggings and a sweater, she hardly fit the princess mode. Her career had taken her across the globe, from jungle to ice, wildland to city. No place seemed as surreal as Tiranistan, with its darkly enchanted forest, doors reaching into cliffs, and government leaders making side comments in a language she didn't understand.

Her eyes moved to Darpan. He'd hardly said a word but managed to engage in the conversation through a grin here and a cocked eyebrow there. The men she'd just met treated him like someone they knew. How long had he been here? What project did he hide in that tent? She still had a longing to photograph that off-limits story.

They went through one course after another of heavy food. After dinner, Andrei asked if she'd like to join them back in the salon. She declined, claiming jet lag.

"Will you have time for photographs tomorrow?" she asked.

"I am busy in the morning." He nodded to the men who hovered around another bottle housing the national drink. "I believe they will leave in the afternoon. After that, I would like to review my wardrobe with you."

As she headed back to her room, she saw Darpan on the balcony. She slipped out a French door and joined him, looking into the black valley below. "You didn't say much at dinner."

He turned his face toward her, the light from the castle illuminating an eyebrow arched over a black eye. It would have made a beautiful photo.

"I tend to be more of a listener than a talker at these dinners."

She sensed meaning beneath his words and wondered if he had reasons to be here beyond helping Andrei with a communications system. At least in her imagination, he made the perfect spy.

"Have you decided where and when you'll photograph his highness?" The smile tickling his lips hinted at a joke, his tone did not.

"We're meeting tomorrow to talk about wardrobe. Hopefully, we'll start shooting the day after."

"Wardrobe. Sounds like you may get to see the hallowed third floor. Definitely take your camera."

"What do you mean? Why?"

"It doesn't exactly match the décor of the rest of the property."

He had her curiosity now. "So, you've seen it?"

"Certainly. I upgraded the Wi-Fi on the property. Especially on the third floor."

"I wish you'd tell me what to expect instead of hinting at it."

His broad grin caught starlight. "That would not be nearly as much fun."

"You are such a puzzle. This whole place has me intrigued."

"As it should. The world is changing at the speed of fiber optic cables. Tiranistan, once left in the past, is fighting its way into the future. We've seen over and over the instability this brings. You can document this."

"How? Sometimes I don't even know what's going on." Bits of story wafted through her head, but nothing firm enough to grab onto. Not yet.

"I encourage you to keep your eyes and ears open and your camera at the ready." He turned fully toward her, leaning against the balcony railing, his angles opening to her, welcoming. "I'd love to continue this conversation. Perhaps we could find a time to meet. I take a basket of pastries and a canteen of strong coffee to the tent in the mornings. Stop by for breakfast whenever you'd like."

"I will, thank you." Her eyes couldn't escape his, except to move slightly lower to where his lips beckoned. She tried to shake off the carnal attraction that overwhelmed her when she was near him.

"Do you have this effect on all women?" The question sprang out of her. a slim protection against his powers. If only she could photograph him and channel this into the kind of love that would bring her an award-winning picture. That thought alone kept danger at bay.

He reached for her hand, sending sparks of electricity up her arm. She stepped closer, wanting to run in the opposite direction. What dangerous magic was this?

"You are like a creature out of a fairytale." He released the words in a whisper.

She inhaled deeply, slowly pulling her hand from his. Two couldn't be trapped in a princess dream. Perhaps it was her blond hair and the blue eyes of princesses past. They could play the game: fairy princess, ogre prince, and intriguing outsider. The safety of the dream allowed her imagination to soar beyond the possible. Real relationships devolved into a sticky mess at best, tragedy at worst. Perhaps they'd write a fun subplot and set the story askew.

As her pale hand dropped from his, her hair swung off her shoulder, and she caught the blond glimmer in the starlight. She created stories every day with her camera. She didn't live them. The love she wanted came from fame and crowds, not an individual.

"I've got to go now. I'll see you in the morning," she said.

Margo trudged across the field the next morning under a steel gray sky. She'd spent the night adrift in her bed, dreaming of princes and castles and love.

Before leaving, she'd asked Radmi about Andrei and learned he and the other men were meeting in the library. Margo had seen the dark room with its towering cases of books. The lack of windows and questionable lighting had her cross it off the list of shoot locations.

In a room without windows, Andrei wouldn't spot her visit to Darpan's tent. Only the staff would see, if they looked. The rain started before she reached the tent. Darpan quickly unzipped it and beckoned her inside.

Larger than she'd expected, the space had four sheetrock walls and a wooden floor. Along one wall sat a bank of electronic equipment. The easels faced the walls, and a lumpy oriental rug, probably hiding cables, covered the floor. A polished wood table laden with pastries and drinks sat just inside the door.

"This is not at all what I expected. Yet one more puzzle."

"Sometimes life is a puzzle. Have you figured out where you will photograph Andropov?"

"Why do you call him that? Surely, he's asked you to call him Andrei." A line of irritation ran up her spine.

"This is a job. He is my boss, not my friend." A shock of hair fell onto his forehead as he spoke, and his calm demeanor didn't match the undercurrent of spite in his voice.

"Perhaps we should call each other by our first names."

"If you'd like."

"Fine." She didn't know where to put her growing frustration. He'd invited her here and now acted like she didn't belong. Of course, her ongoing frustration began in Italy, long before she met Darpan, yet it seemed to grow stronger in his presence. What was she missing?

"Why do you dislike him so much?"

"We've talked about this." He ran a hand through his hair, the muscles in his arm twitching as he did so. He seemed frustrated as well.

"At a UN meeting, he threatened his neighbors. Is there more? Do you know if he plans on carrying through on his threat?" She stared at him, and he returned her gaze but said nothing.

"Are you planning on doing something about it?" she asked.

He looked down at the table, a muscle twitching in his jaw, but said nothing. The air between them grew thick with tension, and she wished she could open the flap of the tent and let it out. Rain beat down a quick tempo, adding to her unease.

"Is there anything I can do?" Her voice, quickly muffled by the rain and small space, sounded small and alone.

"I'd love to keep having these conversations, learn more about when and where you plan to photograph the president." A switch had turned off. His voice was slow and even. Passionless.

She scoffed, an unrecognizable sound escaping from her throat. "This doesn't feel like a conversation."

"Margo." Her first name. "My work here is very sensitive. I can't discuss it. I'm not even sure if Andropov would like it if he knew were talking."

"Why would he care? I'm just here to take his picture."

"Does he know that? Does he really believe it? I know that his trusting me is the key to my being able to do my job."

"Then why did you ask me here?" None of this made sense.

"Two reasons, I guess. I'm curious about what goes on here. I try to talk with the different people he brings in. Perhaps there's a way we can help each other be successful."

"And the second reason?"

He looked at her a long time before answering. "I'm drawn to you. I think about you over there in the castle. I don't know what it is, but it's as if I've known you my whole life when I've never known anyone like you at all."

"I feel that, the pull. But you need to know that this attraction, it's not something I'm looking for. All I really want is to get my career back on track. Start working legitimate jobs again. Take another shot at fame."

"Why fame?" He seemed surprised at her words.

"That's how photographers make it, really good ones anyway. Once they become famous, they can change the world with their art. People love them. People still love my dad, and he died almost three decades ago."

"I'm not sure the love of a crowd is the same as the love between two people."

It was a funny thought, something that had been confused in her head for the longest time. But her dad had found love through fame, and her mom had been consumed by his love. "I think, at least for some people, one follows the other. At least that's what I've seen in my life." The rule she'd lived her life by sounded silly in the stale air.

"Well, I'm certainly not an expert on love."

"Why? Don't your parents love each other?"

"I don't know. Sometimes it seems more like a business relationship. And my parents' love for their children, well, it's laden with expectation. It's something that must be earned. Especially with my mom."

The conversation had dropped to some deeper level, where it flowed more quickly, their tongues loosened by the pain in their past. Margo grabbed it like a life raft. "Losing my dad broke my mom. I think she was truly and deeply in love with him. After he died, she kept searching for that same kind of love. Maybe it only comes around once in a lifetime. I know she never found it again. Each bad relationship broke her a little more."

"I'm sorry. That must have been hard." Darpan laid his hand across hers, squeezed gently.

"So, anyway. I'm not really looking for that traditional kind of love."

"You have no idea how much that makes me want you." His fingers grasped hers even tighter, and his eyes burned with intensity.

"I think that makes you a little odd." She smiled at him from beneath her lashes, his honesty making her shy.

"Definitely. But I've never been one for traditional relationships."

"Have you ever been in love?" she asked.

"No. I've been in like a few times. Short-term passion. That's it. You?"

Margo thought back to high school. The boy she thought she'd loved. At least she'd called it that at seventeen. Then, her first photo love. The popular girl on campus. A cheerleader. All tan skin and voluptuous lines. Margo had huffed through the camera as the girl turned into a woman and then into a goddess through the viewfinder.

The cheerleader had leaned forward with a gleam in her eyes, as if she knew the pristine white tank would show her deep cleavage, catching a shadow of nipple. Margo had timed the sun perfectly. The setting glow burnished brown skin and black hair. When the girl had opened a knee, bold in her beauty despite the short cheerleading skirt, Margo had fallen in love.

She'd shown the photos to her boyfriend first, tried to tell him the story. He'd left Margo that night. She caught him kissing the cheerleader in the parking lot two days later. She wasn't sure which of them she mourned more. But she'd learned how the arrow of love shot from her through the lens to the photo, infecting those on the other side.

"I love best through my photographs," she said to Darpan. "That way, I can share my love with the world. The rest of it is just sex."

The memory stirred passion. It was as if she'd relearned her place in the world. She was a photographer, and she'd save her love for that because it would make her great. But she was also a woman, and her woman's desire needed sating. He had declared photographs off limits, but there were other things she could have. She pulled her sweater over her head.

He stared at her, not saying anything, but she could feel him feasting on her with his eyes. His dark hand rose to her pale skin.

She reached around and unhooked her bra, then let it slide off her shoulders and down her arms.

"You are so beautiful," he said.

She wasn't, but she was powerful. And she knew the eye of the viewer created beauty, not physical perfection. She removed her jeans. Each piece of clothing that fell from her skin raised her temperature a few degrees. She'd never felt desire like this before. Not even with Kirk on a tropical beach.

Stripped to her thong, she finally spoke. "You need to take your clothes off. And do you have a condom?"

"I, I do," he stuttered. He pulled a wallet out of his back pocket and searched, finally removing a foil covered square. She reached for it.

He pulled off his shirt, revealing a tightly muscled torso, thin but strong, with the perfect thatch of dark hair on his chest. She wanted to run her hands through it. Would run her hands through it. His jeans hung loosely, but she could see her effect on him. It perked her nipples, and warmth rushed down from her belly.

"Everything?" he asked.

She nodded. He dropped his jeans, then his boxers. He was lean and erect, and she ached with desire. "Sit." She pointed to a chair.

He obeyed. She removed her thong, her desire overcoming any embarrassment about her body. She'd lost so much lately. Now she would get what she needed. She opened the foil packet and handed the condom to him. When he was ready, she stepped forward, straddled him, and placed her hands gently on his shoulders. He set his hands on her waist, a look of wonder in his black eyes. She slowly lowered herself onto his lap. All the anger she'd felt toward everyone lately, the hate she poured on herself, dissolved.

Their bodies fit together like they were sculpted from the same piece of marble. He reached up and loosened her ponytail, and her blond hair spilled over his dark skin. She looked at his beautiful face, the full lips she'd wanted to photograph for days, and kissed them instead.

After, while her toes still tingled with release, she thanked him.

He smiled at her and touched her cheek. "You cannot thank me. I am speechless at this gift you have given me."

She smiled at his words. "I think we may be better at not talking."

"Talking has never been my talent."

"I can see that," she said. "But you are clearly quite talented."

She dressed. He did the same. She should probably say something, but she didn't want to, didn't want to ruin this perfect moment. Before, when they talked, they'd uncovered old wounds. She'd used his body as a balm to heal some of those hurts, and now she radiated satisfaction.

She glanced at him as he pulled his jeans on. A smile from deep inside touched her lips, and she went to him, buried her hand in the hair at his chest, and kissed him one last time. "Tomorrow?" she asked.

He nodded, and she left the tent.

Chapter 8

Early that afternoon, Margo climbed the stairs to the third floor to help Andrei with his clothing selection. Portrait photographers identified outfits to bring out the best in a client's skin tone or to hide unwanted attributes. Margo didn't so much care. Curiosity more than professionalism pulled her toward his rooms.

Humphries met her at the third-floor landing and led her to the double wooden doors. He knocked twice, then opened it to the strangest room Margo had ever seen.

Tortoise shell wallpaper gleamed in the afternoon sun streaming through the windows. Lush amber and vermillion carpets partially covered black marble floors. A bronze spiral staircase leading to who knows where marked the center of the room. Two black chandeliers dripped smoke-colored crystals like daggers aimed at the floor.

The vibe mixed overwrought bachelor pad with torture chamber. A maroon leather sofa and several uncomfortable looking wooden chairs formed a sitting area on one side of the room. Humphries motioned her toward it, then left her alone.

"Andrei?"

"Margo, come in." His voice came from a room through another set of double doors. She made her way across the first room and stood at the threshold to his bedroom. Before her lay the largest round bed she'd ever seen. Round. The bed sat fully in the center of the room, its curved black velvet headboard caressing one side. She needed to leave.

"Margo, welcome." Andrei sounded excited to see her. "Please, come in here. Radmi has pulled some of my outfits."

At Radmi's name, Margo finally pulled her eyes from the bed.

"You like my room?" Andrei asked, a twinkle in his eye.

"It's, um, a lot."

"Bachelor pad," he said with a smile.

"Yeah. Let's not do any photos here."

He burst out laughing. "No, that would not be a good idea. I am trying to show the world how great my country is. We could photograph here if I looked for a wife."

She followed him into a different room, wondering exactly what kind of wife that bed would attract. They entered an enormous closet lined with racks of clothes and shoes down long walls. Unlike the rest of Andrei's suite, this room was well lit and had a floor to ceiling mirror against the back wall. Radmi stood next to a black and green military uniform, going over it with a lint brush. Other outfits included a tuxedo, an all-white military uniform, and a camo shirt and pants.

"Should we get some pictures of me in the field with a rifle?"

"I'm not sure about that. It doesn't exactly scream dignified." More like murderous terrorist. "The white one, is it Navy?" she asked, knowing the country was landlocked.

"No, formal. Is it too much?"

"I'm not sure yet. I think we want some action photos as well as staid portraits." She told him about her idea of the horse in the field.

"This is why I hired you. Brilliant idea. Also, I can have a pilot uniform made."

"Do you fly?"

"I am an expert at flying drones."

She so wanted to ask why you needed a uniform for that but kept her mouth shut. If he wanted a drone uniform, great. "Maybe we could find a way to make that an action shot."

"I love it!" He clapped. His enthusiasm overwhelmed her. He lit up like a kid with a new toy as he talked about different shots and what he should wear.

Radmi seemed unphased and made suggestions, fitted jackets, and matched shoes. Watching her, Margo became curious about her relationship with Andrei. They almost appeared like an old married couple. She'd have to ask Radmi about it later.

After several hours, they decided on six outfits. Margo had taken each of them to the shoot locations to make sure the colors worked the way she thought they would. Radmi made marks for the tailor, who would come out the next day to perfect the fit. She also arranged for someone to give Andrei a facial and made an appointment for a barber and manicurist to visit the castle.

"Tomorrow afternoon, I will take you to the stables and you can choose which horse you think is best."

"That sounds fine." It might be fun to choose a horse.

"Tonight's dinner will be a small party. I will wear a tuxedo. Did you bring a dress?"

"I have a dress, although I'm not sure it's tuxedo worthy. I will bring my camera so we can get a few candid shots before the dinner."

"That is good." He turned on a high wattage smile. This guy really wanted his photo taken. "Also, we have a selection of women's gowns. Radmi will take you to see them."

Margo brushed off the creepiness of random dresses in a castle and followed Radmi out of the suite. Not far down the hallway, they entered a room with pale blue walls and a daybed pressed against the window. Radmi opened the closet, and Margo spied two dozen colorful gowns sheathed in plastic and hanging against the wall.

"What on earth is this place?" Margo asked.

"We call it the dressing room."

"But why? Why are all these dresses here?"

Radmi's face went carnation red. "Sometimes, there are women here. They need something to wear." She couldn't meet Margo's eyes.

"What kind of women? What are they wearing when they get here? Is this some kind of sex trafficking ring?" Her mind didn't know where to land. Was this common for the ultra-rich or something more nefarious? What happened to the women after they wore these dresses?

"No. It is nothing like that." Radmi shook her head, looking at Margo again. "A lot of times there are government and political people at the estate for dinner. Men. Andrei, President Andropov, he likes to have women come to make the dinners more interesting."

"Where, exactly, do these women come from?"

"The local villages. They like to come up here. It is like a fairy tale. They get to visit the castle, wear beautiful clothes. They eat and drink like they never could at home. It is fun for them." Radmi spun her story, and Margo detected a wistfulness in her words.

She wasn't buying the fable. "Do they have to have sex with the men?"

Radmi colored again. "Sometimes. Maybe they want to. It is boring in the villages." She looked directly into Margo's eyes. "We don't all want the same lives as our mothers and grandmothers. That is why I learned English. I studied so hard. You are so lucky to be an American. Nothing stops you from achieving your dreams. I want to go to America. I want to become famous like Melania."

Oh, shit. Margo had no respect for the former first lady and her rise from model, or whatever, to politician's wife. But the fervor with which Radmi stared at her kept her opinions in check. Judging others became easy when you ignored your own privilege. "I understand."

Margo turned her attention to the garments before her. "I just don't think I'm comfortable wearing one of these dresses. I'm here as a professional photographer, not as eye candy and entertainment for Andrei's guests."

"Yes, you are right." Radmi took her hand and led her out of the closet. "I can order you a new dress. Your own dress."

"You can do that?" Margo had thought of Radmi as a housekeeper. This seemed a step above. "I will take care of it." She walked a slow circle around Margo. "I think I can get the perfect size."

"Thank you. I can pay for it."

"No. It is fine. I will ask Andrei. He will agree."

The awkwardness of the situation tightened her stomach. But Margo didn't have an appropriate dress, even though Andrei had warned her about this before she left New York. At least Radmi had saved her from wearing a dress meant for a far different situation. "Thanks, again, Radmi. Let me know when I can give you your first photography lesson."

"Today is busy, but perhaps you can show me a little bit when I bring your dress?"

"Yes, I would like that." She owed Radmi. Perhaps exposing her to the opportunities behind the lens would make her dreams more realistic.

***

The pale lavender dress differed from anything Margo would have picked out in a shop, but it transformed her when she slid it on. The silk gathered generously at her small bust, held up only by the thinnest spaghetti straps. Below her waist, the fabric gathered at one hip. The overall effect gave her curves she didn't possess, and the color made her pale skin glow.

She'd fixed her hair in a low bun, but Radmi insisted on taking it down and letting it flow over one shoulder. She looked about as good as she could, maybe as good as she did the night of the gala in Italy. The pain of that night always surfaced so quickly.

She taught Radmi the basics of the camera, and the young woman wanted to take her photograph. Margo declined. She had no desire to document this evening. She took Radmi's photo instead, despite her complaints that she needed a fancy dress and a model's pose.

"There are more stories to tell than pretty women selling fancy clothes. Please, let me try." Margo sat Radmi near the window where the evening light illuminated her face. She asked her what she loved most in the world, then her saddest memory. The light played across Radmi's features as she answered, "My country." Her face darkened at the next thought. "Evil."

Could Andrei be the evil that changed Radmi's face? To lighten the mood, Margo turned the back of the camera toward Radmi and showed her the photos. Before Radmi could react, someone rapped on the door.

"Radmila." Humphry's gruff voice pierced the door.

"I'm late." Radmi jumped up and ran out.

Margo grabbed her camera bag and followed Radmi out the door. Down-stairs, neon lights glowed from the patio. A bar sat in the salon, staffed by a person Margo hadn't seen before.

"Margo."

She turned to see Andrei in a perfectly tailored tuxedo. His blond hair appeared darker from the gel that slicked it off his face. He had a charming smile, at least when he wasn't acting creepy.

"You look fantastic. That dress suits you."

"It's lovely, thank you." She couldn't help but think of the closet full of dresses upstairs and the local girls brought in to fill them.

"You are the kind of woman who should dress in silk all the time." His attempt at charm fell flat. She didn't know what kind of woman he spoke of, but she hoped never to be like that. She would never, ever live her life for a man.

"I've got my camera. Do you have time for a couple of shots before the guests arrive?"

"Anything for you. Where would you like me?" He cocked an eyebrow, and his lips hinted at a smile.

She ignored the innuendo. "Let me have you stand on the stairs."

She hid behind the lens and photographed him until people arrived and interrupted them. None of the photos rose to the standard of a formal portrait, but it gave her a chance to work with the angles in his face. His high, broad cheekbones bounced light, and her favorite shot was near the patio doors, where a touch of neon light gave his face an early eighties glow.

She wandered onto the patio, enraptured by the light. Neon bulbs shone from the patio floor, alternating purple and green as light climbed the castle wall, then disappeared into space. An array of small neon globes formed a centerpiece at each table. It was lovely and strange, and she felt the foreignness of it all.

At one point, she turned, feeling eyes on her back. Darpan. Heat rushed to her cheeks, remembering her boldness from the morning, and surged again at the memory of his skin on hers.

He stood twelve feet away, a purple glow playing across his face. He didn't smile, but the intensity of his gaze lit her on fire. She stepped toward him.

"It's nice to see you again," she said.

"You look amazing. So different."

"All dressed up." She felt naked in the thin silk.

"You looked amazing this morning too. I've thought about you all day."

"Me too." She stepped closer, close enough to see the set of his jaw and flare of his nostril. His beauty made her fingers itch for the camera. Or she could run them across his skin. She had to get a hold of herself. He was just a guy. One who struggled with job and family and ambition the way she did. He was like her. "So, am I still invited to your place for breakfast?"

"Absolutely."

"Darpan. Glad you're here. Doesn't Margo look fantastic tonight?"

Andrei approached her and wrapped an arm around her shoulder. Possessive. She struggled not to shrug it away. She still needed the money.

"We had this dress sent up from the city for her today. It is perfect for her. Don't you agree?"

"It's lovely." Darpan's voice portrayed no emotion, but Margo caught the widening of his eyes as Andrei spoke about the dress. Shame knitted its way through her joints. She didn't want to be thought of like those girls. He hadn't bought her, just her talent.

"I think I'm going to get a drink," she said, hoping to escape the heft of Andrei's arm.

"Wonderful, come with me. We'll get you the best in the house." He turned from Darpan and led her back into the estate. Each step seemed to take her closer to a trap she didn't want to enter. It was Italy all over again. Dread that this trip wouldn't end well either crept up her spine.

The bartender opened a bottle of Cristal. Margo took the tiniest of sips, not wanting to drink at all. At least Andrei had removed his arm to shake some man's hand.

Margo surveyed the women in the room. They all seemed to be her age or older, and they also appeared attached to dates. No village girls in dresses, at least none that she could identify.

Andrei rarely left her side as the night wore on. They ate on the patio, and she only glimpsed the back of Darpan's head as he dined at a table far from hers. She wanted to explain things to him, assure him she wasn't Andrei's date. Wasn't his anything, except his photographer.

But she never had the chance. She sat, bored by conversation in a language not her own. Darpan rose from his table and said a few words to his tablemates. Then he left, without even looking her way. Morning couldn't come soon enough.

Chapter 9

The tent flap was closed but unzipped when Margo approached. She'd arrived earlier this morning, before the dull charcoal sky had even a hint of the coming sun. She grabbed one side of the flap and pulled it back, calling Darpan's name.

"Come in."

She entered, dropping the flap behind her. He stood in the middle of the room, facing her in jeans and a white button down. She tried to read his eyes and failed. The desire to stand naked in front of him, then melt into the warmth of his arms, overtook her.

She'd enjoyed sex since high school, thought of it as a tool that guaranteed pleasure. Her pull toward Darpan differed. His body was a refuge, a place to hide from the daily hurts and weirdness of the world and discover some new part of herself. She hoped he felt the same, yet this morning, she struggled to divine his thoughts.

"About last night." She wanted to put her fears about what he thought into words, deny anything he might imagine.

He strode toward her, wrapped his arms around her just the way she'd hoped, and pulled her close. His gaze singed her as he searched the depths of her eyes. His lips dropped to hers, and then the rest of the world faded away.

She brought a hand to the back of his neck, drawing him deeper into the kiss, and met him with an intensity she'd never experienced before. Her entire body should have thrown off sparks with the electricity flowing through it. He finally rose out of the kiss, leaving her gasping.

"I have thought about doing that since you left the tent yesterday. You were so beautiful last night. It was like you'd arrived from another world." He took a step back, his face darkening. "The way he wanted to possess you . . ."

"I know. He's obnoxious, but it's not like that. I promise. The dress. I didn't have anything appropriate, so Radmi ordered it. I didn't know he'd take it as his own contribution. There is nothing between us. I am a professional, and I'm only here to do a job. This—" she waved her hand between them. "I don't know where this came from."

"You might not think he possesses you, but he made it fairly clear last night that he believes he does."

"Then I'll have a talk with him." And say what? She could do this. She must clarify to Andrei that they had a solely professional relationship.

"Be very careful. I think he's a much different person than you realize."

Margo closed her eyes, and the candy-colored, plastic-wrapped dresses floated before them. "I have an idea who he is. I know about the girls he brings up here."

She opened her eyes to Darpan's dark look.

"Yes. It is not uncommon," he said. "That building is a place of secrets. That's why I stay out here most nights. In the capitol's state house, where Andropov lives and works most of the time, cameras are hidden in every room. He trusts no one. Closet doors are rigged with alarms, and every bathroom has spying lenses."

"And here?" Margo's voice barely registered. She didn't really want to know.

"I don't think Andropov wants evidence of what happens here. There are no cameras. The castle is a fortress against this cliff. Only one road leads here from the valley far below. Geography, not technology, keeps this location secure."

"I wish I knew what happened to those women. Radmi seemed okay with it." Was that true? How did a housekeeper know so much, anyway?

"I think you have more to worry about than those women. They serve one purpose. His view of the world and his place in it reminds me of truly evil dictators from past centuries. What Andropov wants from you seems less clear."

"I can make it clear. I will make it clear, but I don't want to talk about him. I am right here. With you." Her little girl voice saying those exact words to her mother echoed through her. She dropped her head into her hands. She shouldn't be here. But when she looked up at him, she wanted to kiss him again. She wanted to crawl into his skin and bury herself in the quiet.

"I don't want you to get hurt," he whispered.

"Are you going to hurt me?" Challenge laced the quiet question.

He dropped his head. "I don't know."

His honesty broke through any barriers that remained. He gave her the choice. She turned to the tent's zippered door and closed it. Then she went to him, took his face in her hands, and kissed him. "I understand."

She trembled when she saw the fire in her words light in his eyes. He lunged into her, kissing her hard and deep. She struggled out of the clothes that constrained her, keeping him from her, then stripped him of his. Naked, she climbed on top of him, wild with desire. She didn't recognize the insatiable woman devouring this man, but she let her have free rein.

Later, they lay side-by-side and drained on an oriental rug. Darpan's breath came deep and strong. "You have no idea what you do to me," he said. "I didn't know these feelings existed. I don't know what I was doing before this."

"Same." She lifted herself off the floor and leaned on his chest. "You are electric, and you make me electric too. I am drawn to you like a magnet. My clothes just go flying." She shook her head. "I'm normally not like this."

"Me either." He sat up, then pulled her onto his lap. "But I need you. I need you now."

She smiled, instantly ready for him.

"We have to talk at some point," he said.

"Talking is overrated."

But they did talk. Eventually. He asked about her schedule and what shots she had planned.

"You want to photograph him on a horse with weapons in the background? You have to be kidding me. That's brilliant." Darpan chuckled easily.

"It is the image he seems to want to project. There are others, though. He wants a photo as a drone pilot."

"Fascinating. I could decorate a drone for him."

"Decorate?"

"Make it look super modern and technologically advanced."

"Well, I can ask him about it."

"No." Darpan's harsh voice stung. "We have to protect you. When he saw you talking to me last night, he wasn't happy. You saw how he reacted. Please, let me handle this."

"I take it you don't want him to know about this." She waved her hand between them.

"I don't think it's smart."

"So, we'll keep this relationship hidden." The thought made her wary, and sad. But she understood. This wasn't real life. She'd dropped into a foreign country and found something with Darpan that probably didn't exist in the real world. And here, they both had jobs to do.

"I have no reason in the world to keep this relationship hidden except to protect you. And, honestly, to protect my own work here."

"I wish I had met you in a bar in New York City." She wanted to pout. With all the travel required by a professional photographer, she'd never had time for a boyfriend. Never really wanted one when casual relationships gave her the release she needed. But she'd have done a lot to keep a connection like this.

Everything about Darpan differed from the horrible men her mother pinned her hopes on. He didn't need her. She didn't need him. Instead, desire and some melding of their minds led to an inevitable meeting of their bodies.

In days, this had become the healthiest relationship she'd ever been in. She'd chased Kirk, wanted the handsome bad boy. Before that, she hadn't had more than three dates with any guy since high school. She hadn't wanted that, had known she'd be happiest with the mass adulation of the crowd, not the individual obsessiveness of normal relationships. The kind of obsessiveness that caused someone to drive off a cliff rather than allow the object of his fixation to leave.

Darpan's sly grin lit his face. "You know, you would have had to find me someplace other than a bar."

"Yeah. I doubt I'd ever have found a nondrinking vegetarian. It's all impossible anyway. But I really like you. This feels like the most normal relationship I've ever had."

With that, he laughed, the noise coming deep from his belly. "I'm afraid I feel the same, and I don't think that says anything good about either of us."

"Well, I never really wanted a serious relationship. I've got other things I need to focus on."

"Exactly. All that pressure to meet someone, get married, start a family. There are things I need to do in the world, and they don't involve a life mate."

"Life mate." She giggled. "That's a pressure I don't have, but I also don't see the need. All people do is hurt each other anyway. This is better. Clean. No expectations."

"I don't know about clean. We did do it on the floor." He grinned, then turned serious. "I wish this fit into my life. I wish I had the time to really get to know you. To learn all the questions I need to ask you." He pushed a strand of hair behind her ear, then let his finger trail down her jaw, her neck. "I would spend a lifetime learning about you."

She leaned forward and gave him the softest of kisses. "And I could spend a lifetime learning every inch of your body and every corner of your mind. Maybe it's the lack of time that makes this so intense."

"Perhaps."

"I've got to go." She whispered the words into his open mouth, sealing them in there with a final kiss.

"Will you be back tomorrow?"

"Yes," she said. "Yes, and yes, and yes."

Margo walked down the main aisle of the barn, watching the different colored heads emerge from the half doors. Andrei had called out to the horses on their arrival and received a quick response. He fed each horse small bits of carrot and rubbed their heads as he made his way through the barn.

The horses were gorgeous. A black steed with a white blazing running the length of his face stuck his nose out the door first. Across the aisle, she saw a chestnut as bright as a copper penny. She thought the dapple gray with the bright white mane and tail might be the most photogenic, although the elegant horse just down from him had the coloring of a Budweiser Clydesdale.

"What beautiful animals. I'm not sure how to choose the best one for the photograph."

"Just wait," he said. He walked to the last stall and clucked to the horse inside. Margo walked toward him. The solid bottom half of the door matched the others, but the upper half had metal bars instead of opening to the aisle.

Inside, she spied a huge white horse. Enormous muscles rounded his thick neck, and his nostrils flared at his gray muzzle. He half reared and lunged toward the door. Margo backed up before she could stop herself. The horse oozed power.

"Is he tame? Can you ride him?" she asked.

"I can, yes. Most people cannot." Andrei's pride rang through his voice.

"He would be amazing in the shoot. His shape, his color, they're tremendous." Margo gazed at the horse from the middle of the barn, staying well away from the blustery stallion.

"I thought you would like him. He is strong like me." Andrei flexed his biceps, and defined muscles rose beneath his fitted black shirt.

"I see that." The way he always tried to pump himself up, sometimes literally, made Margo curious about the background that would lead to this type of self-confidence. "You must spend a lot of time at the gym."

"It is important that a leader be seen as strong. When I was young, I was not so strong. I worked hard to build myself. Now, I am stronger than most men. I studied the strategies of war and the great history of our country. I worked hard and rose to be president. These are great achievements, but this is just the beginning of my story."

"What else do you hope to accomplish? I've heard how you want to restore the ancient borders of your country." A small curl of excitement wound its way up her spine. His true self, whatever lay underneath the cultivated exterior, began to seep out. She needed this closer understanding to take a meaningful photo. For the first time, she longed to capture his inner ambition and whatever long-forgotten traumas led to it.

"It is not for my country alone that we must achieve this. Other powers oppressed my citizens, the true Tiranians, for generations. Dictators stole their country, imposed lies of borders, and ripped families apart. I will right this wrong."

She longed to ask if he was certain the citizens outside the castle boundaries felt foreign oppression, but she'd lose him if she doubted the story he'd constructed. "Why do you think the United Nations opposes your plan?"

"Tyrants lead the United Nations. They are the ones who benefitted from the wrongs of the past. But that is fine. Their countries are failing. The United States, Western Europe, these are failing states. Even Russia and China have seen their best days. Countries like Tiranistan will dominate the future. We will reclaim the greatness of our past."

Andrei had drifted into platitudes instead of closing in on the source of his desire. She brought her camera to her eye and took several shots of the white stallion through the bars. The horse flipped his head up and down at each click of the shutter.

"He's a beautiful horse. He'll be perfect for the shot."

"Yes. The photo you have planned is exactly what the world needs to see. This stallion represents the best of our past. I'm bringing advanced weaponry that speaks to our present capabilities. And I am the future."

He turned and walked down the barn aisle, shoulders squared and with the barn lights bouncing off his blond hair. The horses still had their heads outside the stall doors, as if saluting him. Going through the world with that kind of ego, blindly knowing whatever you desired you would accomplish, astounded Margo.

She had confidence in one small thing, her ability to take beautiful photos. She had honed this skill over many years, always striving to improve, to take that next step forward. For Andrei, the world seemed to lie at his feet, or at least he thought it did. He had so much conceit he thought a mere photo would change the world's perception of him.

How hard would he fall when things didn't go his way?

Chapter 10

Back at the castle, a scrawled note from Radmi rested on Margo's dresser. She'd returned to her village for the night. No other explanation, just her signature. Margo had planned on meeting her for another photography session. After spending time with Andrei in the barn, she had questions for the other woman about Andrei's youth. What had made him the person he was today?

With nothing else to do, she thought she'd find a ride to the nearest village. Perhaps she could ask the locals their opinion of their president. When she questioned Humphries, he let her know that no vehicle would leave the estate for the rest of the day.

"What if I really needed to go somewhere?" she asked. She didn't expect to run out of toiletries or supplies, but she'd never considered not being able to leave when she wanted.

"If you need something not at the estate, I will try to procure it for you."

"But what if I just want to leave? I'm a photographer. I might want to photograph other places," Margo said.

The sour look on Humphries's face told her he couldn't care less. "In that instance, I would suggest you speak with President Andropov."

She gave up and walked out the door, maybe to show him he didn't control her. Or maybe to prove to herself that she could. She walked down to the bridge and crossed the ravine. She wondered if she could walk to a nearby town. It had been a long drive up the mountain, but perhaps going down wouldn't be so bad. Although she'd have to find some way back and the afternoon had already grown late.

On the far side of the bridge, the path rose steeply before entering a thick pine forest. A deep layer of pine needles covered the path, and she bounced along their soft carpet. She enjoyed stretching her legs in the cool shade of the trees. She carried her camera, although for a long while, there was nothing to photograph but trees. In a way, it relieved her not to see the strange ornaments in the forest near Darpan's tent.

The trees ended abruptly in a meadow that led to a small outcropping of rocks. On the far side, a trail dropped steeply to the valley below. Switchback after switchback clung perilously to the side of the mountain. The trail narrowed so much she wondered if it was primarily used by animals. She didn't have a fear of heights but shuddered at the thought of attempting a trail where one misstep could send one off the side of the mountain.

She turned, ready to return to the castle, and saw an enormous deer opposite the meadow near the forest trail. His antlers spread wide toward the sky. The majestic creature stared right at her. She slowly raised her camera, looking down briefly to remove the lens cap. When she looked up, the deer had vanished. Nothing stirred, as if he'd been a figment of her imagination.

She stood in the stillness. All sounds and every movement of air had stopped with the disappearance of the animal. "Hey, where'd you go?" Margo called, mostly to bring the strange moment back into the normal world.

She headed back to the forest trail, hoping the deer wasn't ahead of her, waiting to spear her with his pointy horns. Fairytale. Every time this place started to seem normal, something weird happened. Decorated trees, magical disappearing animals. She would love to capture the strangeness in a photo. She might not find the deer again, but she could return to Darpan's forest.

She trudged down the pine needle path, the trek seeming longer as the day plunged rapidly toward evening. The skin on her arms chilled as the temperature dropped. She broke into a light jog. At last, she cleared the forest and trotted down the path to the bridge. She stopped midway across, catching her breath and looking into the stream far below.

The shadows cast by the cliff and the castle stretched toward the bridge, sending a chill up her spine. The skin on her arms prickled in response. She looked toward Darpan's tent, hoping to see him. It would be nice to visit him. Just thinking of him warmed her.

But the tent looked shut tight. At least she'd likely see him for dinner. At the thought, her stomach growled. Hopefully, there'd be no visitors, no events. Perhaps she'd even get to have dinner alone with Darpan like when she first arrived.

When she turned toward the castle, it looked brighter. The patio where they'd sat invited her, and she strode purposefully toward the building.

Strangely, Humphries waited near the door and opened it the moment she got close. She entered the foyer just as Andrei strode in from the salon.

"Where have you been?" Andrei's cross voice surprised her.

"I went for a walk. I saw a beautiful deer."

"You must let us know where you are at all times." He crossed his arms, addressing her like a child. "We are responsible for you. You can't just run off. Something might happen to you."

"What on earth would happen to me? I am an adult, and I don't need to feel trapped here. I also don't need you checking up on me."

"While you are here, in my employ, you will let someone know when you leave and where you are going."

She bristled at his words. But she was indeed in his employ. "Fine. But I would like to be able to go into town and photograph nearby communities. I do not want to feel like a prisoner here."

Andrei relaxed his arms, and his face rearranged itself from scowl to smile. Margo wondered what the effort had cost him. "Of course. You are not a prisoner, and I would appreciate such a renowned photographer taking an interest in our villages. I will arrange something. In the meantime, I would like you to dine with me tonight."

"Of course. Will there be any other guests visiting the castle for dinner?"

"No guests. I will have Humphries set up a table in my suite. Seven-thirty?"

"You want me to eat in your suite?"

"Yes, and I would appreciate it if you would wear a dress. I am not used to the casual clothing of Americans."

She hoped he understood she would never have anything but a business dinner with him. Part of her wanted to address it immediately, but she couldn't help noticing the stoic curiosity on Humphries's face. It wouldn't do to embarrass Andrei in front of the staff.

Andrei seemed to await her response. "Fine. Business dinner. Seven-thirty. Third floor. I look forward to seeing you then." She inwardly cringed at the awkward response, but she'd taken the best way out of a bad situation.

———

At the appointed hour, Margo knocked on the door of the third-floor suite. As requested, she wore the one dress she'd brought, a body-hugging maroon knit piece that had been her travel go to for years.

Without the sun brightening the room, the tortoiseshell walls shimmered faintly under the glow of the two chandeliers. The word *moody* popped into her brain.

"Welcome," Andrei said. His lapis blue sweater brought out the color in his eyes.

"I'll be right back. I've got to get my camera. The light in this room is uncanny."

She returned to the tawdry room, hoping actual turtles hadn't been harmed in the making of the walls. She directed Andrei to sit on the black leather sofa, but the dark furniture stole all the light. She pointed to the square table, clearly set with their dinner in mind. Three tea candles in glass orbs brought flickering light to his face. The severe shadows the lens picked up created a menacing look, even when he tried to smile.

Finally, she had him stand against the wall opposite his bedroom. She opened the double doors and turned the light on, trying to ignore the giant round bed. The perfect light bounced off his features and brought them to life through the viewfinder.

An excellent model, he gave her every look she asked. Brooding, charming, relaxed, as if in a room full of friends.

"Let's go for sexy." The second the words left her mouth, she wanted them back. She hadn't been thinking about him, the ambitious dictator with candy-colored dresses hidden in a closet, she'd only had eyes for the next shot. At least she could hide her emotions behind the camera.

"That is easy," he said and gave her his best smoldering look.

Finally, they dined. He seemed to be on a high from the photo shoot, smiling and gazing at her from under his brow.

"What has you so happy?" she finally asked.

"I think you fell in love with me a little when you photographed me."

Oh dear god, not this again. "I told you, it doesn't have to work like that. It's not going to work like that. But I think I got some good photos."

"In time, you will be in love with me. I am sure of it. You will fall in love, and then the world will fall for me when they see your photos. I understand how photographs change the world. It has happened before and will happen again."

"Andrei, I'm afraid you expect too much." His words disturbed her far more than she let on. His talk about the world falling in love with him landed too close to her own desire for adulation.

"Do not worry, this will happen." He sat back in his chair and swirled a deep red wine around his glass. "I have plans for you."

He looked like he had the world by the balls. What would give a person that kind of confidence? "What was it like growing up in Tiranistan?" she asked.

The impenetrable mask of a leader settled upon his face. "I had a difficult childhood. I do not know if you have read about this, but I grew up as an orphan."

"Oh. No, I'm sorry. I didn't know." Her heart went out to him. For all the troubles of her childhood, at least she'd had people who loved her. The memory of her grandmother's caring eyes stirred a longing in her breast. "I never knew my father. He died before I was born, but I grew up with my mother and my grandparents."

"I do not know who my parents are. I am truly a son of this country. Tiranistan is both my mother and my father." He said it with pride.

No wonder he believed he should rule the country, should bring it to greatness.

"How? How did you grow up?"

"I grew up in an orphanage in the capital. My life was hard, but I was strong. I have overcome my past, just like my country will."

Again, that confidence. He'd had nothing but institutional support, and she doubted that meant much here. It's likely he lived a life far harder than he'd ever admit. Far harder than hers with one parent. Her mom may have been an emotional mess, but she was there. And her grandparents did their best to protect her from her mom's flighty behavior and unsavory boyfriends.

She and Andrei had childhoods as different as she and Darpan did. He had two parents who doted on him perhaps too much. According to him, they expected so much of him he now rarely visited, certain of their ongoing disapproval. Margo's mother didn't expect much from her. Strangely, her father drove her from beyond the grave. From the first time she'd picked up a camera, maybe before, she'd wanted to be like him, have his level of career. But that ambition turned to smoke when compared to Andrei. The man in front of her wanted to literally change the boundaries of the world. He might start a war to make that happen.

"What are you thinking about?" he asked.

She stared into his intense blue eyes, trying to parse what made him different from other men. "I'm thinking about your bold plans for your country and how you relate that back to your past."

"I have bold plans for you as well." He ignored her question. Nothing changed in his intent gaze. He would invade his neighbors. He had plans for her.

"Andrei, I am here to do a job. Nothing more."

"I know that you believe that now. But it will change. You will fall in love with me, take a remarkable photo. I am a wonderful lover."

"No. That would be against my professional ethics. I don't think you understand. When I fall in love with a subject, it can be an animal, a landscape. It is not sexual." She hated saying the words. It made her feel dirty. Especially since it had been sexual once. That first time, before she understood the true connection between love and photography.

"But I am here, and you are here. We are both attractive people. It will happen."

"No. It won't." I'm already sleeping with Darpan, she wanted to scream. He's the one. In some very important way I don't understand, he's the one. But she would never let Andrei know. It would ruin her assignment and Darpan's. Or worse. After all, a man willing to start a war, to kill people over politics, might be dangerous in other ways.

"Give it time," he said. "You will see."

She ended her protest. She might as well talk to a wall. Tortoiseshell wavered like something out of a horror movie. She excused herself, leaving half her meal uneaten.

"You do not need to go," he said. "You have nothing to fear. I will not force you. I believe you will come willingly to my bed."

"You have got to stop saying that." Margo stood and threw her napkin on the table. "If you cannot accept this as a professional relationship, then I need to leave."

"Please, stay. I must show you something." He rose and walked toward a mirror along one wall. He slid it sideways a few inches and revealed a button. After he pushed it, a hidden door in the tortoise wall opened.

What kind of freak show was this? Margo stepped toward the secret room, drawn by walls filled with photographs. She stepped through the doorway, praying this wasn't some teenage slasher movie where she wouldn't escape the evil villain.

Time slowed. She recognized some of the photos. War photos. Her father's photos.

"What's going on?" she whispered, fearing the answer.

"Your father was the greatest photographer in a generation, maybe ever. He captured the truth. Did you know he took pictures in my country?"

"No." A chill ran up her spine, but she wouldn't leave. Instead, she moved from photo to photo, measuring her father's brilliance.

"He filmed the military coup in Tiranistan. He was here three days, and his photos landed on the front page of the world's newspapers. The images fueled the military's ire and self-righteousness." Andrei's voice had grown low, robotic.

"I didn't know." But she did. She knew what photo waited when she turned to face the next wall. He'd photographed the execution of a dictator. She'd never seen that particular image in her childhood home. She'd found it online once. And she hated it. Brutal. Destructive. The image portrayed the depravity of human nature.

"Look at the photo," Andrei commanded.

She did, even though it turned her gut. She should have put all this together. Instead of researching her destination like usual, she'd wallowed in recovering from the shame of Italy.

"Your father showed the world the worst of my country. You will show them the best." His quiet tone had none of the arrogance of earlier, but steel lay underneath it. "Tomorrow morning you will take my photograph with the horse and weapons more advanced than any in your country. Then we will schedule other photos. I promise, you are here to work."

Every cell in her body told her to escape. She took a deep breath. *Get your head back in the game.* She wouldn't let his manipulation beat her. Take the money and the photos, then leave. "Let's take outside shots at dawn and dusk and save the interior shots for the day."

"That will be good." His voice had turned smooth again. "After that, I must be gone for two days. We can take the photo with the drone after that. The drone pilot's uniform will be ready when I return, and I am having a specialized drone built."

"Fine. That gives me time to look through the photos we take first and run a few by you." Proud of herself for turning the conversation back to business and only trembling on the inside, she turned to leave.

By the time she closed the door to her room, the unease of vulnerability had seeped back into her veins. She pulled a high-back chair in front of the door. She didn't expect trouble, but she didn't want any middle of the night surprises.

The rooms she'd once thought beautiful seemed cold and lonely. She wouldn't sleep well now that she knew about Andrei's shrine to her father. Andrei hadn't chosen her because she was good, at least not entirely. He wanted the connection to her father to help him rewrite history.

She wished she had a way to get word to Darpan. She wanted to talk to him about her father and Andrei, but she couldn't sneak out and wouldn't meet him in the morning. She could not waste the dawn light. The glow the rising sun cast on the dark cliffs would provide the perfect backdrop to a photo with an alabaster horse.

Chapter 11

Margo rose before dawn and headed straight for the coffee. She'd woken thinking of her father's photos in Andrei's hidden room. They warned her of danger and some deeper hidden story she didn't quite comprehend. As soon as possible, she needed to finish this job and leave.

She heard a large vehicle and looked out to see a truck and trailer. Two men backed the white stallion out of the trailer. Plumes of steam escaped the horse's nostrils, making him look like a creature of legend.

Thirty minutes later, Margo stood outside in the cool morning. A saddle the color of blackstrap molasses adorned the animal. Beneath it lay a navy blanket embroidered with the flag of Tiranistan. A bit with long silver shanks had been placed in the animal's mouth, and as he tossed his head, a fine rope of silver braided into his reins glinted in the new sun.

Also glowing in the dawn light, four evil-looking silver missiles lay in a metal contraption ready to launch them toward death and destruction. They had taken over part of the field on the way to Darpan's tent where a break in the trees made the cliff the perfect backdrop.

Margo tried to ignore Darpan, who chatted with the horse's handlers. Finally, Andrei emerged from the castle in his military finery. Polished mahogany boots, white breeches, a navy jacket with gold bands across the front and on the forearms, and a tall hat adorned with a gold badge. He looked like someone from another century.

The glimmer in his eye and the set of his jaw showed his self-esteem. He loved this. Which did he love more, ruling or crawling his way to the top, the very upper echelon of his country? Orphan to president. And now that he'd accomplished that, he'd set his target on neighboring countries. Where would it stop?

The metal sheaths with their pointed tips and winglets screamed death machines. Andrei told her their sophistication surpassed anything her country had and could rain terror on the world. He said it with joy.

She glimpsed Humphries scurrying through the garden. Something large lay across both hands.

Andrei approached the stallion, took the reins from the handler, and swung himself into the saddle. Humphries handed the man near the horse what Margo now saw was a sword.

She raised her camera to her face. Her skin prickled with the beauty and tragedy the shot represented. She clicked the shutter, not giving direction but capturing the action as it unfolded. The handler passed the sword to Andrei as Margo's finger closed on photo after photo. She hated what she was doing. She loved what she was doing.

Andrei looked right at her, his eyes searing through the lens with pride. The handler and Humphries backed out of the shot. Just the two of them remained, the conqueror and his storyteller.

The horse glowed in the light of the sun. Metal gleamed. The missiles pointed south, threatening. The horse reared, soaring upward. Andrei beamed with pure energy and ego. Alexander, Genghis, Caesar. His ambition underscored every shot. Margo captured it again and again, digitizing it, making it permanent.

"That's it," she finally called when the soft sun turned harsh. She packed her gear, exhaustion pulling at her. Sometimes a shoot left her as high as any drug. Other times, like today, the mental fatigue of constant focus drained her. Today, she wanted to crawl into a hole or rip the metal door from its hinges and hide inside the cliff. The photos would be excellent, and she hated herself for it.

She collapsed her tripod, shouldered her bag, and headed toward the house. Andrei, no longer on the horse, spoke with Darpan. Margo looked away. Did Darpan ever feel like this? Would they be judged for being on the wrong side of history if Andrei carried out his destructive plans?

Margo stayed in her room until evening when she had scheduled additional photographs with Andrei. She photographed him in a different military uniform and in a tuxedo, but the light didn't cooperate. She'd hoped for dramatic shadows, but with the castle snuggled into the cliff on the west side of the valley, the light merely tinged sepia shortly before the sun disappeared behind the mountain walls.

Andrei preened in front of the camera, telling her to keep shooting long after she wanted to stop. He played some wicked game she didn't understand, demanding photo after photo. It was as if he had to prove his control over her, demanding she keep shooting and reminding her how much he'd paid her.

Finally, she put her camera away. She told Andrei they'd have to try again in the morning, but he reminded her would be out of town. Half relieved and half disappointed, the welcome break kept her further from her return to New York. After watching his ego through the lens, she wanted to put as many miles as possible between herself and this dictator.

———

The next morning, Margo trudged through the field in the same golden light she'd shot in yesterday. It felt like a crime scene. Her photographs alone weren't enough to sway the public's opinion of a man, but they might contribute. Her photos, Darpan's communications network, who knew who else Andrei had hired to put their tiny piece of the puzzle into place. When, if, he achieved his goals, they could all pretend it hadn't been their fault. But she'd seen the completed puzzle in the light of his eyes. A world remade with him at the center. Her piece made her complicit.

She stood outside Darpan's tent, wondering why she'd come. She didn't want sex, not when guilt had replaced desire.

"Darpan?" she halfheartedly called.

He opened the flap immediately, as if he'd been waiting. She watched anticipation fall from his face, replaced with concern.

"Come in." He held the tent flap back, gesturing her inside.

He'd arranged a pallet of blankets on the floor. She was such a jerk. "I'm sorry. I can't . . ."

"No, no. I'm sorry. Quite sorry, and quite ridiculous. I shouldn't have assumed. Please, sit."

He busied himself with making tea. She sat, numb and not knowing how to start the conversation.

"How do you work with him when you know what he wants to do?" she asked as Darpan brought two cups to the table. "He'll take over the world if he can. He's that ambitious."

"Yes, I think he is." Darpan offered her sugar. "If it helps, he doesn't have the capacity to take over the world. The larger countries can take out his military if they get involved."

"But until that point, people will die."

"Yes."

The awfulness of the situation sank through her. She took pictures. Her realm was art and beauty. She used her photos to explain the world, the beauty and importance of wildlife, the trauma and tragedy humanity faced. But this. These photos would promote violence and death, not record its aftermath.

"I should leave. I should pay him back and leave." She wouldn't meet his eyes and instead looked at where his hand had reached out to clasp hers. "Only, I don't have the money to pay him back."

"It's going to be okay." He squeezed her hand, shifted his chair closer. "You didn't know. And there are people who will combat this."

She had expected him to say it was just a photo, that she shouldn't worry about it. But he didn't deliver that kind of comfort. Instead, he respected what she did, understood she had power, even if just a puzzle piece's worth.

"How much more do you have to do here?" he asked. "You should get away, go back to a normal life."

"But I'll always know what I've done. How do you deal with it?" She finally looked him in the eyes.

"I have a job to do." His face closed down, shutting her out.

"That's what I used to tell myself. I probably shouldn't be here." But she didn't want to leave. The warmth of his hand comforted her, and the smoke of their earlier passion wafted through the air.

"Stay." His word broke like a river, washing through her.

She had screwed up her life completely, and now she had to live with the consequences. She had no way out of this decision, had already done the wrong thing. It might not mean much in the big scheme of things, but it meant something to her. She'd had a moral compass, an artistic compass. And she'd sold it for a hundred thousand dollars.

At least I'm not cheap. She caught the irony as she reached toward Darpan, wanting to use him to erase her thoughts.

It almost worked. Or at least it worked for a while. But eventually they had to get up, get dressed, and return to their work. Her thoughts reverted to Andrei.

"What causes a man to become so power hungry?" she asked. "Is it because he was orphaned? I imagine that is especially difficult here."

"Orphaned?" Darpan seemed surprised.

"He told me he grew up in an orphanage." Margo grabbed the back of a chair to steady herself, the ground beneath her built on lies.

"Well, he did spend time in an orphanage. I'd be happy to provide you with a little more background. Maybe tonight."

"I'd like that." The changing story rattled her. She blamed her lack of preparation. She'd been so blinded by the money and the quick solution to repaying her aunt that she'd failed to prepare. The simple portrait had morphed into quicksand she longed to escape. As soon as Andrei returned, she'd take the final photos and get the hell out of here.

———

Engrossed in editing the shots she'd taken of Andrei, Margo started when she heard a knock on the door that afternoon. She looked up as Radmi entered.

"I was wondering what happened to you." Margo stood and picked up her camera, figuring the woman would want another lesson. "You went back to your village?"

"Yes, I needed to be gone for a couple of days."

As she neared, Margo spied the telltale sign of a bruise still colorful enough that heavy makeup couldn't completely obscure it. Evidence of light swelling ran across her cheekbone and up her temple.

"What happened?"

"Oh, it is nothing, just a little accident." Radmi's voice ran low, as if she feared being overhead.

Margo lowered her voice to match. "That is not an accident. I found plenty of those on my mother over the years."

"I am very sorry to hear that. Your father?"

"No." Margo shook her head, wishing she could shake away the thoughts. "Bad boyfriends. It's over now. She died. But you can't let people do this to you."

"I will be fine," Radmi said. "Please do not worry." She placed a hand on Margo's shoulder.

The gesture offered no comfort. "Did it happen here? Is that why you went away? It doesn't look new."

"This is not important." Radmi touched her cheekbone. "How are things going for you here? Is everything all right?"

Margo released a heavy sigh. "The tension in this place builds daily, although it's nice to have time without Andrei here. He seems excited about the photo shoots, but I'm afraid he's looking for more from me than just pretty pictures."

"That is a hazard that comes with the territory."

Margo caught Radmi's set jaw as she turned away. Not for the first time, she wondered why such a beautiful woman had agreed to work here as a glorified housekeeper. There might not be a lot of opportunities in the villages, but the bruise on her eye warned of significant dangers.

"Is that what happened to you?" Margo asked.

Radmi turned back to her. "Please, let's not discuss this. Would you show me more about the camera?"

Margo acquiesced, and Radmi visibly relaxed into learning about light and shutter speed and all the things so familiar they were more like breathing than breath itself. Margo lost herself for an hour and found joy in how quickly Radmi learned to frame shots.

"You'll be a good photographer someday. Keep practicing. If you ever make it to the States, get in touch with me. I know a few fashion photographers, but perhaps you could shoot on the side, even set up a little business. It's usually quite safe."

Radmi moved the camera from her face and looked into Margo's eyes. "Thank you. You are a good person."

It seemed a strange comment. But maybe here in a tucked-away castle with a power-hungry would-be king, kindness was rare. She hoped not, hoped this young woman would find a different situation. She hoped she would as well.

Each day, the walls of the castle closed a little more. Hardly noticeable at first, the compressed air had become thick with tension. Her imagination spun stories where she'd never escape but would be buried within these walls in a candy-colored dress.

Radmi held the camera out to her. "Are you okay?"

"I'm fine. Sometimes I just get the feeling that something bad will happen here, and I've unwittingly become a part of it."

"But you won't be here much longer, will you?"

"I hope not, just a few more photos." She had to keep telling herself that. Just a few more photos, a few more days.

Chapter 12

Andrei returned the following afternoon with a raft of military men dressed in green. They disappeared into the third floor, and when Margo learned they'd stay there for dinner, relief washed through her. She had hated the night Andrei had displayed his purchase in a lavender dress. She hoped to avoid a similar situation for the rest of her stay.

Instead, she had dinner in the salon with Darpan. With him, the world quieted, and her fear receded. They had meandering conversations about their childhoods. She wished she'd met his siblings and run wild in the jungles of central India as a child. He thought Aunt Joyce deserved a special place in heaven for not pinning her own desires on Margo, as would have happened if he'd had to go live with one of his aunties.

She still wanted to photograph him with an urge that embarrassed her. Now that she knew the electric touch of his fingers, the hot suede of his lips, she wanted to transform those feelings into art. He steadily refused to be her subject, but he opened to her in every other way possible.

"Radmi's back," Margo said, once Humphries had delivered their entrees and then retreated. "I gave her another photography lesson today. I wish I had a camera to leave her."

"That's fantastic. Maybe I can get her a camera the next time I order supplies."

"That would be amazing. She shows a lot of promise. How much longer do you think you'll be here?" They hadn't discussed who would leave first, and when. Margo hadn't wanted to talk about an impossible future. But after less than a week, she didn't want to give him up. He steadied her, didn't judge, gave her hope.

"I'm not sure. A few weeks. We're getting close."

"Where do you think you'll go next? Do you have a job lined up?" Maybe one where a photographer could tag along. She'd never say that, but every neuron in her body wanted to.

"I'm not sure what's next. I've got a couple of offers to consider. What about you? Where will you go?" His eyes peered into her like he could see into her soul.

"I don't know. I've been living on my friend's couch since the Italy disaster. I guess I'll go back there. She might not even be there. Her grandmother's birthday is coming up, and she planned to go to El Paso for a while."

"Have you thought about going back to visit your aunt?"

"No. Not at all. Why?"

"Since I've met you, I've probably thought more about family than in the last ten years."

"Why?" How could she, of all people, inspire anyone to think about family?

"I'm not sure the life I've been living can last forever," he said. "I don't usually consider things like this, but without this job, who am I? What do I have? I'm not sure I want a job to define the rest of my life, even one I'm passionate about."

"That's pretty deep." The air stilled around her. She had never considered stepping off her path. Even when that path was ripped away, she'd only thought of finding her way back. She defined herself by her art. "I don't think I can do anything else. I am the photos I take. It's the one thing I do well."

"I bet Radmi would say you're a good teacher. I bet you're good at lots of things."

"Teaching Radmi was nothing. I just transferred a little knowledge. And I'm not good at lots of things. I've wanted to be a famous photographer from my earliest memories."

"Famous? Like your father?"

"Yeah. It sounds silly, but I wanted to follow in his footsteps." The drive that once filled her chest had been pierced by a room full of photos. She wanted to think about anything other than the crazy reason Andrei chose her to photograph him. He seemed to be looking for her to rebuild respect for his country. And he seemed to blame her father for the state of the country since the last dictator's fall. His bizarre desire to blame her father for showing the truth touched the edges of sanity. It made her fear Andrei.

"Do you ever think about having your own family?" Darpan asked. He didn't meet her eyes directly, as if he knew he asked for a truth that might destroy whatever they'd built.

"I've thought about it. It's not likely." Margo picked up a water glass, and her trembling hand sent a small wave over the side. She set it back on the table. "I loved my mother, but she was broken. I think she loved my dad too hard, wrapped up everything she thought she was in him. When he died, she tried to recover that love in every jerk who asked her on a date. It was horrible to watch."

"Why on earth do you think you'd be the same? You are strong. You have built a career, figured out how to get your life back when it was stolen from you. I'm quite impressed."

"That's not the woman I see in the mirror. I've chased stardom, not a single love." The ridiculous statement embarrassed her. She looked across the table at Darpan, his unruly hair, quiet demeanor, and the light shining out of his dark eyes. Suddenly, she understood. The hundred suns she'd searched for could be found in one person. "At least, until now."

"Excuse me," Humphries stood at the door. "Mr. Yadav, President Andropov requests your presence on the third floor."

"Of course," said Darpan. "Ms. McAllister, nice to see you again." He left the room without looking back at her.

Her heart left the room with him. Lost in a quagmire, her mind tried to figure out what was next. The fairytale had thrown her life into chaos, rewritten the happy ending. Had Darpan opened a door to something more, something she'd never wanted? Her desire shifted the world into a different dimension. A world where love was possible.

———

Pounding pulled her from sleep. "Margo, Margo, wake up." Andrei's voice yelled through the wooden door. He tried the handle, but she'd locked it. And put a chair in front of it.

"Margo, I want to see you. It is time." The slur of alcohol ran through his voice.

She sat up in the bed, hiding her body with the duvet, as if he could see through the door. "Andrei, we have a photo shoot first thing in the morning. If you want me to do a good job, and if you want to look good in the pictures, you need to go to bed now."

"Margo. Why do you make me wait?"

"The photos, Andrei. The photos are important."

"Tomorrow then."

Heavy footsteps walked away. She buried herself under her covers and trembled with fear. She had to get away.

———

The next morning, twelve government leaders flanked Andrei on the steps of the castle. Exhausted, Margo had hardly slept after Andrei's late-night visit. She hated vulnerability, but it lodged itself under her skin anyway.

Photographing them made her angry. Navy uniforms, chests full of medals. She would never love any of this. Yet they would use her photos to bully their neighbors and to project an image of success. And power. And she would help them, a mere pawn in a game she couldn't influence. She wished she could find a way to manipulate the photos and tell the world to beware.

If only she could embed an SOS in every pixel. She needed saving, and she needed to save others. She just had to find a way to hold him off one more night, maybe two. After that, she'd be done. He'd have no reason to keep her here, and she would leave, forget this sorry part of her life. Except, of course, for Darpan.

The men on the other side of the camera looked stern. They put swords on their outfits and took them off. She arranged them wide and then again deep. Always with Andrei front and center. He looked the same as ever, no worse for drink and a late-night visit.

Her rage grew. She had fallen in love with her subjects before. Today she experienced falling in hate. She captured his arrogance, the bully buried beneath a smooth veneer. His pride radiated through the lens, imprinting on her mind. It would be in the photos, and he would love them. She prayed, then, to the god of everything good and everything evil. She prayed the images wouldn't betray her and turn her hate into something others could love.

Finally, the sun rose high enough to cast stark shadows. She stopped. Stopped documenting the story this man made up and fully believed. Stopped taking photos that furthered the lie that he deserved respect. Darpan had warned her about his lust for power. The power Andrei craved ranged from global to extremely personal. Anger burned through her.

"Margo," Andrei said walking toward her. "You will come to my room this afternoon and show me the photos."

"That's not how this works." Flames licked her words. If only she could make them real and burn him to the ground. "I have taken hundreds of shots. It will take me all day and into the night to find the right images and edit them properly. If you want great photos, you must let me do my job."

An eyebrow arched over his cold blue eye. She faced him, immobile. She had many reasons not to want to spend time with him, but she clung the hardest to not letting him tell her how to do her job. Whatever it took.

"Tomorrow then." His voice was low and coated with steel.

"Yes. We shoot the drone photos at dawn, correct?" She reined back the anger. She had a day's reprieve.

"Yes, the uniform will be delivered today, and I believe Darpan has finished the drone. Until then." He gave her a curt nod, then turned on his heel to face his men.

Margo kept her head down while putting her equipment away. Her emotions threatened to incinerate her, and frankly, if she had to stay here much longer, she'd welcome it.

Margo asked Radmi to bring her meals to her room. All day she looked through photos, pulled out the best ones, enhanced them. She had over sixty images to show Andrei, and she thought he would love him. It disgusted her. But at least she'd finish soon.

Eventually, she heard the clinks of cutlery and overlapping voices that signaled dinner service. She'd finished the photos, but nothing would have made her join the shark-infested waters of the salon. Footsteps approached, and she heard a light knock at the door.

"Margo, I have your dinner." Radmi's voice whispered through the door.

Margo removed the chair from the door and invited her in. Radmi swept through the room carrying a tray and set it on a small table.

"How are you?" Radmi asked. "I'm worried about you in here."

"It's okay. I needed to finish the photos. The sooner I can leave here, the better. Tomorrow is the last photo shoot. I need to get home." Margo wished she could slip away now, not have to face Andrei again. "I am afraid of what Andrei wants from me."

"Are you ready to go when the time comes? Do you have your passport someplace safe?"

"Yes, of course. It's in my camera bag. Who do I need to tell that I want to go? My ticket is open-ended."

"You must talk to Andrei. It is the only way."

"The only way forward is through. Great." It's not like a housekeeper could help her. She sighed. "I'm photographing him again first thing tomorrow and then reviewing photos with him tomorrow afternoon. How quickly can I get out of here if we wrap up tomorrow?"

"It just depends. Flights leave the capital every day. I'm sorry, I wish I knew how to help you. You seem so much more tense than when you arrived."

"I apologize. I shouldn't burden you with this. By the way, is Darpan at the dinner tonight?" She hadn't wanted to ask but couldn't stop herself. The cautionary look on Radmi's face told her she should have left the words unspoken.

"He is. You should be careful with that one."

"Oh, he's just a friend. It's nice to have someone to talk to." She waved away the importance of her question with a gesture.

"I'll leave you now." Radmi breezed out of the room, leaving Margo with her thoughts.

She moved the chair back under the door handle, locking herself in her fancy prison. She wished she could get word to Darpan since she wouldn't see him in the morning.

Finally, she had nothing to do but sleep. She woke constantly, every sound a threat. She had double-checked her passport after Radmi's comment, repeatedly made sure she'd secured the door, did everything she could think of, but nothing made her safe.

She worried about leaving. He wanted more than photography, but that wouldn't happen. She hated bullies, men who thought they had the right to everything they desired. He wanted her, when he had towns full of women. He wanted the world's respect but didn't want to earn it by being respectful.

She'd have to talk her way out of this one. Perhaps she could convince him the photos needed to be printed, and no place had better print shops than New York. She'd tell him she had another job.

She woke long before dawn and retrieved her computer. Her cell phone had been useless here, leaving her disconnected from her friends. Occasionally, when Andrei was at the castle, she had Wi-Fi. She checked and found it working.

She emailed Liliana and told her she only had a day or two left on the job and hoped to be back in New York soon. She wanted to spill her guts about her fears and her growing desperation but worried her message would be intercepted. She couldn't wait for the day when she sat on Liliana's green couch and told her about Darpan, who seemed so much like her, even though their backgrounds couldn't be further apart.

If she got back, when she got back, different forces would drive her. Here, she'd become friends with fear, opened to love, glimpsed depravity. She'd worry about different things moving forward. Her life needed to mean more than documenting the world. She needed to act.

She wanted to promise someone, maybe Liliana, maybe Aunt Joyce, maybe herself, that she had learned something from this experience. Her path to wherever she thought she'd been headed seemed both selfish and trite. Real good and actual evil existed in this world. And through her photos, she needed to tell the truth so people could make good decisions. This is what her father had done. He didn't photograph for fame or love, he tried to show the world to itself, so people understood the repercussions of war. Why hadn't she realized this before?

She had to tell Darpan what she had discovered. This was bigger than both of them. This was how you were supposed to exist in the world. Always be part of the solution. Work to make the world a better place. Her gut told her Darpan already understood, but perhaps, like her, he was afraid to act on what was right. Why else would he work for someone like Andrei? The world needed their skills.

She looked at the clock. Five thirty. She had no idea what time he got to the tent, but he'd always been there when she'd arrived. Any sane person would be asleep right now. But she had to try. In one hour, she'd set up for Andrei's final photos. With the best of luck, she'd head to the airport that evening, without time to say goodbye to Darpan. Without luck, she'd stay longer. And Andrei would become a much greater danger.

She slid into her clothes and as quietly as possible left her room and snuck out of the house. The brisk air outside filled her lungs with hope. The last twenty hours locked in her room had done the opposite. She needed to remember this, needed to make sure she acted instead of hid when the time came.

She crossed the field under a starry sky, much like the night Darpan first showed her the tower. How had she become so entrapped in such a short time?

"Darpan," she called as she neared the tent. The zippered opening was undone. She pulled it back to see the closed door behind it. He must be at the castle, deep in sleep. She knocked softly anyway. "Darpan, it's me, Margo."

"Just a minute." Seconds later he opened the door. His rumpled hair and squinting eyes told her she'd woken him.

She wondered why he'd slept in the tent. "I'm sorry for coming so early. I wasn't sure I'd get to see you again."

"Please, come in." He shut the door behind her, then turned on a light. "It's great to see you. I was hoping to see you at dinner last night."

"I couldn't go. Things with Andrei, well, they aren't going well. I'm hoping to leave very soon. We've only got one more shoot, this morning."

"Ah, yes. The drone shot. Do you remember the etching I showed you in the titanium band that wraps around the drone? If you can get a shot of that, it would be amazing."

"Of the etching?"

"Yes. If you can. And I hope you're right and you get to leave soon. It's getting dangerous here. He's moving closer to war."

"Believe me, I feel the danger. You have no idea. I'm scared to death."

He hugged her then. Wrapped his arms around her and absorbed her swirling fear into himself. She closed her eyes, focused on his breath, and matched hers to its slow pace. She became solid again.

"Thank you," she said, pulling back from him.

"I do not know what the next few days hold, but you are right. If he starts a war, departing the country will become difficult. Do whatever you can to leave as soon as possible."

"I hope I will see you again someday." Sadness and hope combined in a single comment.

"You will. I promise. I don't know where or when. But sometime. After all of this." He swung his hand around the tent.

"I've been thinking. Well, actually, I've been holed up in my room working, furiously scared or frighteningly angry. Both, I think. I may not have a big role to play in whatever this king-killer has planned, but I am enabling him. You are too. We are better than this. We need to use our talents for good."

"Indeed." He let out a chuckle. "I couldn't agree with you more. Let's meet on the other side and work on that."

She met his smile with her own. For the first time since she'd woken up in a trashed hotel room in Italy, her future held light. She might still have a tunnel to get through to reach it, but it existed.

"I would love for you to stay, but you can't be seen here. Last night at dinner, Andropov commented about us being together."

A shudder went through her. "What did he say?"

"It's not important, just a little ribbing. But we don't need to give him a reason to doubt us. Not when we're so close to the end."

She said goodbye, then walked back into the cold morning, keeping to the tree line now that she had to worry about being seen. Twelve hours. Maybe twenty-four. Just make it until then.

Chapter 13

Andrei stood before Margo, palming a drone the size of a sourdough loaf. He stared at it like a lover. He wore his ridiculous uniform with pride. A dark pilot's jumpsuit covered him, its metal zippers and bands the same dripping onyx color as the drone's band. The band with the etchings.

The exhaustion of almost no sleep made her better. Everything else she might have thought about—the weather, Darpan, whether she'd survive the night without being raped—disappeared. The world narrowed to angles, light, and color.

"Let me check the light," she said and took a reading near the drone. "Now some practice shots. Rotate the drone toward the ground and then up so I can see how it photographs best."

Andrei followed her directions, and she shot and shot and shot. She clicked back through the photos. The light needed to crest the far ridge to give her glint on metal. "We need a couple more minutes. Maybe a little powder?"

Each time she'd photographed Andrei, an audience had accompanied them. This morning only Andrei and Radmi joined her on the field. Radmi carried a case with makeup, hairspray, several pairs of sunglasses, and a thermos of coffee. She attended to Andrei while Margo looked through the photos again. When she enlarged the photo, she could just make out the etching, sometimes. The strange hieroglyphic enthralled her. She hadn't asked what it meant, but for Darpan, she'd try to get it in the shot.

She looked to the far side of the valley where a yellow glow brightened the gray sky against a knife blade of mountain. "It's time."

She focused her energy on the lens. She gave Andrei direction after direction on the drone. He held it different ways, knelt by it on the ground, looked serious, happy, triumphant. He switched from gaming glasses to aviators to his cold blue eyes. She saw the joy there, like a kid at Christmas who was about to use his new toy to kill the neighbor's cat.

And all the while, like a third eye, a sliver of her consciousness focused on the drone's band.

She moved Andrei across the field, from dark uniform and drone with a black cliff background, only his blond hair glowing in the rising sun, to a background of forest, and finally, to the pool with its multicolored tiles.

She loved the strange beauty of the colors contrasting with the futuristic, insect-like architecture of the drone's exoskeleton. And the sheer confidence with which Andrei peered at the drone and surveyed his kingdom. It was beautiful, in the frighteningly deadly way that megalomaniacs stared at their prey. It was as if she'd entered a new dimension, one that before had only existed in Ursula le Guin novels or the depths of the human imagination.

She clicked the shutter button over and over. Andrei set the drone on the ground and took the controls from Radmi. He made the device rise, then hover. He spun it around him, then shot it straight up into the air until its noise disappeared and the drone itself became a mere speck in the sky.

He returned it to eye level, the sun glinting perfectly off titanium. Then slowly, he maneuvered it directly toward her. She clicked the shutter, capturing the drone in perfect focus and Andrei behind, a bit blurred, like a monster or a ghost. Then she switched focus, the drone an approaching mass and Andrei sharp and clear, enraptured with his power. And she understood that he loved himself more than anyone else ever could.

He'd had no one to love him, so he'd built his own world in the shape of himself. He had an entire country take on his identity. He made up for every loss, every grief, every sin, with ambition, power, and glory he created from whole cloth, a world anew. And it was beautiful, and terrifying, and in that moment of understanding, his power awed her. And she captured it.

"I got it," she yelled. "That's a wrap."

Yet still the drone closed in. It darted in at her, just inches from her face, then backed away.

"Hey, knock it off," she yelled over the machine's incessant noise.

It dove at her again, its wind kicking up her hair. It backed off, then rose, circling above her head. "If I drop this camera, your photos are ruined!" she screamed.

Andrei flew the drone out over the valley. He had a broad smile on his lips. "I am surprised. I thought you were stronger than that."

"I'm a photographer. I don't ever want to be attacked while holding my camera." So much rage filled her. She barely contained it. This bastard.

"Keep taking photos. I will show you something really spectacular now." He worked the controls, and Margo heard the drone getting closer.

"Both of you, come with me." He walked them into the field toward Darpan's tent until they were thirty yards from the pool. "Keep photographing the drone. Don't stop."

Margo turned her camera on the device. "If you want me to capture it, you need to go slower, or I need a different lens."

He slowed the drone. Its engine whined as it made its way back to them. Margo captured it with blue sky behind it, then it came lower and swung in front of the castle, far enough away that its whine just whispered on the wind. Menacing. It practically wrote the word in the air as it flew past.

Andrei brought it toward them again and made the machine hover over the iridescent pool, ten feet above the water. It rose straight up, twenty feet, thirty, forty. Margo dutifully took photos, wondering when the game would finally bore him. She'd tired of it long ago.

She heard a loud beep come from the controls, then faster than she could follow, something dropped from the drone.

The pool exploded in a blast of water that sent tile and concrete through the air. Margo fell to the ground and turned her back to the blast while curling around her camera. Someone screamed. It might have been her. Someone laughed. Andrei. She stayed in a tight ball, the camera its center.

"Take photos." Andrei's demanding voice made it past the ringing in her ears. "Turn around look at this. Take photos."

"What the fuck!" Margo turned on him. "What the hell do you think you're doing? You tried to kill us."

"No." He laughed, an eerie, taunting sound. "I wanted to show you the power of the drone." His smile cracked his whole face in two.

Andrei still had the controls in his hand and brought the drone close.

"Get that fucking thing away from me." Margo looked around for someone sane, someone who could convince Andrei to keep the bomb-laden machine far from her.

Radmi stood nearby, seemingly unfazed by the explosion. Margo shook her head at the woman. Radmi merely raised an eyebrow and almost imperceptibly shrugged her shoulders. Darpan emerged from his tent and walked toward them.

She turned back toward Andrei who had the drone in front of him, just a couple of feet off the ground. She hoped another bomb would explode at that moment. It'd be worth whatever injuries she sustained to get rid of this asshole.

The drone landed and went silent. Margo hardly breathed as Andrei leaned over and lifted it up. He looked at her, his face growing serious. "Are you still afraid?" he asked. "Everything is fine."

"How the hell do I know that? You could blow something else up right now. You're crazy."

Margo watched his face transform into something ugly. "Do not ever say that again, or you will see something else blow up. I am only showing you the capability of our military. That is part of what you are here to document."

Darpan joined them near the drone. Andrei turned toward him. "You can go now. Take the drone with you. Margo, photograph the damage, then meet me inside." He turned to Radmi. "Let's go." Then he strode toward the castle.

Margo's hands shook as she brought the camera to her face. One look through the viewfinder and she realized she needed to clean the lens. Miraculously, it wasn't scratched. She lifted fingers to her throbbing temple. They came away bloody. She wiped her temple with a sleeve. There wasn't much blood, but she'd been nicked near her hairline.

She looked over at Darpan as he bent toward the drone. "Be careful with that thing," she said.

"He deployed the only bomb. I'm really sorry about that. I had no idea that's what he wanted to do."

Margo just shook her head and walked to the pit where the beautiful pool used to be and started photographing. This job wasn't worth any amount of money. She'd keep her priorities straight in the future.

She finished and gathered her dust-encrusted gear. The walk to the castle reminded her of making it to the next stage of a video game. She may have made it through one tier, but several stages remained before she'd win. And she'd never been much of a gamer.

She climbed the stairs. Humphries opened the door before she reached it. That didn't bode well.

"President Andropov is waiting for you in the reading room," Humphries said. "Follow me."

She had considered the reading room for a photo, but its blood-red walls would have been the focal point of any shot. Andrei sat on a cordovan leather sofa, eating a plate of sliced sausages and hard-boiled eggs. Margo's stomach clenched.

"Sit." He gestured toward the other end of the sofa.

Margo perched on the edge. Dust iced her turtleneck, vest, and leggings. Probably her face as well. He had shed his uniform for clean slacks and a turtleneck. He took a long sip of coffee but offered her nothing.

"When will you finish editing today's photos?"

"I'd prefer to return home and finish the editing in New York."

He chuckled. "That is not our deal. Can you get me the photos by today?"

"It might be possible, but I'll need to cull then edit them. It's a long job."

He looked at his watch. "It is not even eight o'clock. Can you have them to me by four?"

"If I get them to you by four, can I leave tonight?"

"Certainly not. There is a gala here tonight, and I want you at my table as my guest."

"I am here as a professional photographer. I have no other duty to you."

"Margo, Margo. I think you misunderstand the terms of our agreement. While you are here, you will do the things I need you to do. You will be at the dinner tonight. There is a new dress waiting in your room. Gold, my favorite color. After that, we'll see." He crossed his legs and poured more coffee into his cup, adding sugar, then stirring before sitting back to look at her.

Margo looked him in the eye and summoned every ounce of courage she had. "And if I refuse?"

"I do not think you understand the power balance here. I will get what I want whether you are willing or not. Like in Italy."

Dread roiled in her gut. "What do you mean?" But she knew. Like rotating the lens to zoom in on a shot, everything fell into focus. "Those were your guys who destroyed the room." A foggy memory from that night recalled the man who picked her up at the airport.

"Of course. And your little friend, the photographer, was only too happy to be paid off to spike your drink."

Disappointment, disgust, and fear pumped through her veins, leaving her half sick and cold as ice. "How much did you pay him?"

"Not nearly as much as I'm paying you."

"Why? Why me?"

"The photos your father took harmed my country. They set us back decades. You will do the opposite."

"My father?" It didn't make sense. They were just war photos. They showed the truth.

"Your father came here during a period of civil unrest. The president wanted to bring the country together. Your father undermined that by showing necessary actions that he claimed were brutality. People believed him. After the world saw those photos, spies who had infiltrated our country caused the people to rise up. They took the president hostage and executed him in the main square at dawn. Your father documented that, won awards for it, and trashed our country in the process. He never paid for the harm he caused."

Andrei leaned forward on the couch until his leg touched hers. She wanted to flee. She froze instead.

"Our country fell into darkness, and it has taken decades to recover. Your bloodline has much to atone for." Andrei's voice resonated with emotion, and his eyes bored into her, the lust replaced by hate.

She couldn't speak and pressed her hands into her sides to hide the tremor that shook her body. She'd stumbled into a trap, and the steel jaws had snapped shut.

"Return here at four, and the photos better be done. Dinner is at seven. We are done here."

She had no bold response. He would do anything to get what he wanted. She was a pawn, and he'd just run the board.

———

The photos were good. Too good. She could hardly remove her eyes from the one where the drone approached her, a blurred, menacing mass, while Andrei stood in the background, controls in hand, basking in her defeat. He would love the photo, and the world needed to see it.

How could he have flown that drone at her, hovered it inches from her, when he knew it had a bomb? The thought caused bile to rise in her throat.

She hated war, had never been as terrified as when embedded with a US Army division in Afghanistan. At least until now. As much as she wanted to follow in her father's footsteps, she didn't have the stomach for gore.

But Kirk did. A cub photographer along with her on that trip, he reveled in war. Perhaps it was the machismo band-of-brothers thing that she never really understood. Perhaps she couldn't find beauty in a war zone bereft of love.

Kirk quickly became the dashing center of attention in the horrible place. When he befriended her, she'd been grateful. She felt safer just being near him, as if he repelled the ugliness of war.

They both lived in New York, met up occasionally, became friends, she thought. Soon they became more than friends, but never anything permanent. They slept together, took a few trips together, often ended up in each other's beds when they happened to be in the same locale. Beyond Liliana, she probably would have counted him as her closest friend, all the while knowing he wouldn't have done the same.

But for him to have taken money to drug her and let others ruin her life, all while he stood to gain professionally, was a far leap beyond what she could have imagined from him. How could she be so naïve?

Everything she'd thought of as bedrock had crumbled. Her career, her so-called friendship with Kirk, her safety. When she looked back at her life, it seemed so ridiculous. Her quest for fame was as useless as her mother's quest for love. Except for the photographs. She had created beauty.

And now, she used her lone gift to promote a man who didn't deserve it. A dam inside her cracked. The trickle of hate that had always pushed her to be better, to chase her father's glory, gain her mother's love, became a torrent. It spilled its blackness through every cell in her body, filling her with self-loathing.

She deserved whatever punishment Andrei meted out today. Yes, drugging her in Italy was unfair, but what had she been doing with her life, anyway? She'd chased fame and landed infamy. Wanted adulation and earned self-disgust. Poor lonely little girl. Her father died before she was born and owed her nothing. Her mother preferred the love of drunks and abusers to the daughter standing at her feet. And her mother was dead. There was no redemption.

Margo wiped the tears from her eyes and tried to leave the past behind. She saved her favorite edited photos to a file on her laptop. She quickly saved that file onto the SD card that had been in her camera then removed it from the computer and slipped it into a drawer. She'd decide whether to reformat the card some other time. She didn't want to be late meeting Andrei and give him another reason to punish her instead of letting her go. Then she closed her computer and went to him.

His earlier animosity had vanished. They spent the next hour going through photos. He loved them even more than she thought he would. He never tired of looking at himself.

Margo mostly sat there, letting him revel in his own image. Occasionally she pointed out a particular feature or told him which photo she preferred when asked. Otherwise, she counted the seconds as they slowly ticked away.

"You have done well. Excellent. Thank you for these." Andrei closed the laptop and slid it under his arm.

"I need the laptop back. How would you like me to get you the photos?"

"I will keep the laptop. I've asked Humphries to remove your camera from your room as well." Andrei's arched eyebrow and smug voice challenged her to confront him.

"My camera? You don't need my camera. That's not how this works." Her mind flew to the new SD card she'd installed on the device and the one with Andrei's photos in a desk drawer. Why did he think he needed to confiscate all the photos?

"I have paid you enough to purchase another camera. Now, go put on your dress and get ready for the party."

"No." Fuck him.

His hand snaked toward her so fast she didn't have time to pull back. The slap on her jaw slammed her teeth together in a pain that pulsed straight through her brain. She tried to stand and leave, but he grabbed her by the wrist and yanked her back to the sofa.

"When will you understand that you must do everything I ask? I have told you there are consequences for disobeying me." He pressed a button on his phone. "Humphries, please come escort Miss McAllister back to her room."

Soon Humphries walked by her side, deep inside her personal space, all the way back to her room. If she tried to run, he would grab her halfway through her first step.

"Dinner is at seven," he said when they arrived at her door.

"I want my camera back." Margo spat the words at him.

"I am afraid that is impossible." He opened the door for her, and she stepped inside.

All of her camera equipment was gone. The camera bag with her passport hidden in its sleeve, the camera itself, even her tripod had vanished. She turned to complain just as the door swung closed. She heard a lock click—the handle, not the deadbolt which she could lock from the inside. Ice crawled through her veins. She'd just become a prisoner in a castle.

She looked through the room, taking inventory. Only her camera gear was gone. Of course, that represented thousands of dollars. She didn't want new equipment. She wanted the things she'd collected over the years. The equipment that worked best for her. She opened the desk drawer and saw the drive she'd removed earlier. It had all the photos she'd shown Andrei. It was proof she'd been here. She looked for a place to hide it and ended up slipping under the insole of her sneakers. It might not be valuable, but it was one thing she had left.

She did not want to attend the party. Her only hope was perhaps Darpan or Radmi could find some way to help her. She showered and donned the skimpy gold dress. Gaudy. She prayed Radmi would come help her with her hair and makeup like the last time. At six forty-five, she got herself ready. The door unlocked at seven sharp. Humphries.

She straightened her back, raised her chin, and followed him out the door. The night ahead might be terrifying, but she wouldn't show her fear.

The classical music contrasted with the rage and hate coursing through her. Heavy metal would have been more appropriate. The twinkle lights sparkled sweetly where black would have matched her mood. It should look, feel, and sound like the setting for a battle.

Andrei spied her from across the room and motioned her over. He stood among a group of men, most of whom Margo recognized from an earlier photo shoot. The cool room sent prickles across her skin, as did the stares from the men as she walked toward them. Andrei wore a perfectly cut tuxedo, the others military uniforms. She felt naked in comparison and on display.

Andrei retrieved two glasses of champagne from a tray. He handed one to Margo and raised the other toward her, saying something in his language that she didn't understand. The men laughed.

He fixed his eyes to hers, demanding a response. Her arm rose, clinked her crystal to his. She kept a piece of her scared and tired mind back from the party but let her body be there. It smiled, brought the champagne to her lips, let it tickle her nose. She did not drink but swallowed as if she had.

She stood by Andrei's side, his hand occasionally falling to the skin on her back left open by the plunging dress. She stiffened each time, but he didn't seem to notice. His focus remained on whoever these men were. They spoke excitedly, and a frenetic energy bounced around the room.

Margo surveyed the party. Middle-aged men predominated, and there had to be at least fifty of them. She only saw a few women, all of them young and beautiful. They tended to cling close to one man. Her stomach turned as she realized they'd think the same of her and Andrei.

She did not see Darpan in the crowd. She looked again and again. Margo glimpsed Radmi when she'd arrived, but no Darpan. Just a glance at his strong jaw and intense eyes would have calmed her.

Andrei leaned in close, his lips almost touching her ear. "Your boyfriend isn't here. I sent him away."

She became stone, unwilling to feel anything, to let any emotion betray her. Andrei turned his chin to her, stared directly into her eyes. She kept them blank, as if drugged.

"I know about your indiscretion. How you visited him in the mornings. I hope you said goodbye because you will not see him again." Still holding her chin, he placed a hard kiss on her lips. She wanted to retch.

He turned back to the crowd, said something loud she didn't understand. She prayed it wasn't about her. She just had to survive this night and figure out how to get the hell out of this nightmare.

His words weren't about her. He turned and raised his glass toward the stairs, and every other person in the room began clapping. A line of young women, many of them had to be teenagers, descended. A pink dress, yellow, cobalt blue. The girls had hot-iron curled hair and lots of glittery makeup. It made them appear younger instead of sophisticated.

Radmi followed them down the stairs. Margo stared at her, hoping to see guilt on her face. She had prepared these young women for the coming slaughter. But Radmi's face was steel, no trace of emotion.

Could this evening get any worse? A cold ball in the pit of her stomach reminded her that it could, indeed, get very, very much worse. She wanted to down her champagne, then another and another until she ceased to feel, to know, to understand. But some morsel of self-preservation kept her sober.

Andrei made her sit beside him at dinner. She pushed the food around on her plate, unwilling to eat or drink. He could so easily have had someone drug her. He'd done it before. She looked at Radmi, refilling waters, and wondered if she'd participate in drugging Margo. Probably. God knows what she did to those girls.

"You must eat," Andrei said, leaning toward her. "Do not be afraid."

"What do you do with those girls?" Margo couldn't keep the accusation from her voice.

He smiled a wide grin. "Tonight, nothing. Tonight, I have you. You cannot tell me you are not in love with me. I will not believe it. I saw the photos you took, and they are magnificent. Now the world will understand what a great and benevolent leader I am."

Margo closed her eyes, each of his words more ridiculous and threatening than the last. She couldn't stay here but didn't know how to escape.

Andrei took a finger and touched her behind her ear. He slowly ran the finger down her neck, over her shoulder and down the length of her back. His entire hand curved around her hip and traveled down her thigh. He squeezed her knee, then his hand started the inward journey back up her thigh.

Margo snapped her legs together. This could not happen.

He laughed, long and easy and evil. "You will be mine tonight. Eat. Drink. You will need the energy."

Margo sat at the table, forcing herself to take one breath after another. No one would save her. Darpan was gone. Radmi. She didn't want to think of Radmi's sins. She looked around the tables. The young women didn't seem distressed. In fact, they seemed to enjoy their glasses of champagne and plates of meat. Her stomach cramped hard at the thought.

"Are you okay?" Andrei asked.

"Yes, perfectly. I just need to excuse myself for a moment." She started to get up, then turned to Andrei. "If I give you everything you want tonight, may I go home tomorrow?"

"Perhaps. If you are really, really good. Convince me you love me the way your photos tell me you do."

"Okay. That's a deal." She rose from the table. "I'll be right back."

Margo strode across the ballroom packed with tables with her head held high. She refused to look Radmi in the eye as she passed. Hopefully, she would never see that woman again. She slipped out the door, then trotted to her room. She would not spend one more second in this perverse, haunted castle.

Chapter 14

The moment Margo turned into the hallway, she dashed for her room. As quickly as possible, she slipped off her dress and pulled on leggings and a jacket, trading her heels for sneakers. She grabbed her wallet but left her phone. She didn't understand how tracking worked and didn't want to take any chances.

Heart thrashing, she opened the door and peered down the hallway. Seeing no one, she jogged to the side door and snuck out. She kept to the woods near the cliff, bypassing the open meadow. Once she passed Darpan's tent, she entered the haunted wood, praying she didn't trip over some artifact or knock herself out on something nailed into a tree. Finally, she turned toward the bridge.

The forest thinned, then disappeared, and she ran toward the bridge, hoping no one would see her in the moonlight. All these days with no moon, and now suddenly it lit her path and made her an easy target.

She sped across the bridge, her footsteps thundering in a sound that must have filled the valley. Then she scrambled up the rocky path on the far side and ducked into the forest again. She stopped, her ragged breath tearing through her. She glanced back at the path behind her and could see all the way to the brightly lit castle. No one followed. Yet.

A small flame of hope came to life. So many things ahead could put it out. She didn't know where she was going, whether anyone in the small village at the bottom of the valley would help her, or if they would just deliver her to Andrei once again. But for now, she had escaped. Freedom tasted like pine needles and cold air, and she loved it.

She wanted to run as fast as possible, but the forest path, dark during the day, had turned black. She made her way as quickly as possible, often stumbling over roots and stones. It seemed like hours before the forest parted, and she entered the small meadow where she'd seen the deer.

She crossed, then stood for a moment at the trailhead that led to the valley. Even with the help of the moon, the treacherous path seemed impossible. But going back meant a fate worse than falling from a mountain. She stepped forward and immediately slipped on the loose rocks. It didn't matter. *Just keep moving.*

She picked her way down the precarious trail. Every sound turned into someone about to capture her. Every slip of the foot taunted death. But she kept going, sometimes pressing her hands against the mountain when the trail became too steep to navigate on just her feet.

Her breath heaved onto the stones with each slow step. How many hours had passed since she left the castle? They had to know she'd escaped. She imagined Andrei, enraged. He'd have people looking for her. Heck, he had a whole roomful of people at his command. She wouldn't let her thoughts go further down that path. She had to keep her feet on the one beneath her. Just one step after another.

Eventually, after a journey so long she couldn't believe the sky remained dark, the track flattened out. Soon, she was back among the trees. She crossed a small creek, the icy water soaking her shoes. Then the trail rose to a road.

She almost ran into the car parked at the trailhead. She jerked to stop as the car door opened, then turned to scramble back down the dirt. Escape blared in her ears, urging her to run, but she tripped and fell.

"Margo, it's me." Radmi's voice filled the night.

No. She wouldn't go back. She refused to become one of the girls Radmi dressed and painted to be taken advantage of by a roomful of men. If only the ground would open and swallow her. She rose, prepared to run.

"I'm here to help you escape. Hurry. We don't have much time."

Margo paused, unsure whether to run toward Radmi or back into the forest. "But the girls. You work for him."

"Please, I'll explain in the car. I'm your only chance, but we have to hurry."

It was torture choosing Radmi. She might be driven right back to the castle. To the hell that awaited there. But hiding in the forest only prolonged that destiny, especially since Radmi knew her location. How easy it would be to bring the others to her. She stood and walked toward the car.

Radmi drove without headlights. Or heat. For the first time, the night's chill sunk into Margo's skin. Her rock-scratched hands stung, and her feet and much-twisted ankles ached.

"We will try to keep you safe and get you out of the country this morning." Radmi's voice had aged, and tension crackled through it.

"How can you get me out?"

"You'll have to trust me, and I won't answer your questions. The less you know, the better for both of us." Radmi paused and sighed heavily.

"You said you'd explain." If she didn't understand, how could she trust?

Tension radiated off Radmi. Still, she seemed calm and determined, as far from the curious housekeeper as Margo could imagine. "You're not a maid."

"Technically, I am employed by Andrei as an attendant. You need to focus on yourself, not on me. Andrei may send people after you. If you get out of Tiranistan, find a place to hide where no one knows you. Do not go to friends or family for help. You may endanger them."

"So, just disappear? For how long? How do I live?" The implications ran through her head. No money, no support. Not that she had a lot of friends. Or family.

"Margo, if we succeed, you live." Radmi took her eyes off the road just for a moment and glanced at Margo as if to drive the point home.

The words sank in. To survive, she'd have to give up everything. Dreams of fame and adulation. Liliana, her best friend. Any hope of working for the magazine. Her aunt pushed her way into her thoughts. Margo should have been nicer, should have stayed in touch. Now her aunt would lose her and never know why.

The drive continued through the black night. Radmi steered carefully around mountainous bends. It gave Margo time to think.

She'd lose photography, the one thing she did well. She could still take pictures, maybe become a wedding photographer under an assumed name. But that had never been her dream. She closed her eyes. She'd sort all that out later. Now she needed to concentrate on escaping.

Radmi had warned her not to ask, but Margo wanted to understand. "Why are you helping me?" After all, Radmi worked for Andrei and had some kind of weird relationship with him. Margo had wondered if they were lovers.

"I will not answer your questions."

"About the girls. What's going on there, and why do you help with that?" Margo bit the hand that might free her, but she had to know.

"I have a job to do." A stated fact without emotion.

"But those men, I don't even want to imagine what they do to those girls. It makes me think of sex trafficking."

"Those women volunteer to come to the castle, to get dressed up and . . ." She stopped speaking for long seconds. "Sometimes, there are more important objectives."

"What does that mean? What could possibly be more important than the lives of those girls?"

"War. People dying. A cruel dictator governing even more of the world. Tiranistan may well become a flash point for the next world war. There are many things more important than protecting a few stupid women who should have stayed in their villages." Radmi shook her head, her voice filled with regret.

Margo finally put the pieces together. Radmi's mastery of English rivaled her own. She wasn't a housekeeper wanting to make her way to the US to become a famous model. That was her cover. How could she have been so naïve? She'd thought Darpan had perhaps been a spy, but never Radmi. She'd perfected the village girl persona.

As Margo's thoughts spun to Darpan, she couldn't help the next question. "Andrei said he'd sent Darpan away. Do you know what happened to him?"

"I'm sure Darpan can take care of himself." Rancor laced Radmi's voice, stoking Margo's curiosity about their relationship. Then Radmi sighed. "I know you had a special relationship with him, and I don't know where he is. I'm sorry."

"It's fine. Thank you for rescuing me."

"You are not safe yet. You may not be safe for a long time."

They'd driven far down the valley when Radmi pulled into a long gravel drive that ended at a small wooden cottage. A man stood outside, next to a beat-up old car.

"Don't ask anyone's name, just do whatever they tell you."

"You're not coming with me?" Fear thundered back after such a short reprieve.

"No. I must get back immediately. I'm supposed to be searching for you. It is dangerous for me to be here. Do you have a way to buy a plane ticket?"

"Yes, I have my wallet. But my passport was in my camera bag." She couldn't get out of the country without the passport. Despair rose in her gut like bile. She clasped her hands together to keep them from shaking.

"Here is your passport." Radmi pulled the book from her back pocket.

"Oh, my god, thank you."

"Leave. Go with him." Radmi gestured to the waiting man. "Good luck."

Margo wanted to hug her, but Radmi had changed into someone she didn't know, someone supremely confident but not nearly as friendly as the woman from the castle.

She left Radmi, and the man opened the passenger door of the ratty car as she neared. Radmi disappeared into the dark night before Margo was seated.

The man proceeded down the gravel drive, then continued down the valley. The forested gorge and winding road which had struck her as beautiful just days ago had become ominous. She didn't say a word to the man, didn't know if he spoke English. He remained silent.

Long minutes stretched into an hour, and Margo began to see glimpses of the capital below. At one point the lights of an airplane landing blinked across the sky. She wished she were on it, hoped to be outbound soon. When she looked back over the past weeks, she didn't understand how her life had unraveled so quickly. And yet, hadn't it been unraveling for years now, even decades?

She'd been like a stuck weathervane, always pointing one direction, regardless of the wind and her own desires. Why had she taken a warped version of her father's dream as her own? Had she ever really thought about what she wanted?

She couldn't remember who'd first put a camera in her hands, perhaps her grandfather. Her mother had looked at her with such love that day, a version of her father come back to life.

Every photo for years tried to regain that love. And when that love didn't materialize, Margo created her own. If she loved the subject in front of the lens enough, she didn't need her mother's love quite so much.

Now the path had ended. Radmi said she needed to hide, and Margo would do anything to stay out of Andrei's clutches. The thought of what he would have done to her this very night made her shiver.

The driver glanced at her. She wrapped her arms around herself as if she needed to keep warm. She needed so much more than that. She needed a crystal ball to tell her the future. She needed a plane ticket out of this depraved country. She needed to go home, but she had no home.

She closed her eyes and took a deep breath. She must save despair for later. Despite the moderate safety of the vehicle, danger danced all around her. How many days or months or years would pass before she felt safe again? Would she have to wait until that monster died?

But at least she was here in this car driving away from Andrei, unlike those young women at the castle tonight. The urgent need to save herself didn't stop her from wanting to protect them. Despite Radmi's remarks, Margo couldn't believe all of them understood what they faced. Who they faced. After all, Andrei had threatened to drug her and have his way with her. Being relatively well known and American should have protected her. Those women had no protection at all.

She was lucky. Each spin of the tires moved her away from the castle. She palmed her passport, hardly believing it existed. Hope, hope, hope. However bleak, a future awaited if she could get out of the country and lie low.

They entered the capital city. The car pulled to a stop at the airport terminal.

"How long will I be here?"

"The flight to New York leaves in three hours. You must buy a ticket for it." His English had a heavy local accent.

"What if it's sold out?

"If you cannot get on the New York flight, try to get to London or Amsterdam. Those flights are later in the day. The earlier flight is much safer. They will look for you here."

"What if he comes? What if they stop me? Will you hide me again?" Panic surged just under her skin and came out in her words.

"I will leave you now. You will not see me again. You must get on a flight."

"If he finds me, he'll be furious." He'd punish her. She wanted this man to turn the car back on, to drive away from the oily smelling airport. Keep driving until they were hundreds or thousands of miles away.

"You can try to get the attention of bystanders, perhaps ask someone to call the US embassy."

"That's it. Take me to the embassy. They'll help me."

"Radmi wanted you to leave the country. I can take you to the embassy, but you'd still be in Tiranistan. It is safer if you leave." No emotion crossed his face.

He stared at her, waiting for her to depart. In the breaking dawn, he didn't look like a bad guy. His shaggy dark blond hair matched scraggly facial hair somewhere between stubble and an actual beard. Hazel eyes briefly met hers. He looked like he'd seen too much, even though he had to be about her age. She disengaged, opened the car door, and left another person behind.

She passed through the sliding doors with no duffel, no camera bag, none of the trappings of any photographer, tourist, or traveler she'd even seen. She'd never thought of luggage as armor, but it shielded one from being different. Now it seemed like everyone would look at her, question her. She stiffened her spine. This would work or it wouldn't, but she had to at least try.

In line at the ticket counter, terror ran through her. The plan wouldn't work. But it did. She put the cost of an exorbitant coach ticket to New York on her credit card.

"Luggage?" the gate agent asked.

"No. My stuff got stolen." She didn't know why she told the lie. But she needed some excuse and that one rolled off her tongue first.

The agent gave her a strange look but handed her the ticket. Three hours until boarding. Margo went to the restroom and tried to wash the filth from the mountain, from the adrenaline, from the fear from her hands. She rinsed her face. Then, afraid to do anything else, she hid in a stall until boarding.

Every time someone entered, she feared discovery. At the gate, the certainty that she'd be stopped almost sent her back to her hiding place in the restroom. Even sitting on the plane, squashed between two men in suits who must have bathed in cologne, she couldn't believe she wouldn't be stopped. It wasn't until the plane left the ground that relief overwhelmed her. She sobbed, making the men beside her nervous, until sleep finally took the fear away.

Chapter 15

Hours later, she awoke. Now, the men beside her slept. For a moment, she panicked, trapped between them. Then she recalled everything she'd been through. She'd survived so much more than this. She shoved herself past the man on the aisle and went to find water and something to eat.

Back in her seat, loaded up with pretzels and a can of club soda, she considered her next steps. First, she'd go to her bank and withdraw all the money she could. Part of her wanted to believe Andrei couldn't reach her in America, but if he had thugs in Italy, he probably had them everywhere, especially New York. She took Radmi's warning seriously and would do her best to lie low.

She could get a room in the Westside YWCA for less than a hundred dollars a night, an old trick she'd learned in college. She needed to get in touch with Liliana to get some of her things. Radmi had told her not to contact friends and family, but if she called Liliana on her work landline and met her somewhere they'd never been, maybe it would be okay. She'd ask her first.

Then what? Where? She had no idea. She had visions of disappearing into the wilds of Tanzania, getting lost in the narrow streets of the Ciutat Vella in Barcelona, or taking a boat to the island of Chiloe in southern Chile. Surely, no one could find her at one of the ends of the earth. But all those dreams, all places she'd photographed, would require passports, travel, and too short a stay.

She needed a place under the radar. Perhaps a diner in North Dakota would hire her under the table and she could live in a trailer. She thought she'd seen that in a movie once. She might be able to get a job taking wedding photos somewhere. She had a couple of old cameras stashed at Liliana's.

The thought of picking up the camera, taking a portrait, made her stop. A weighted blanket descended on her soul and provided no comfort. She had defined herself by one word: photographer. She'd rather not pick up the camera again than use it the wrong way. Trading her skill for money had gotten her into this mess. She might not ever take another photo. It seemed a far better option to let Margo the photographer go, let her fade away. Better to search for the opposite of her father's violent death than to revisit her shattered dream.

The blanket expanded to cover her chest, pressing down and making it hard to breathe. She had ruined everything. Her eyes overflowed, but she didn't sob, her despair knifed too deep for that. Life, as she knew it, was gone.

———

The wheels touched down and woke her from a deep sleep. Still groggy, she looked for her bags when she exited the plane, then remembered she had none. She had nothing but a couple thousand dollars in her bank and a madman on her heels.

She took the long subway ride into Manhattan. She had nothing to read, no phone to peruse, so she looked at people. Over and over, she caught herself wanting to reach for her camera to capture a face or a pair of hands. She tried to replace that longing with hate. If she hated it, she could become a different person.

She withdrew three thousand of the thirty-seven hundred that remained in her account. A room at the Y cost eighty-five dollars. She reserved it for one night. She'd be gone tomorrow. Tomorrow, she'd go to the Greyhound station and get on the next departing bus. It seemed easier than picking a place she wanted to go. What she really wanted was her life back, but that wouldn't happen.

She couldn't walk down the street without the hair rising on the back of her neck. Surely someone watched her. She must have ducked into half a dozen shops between the bank and the Y, always sure a man on the sidewalk looked like someone she'd seen in Tiranistan. She'd taken the first flight out, but it wouldn't be long before Andrei's goons would be here, searching for her. Margo wondered what had happened to Darpan, wondered if Radmi was safe.

At a store, she purchased a phone with a prepaid SIM card. Then she called Liliana, who suggested a restaurant in Chinatown. They'd never been there before, but someone in Liliana's office recommended it. Margo arrived thirty minutes early and watched everyone who went by. Once, a large dark-haired man peered in the window. She was sure she'd been caught. But he never came in.

Half a dozen times she almost left, scared for Liliana. When her friend entered with a travel bag and a backpack filled with Margo's things, she burst into tears.

"Hey, hey, what's going on?" Liliana asked, after dropping the bags and wrapping her arms around Margo.

"I can't talk about it. I'm putting you in danger just by meeting with you. I'm so sorry." Sobs wracked her body anew. This might be the last time she saw Liliana. The emotion seemed overly dramatic for the red vinyl booths and Formica tabletops, but the fear embedded in her bones from the day of her escape might never let her believe in safety.

"Hey, everything's going to be fine. I told you on the phone I'm not afraid of this guy. Tell me what happened." Liliana unwrapped her from the hug and slid into the booth.

Margo laid her hands flat on the table to keep them from shaking. Something about seeing someone from her prior life brought the trauma back stronger than ever.

"I shouldn't have gone to Tiranistan. Andrei is a really bad guy. He's the one who had me drugged and had my hotel room trashed. He threatened to drug me again and . . ." She shook her head. She didn't want her mind to return to that night. "Plus, he's planning a war on his neighbors. He's going to use my photos to make him seem normal, deserving even, but he's not."

"Oh, sweetie. I don't know if your photos will make a difference in that."

"You don't understand. He's created this whole legend around himself, and I told the story in photos."

"Okay. But you're back. Everything is fine now."

"No." The tears returned. "I left, escaped, in the middle of the night. Someone helped me. I thought she was a housekeeper, but now I think she's probably a spy. She told me I had to disappear, that he'd come for me. I'm also supposed to stay away from friends and family."

"I'm here for you. I am not afraid." Liliana spoke breezily.

"He exploded a drone bomb in front of me." She touched the scab on her temple. It burned with hate. "After he threatened me with it."

"Fuck. Seriously? That dude is crazy." Liliana's eyes grew big.

"That's what I'm trying to tell you."

A waiter approached. Margo glanced at him. She needed to make this fast and didn't want him hanging around. "Fried rice with tofu and iced tea."

"Same," said Liliana.

"Where are you staying?" Liliana asked as soon as the waiter left. "You can stay with me. I think it will be okay."

"No way. This is it. After today, no contact."

"That's crazy. Until when?" Liliana crossed her arms, her expression frosty.

"I don't think you understand how dangerous this guy is, and he has people everywhere."

"Do you really think he was behind what happened in Italy? That kind of makes sense. I've never known you to get pass-out drunk, and you're definitely not the destroy a hotel room type."

"Yeah. Once he told me, it made sense. I think one of the guys from that night is a driver for him. It's still a little blurry. He also said he paid Kirk to drug me."

"Oh, I'm gonna kill that motherfucker. I knew Kirk was too pretty."

"That, I'd be fine with." It still hurt, but her relationship with Kirk had been two egotistical children playing with each other. She sent a prayer to the universe for Darpan's safety.

The waiter brought their drinks. Margo looked at her beautiful friend and took a mental photo of her. How long until she saw Liliana again? She closed her eyes, wishing the thought away. That way lay sadness and a loss of sanity. She had to act with determination.

"So, what's your plan?" Liliana asked.

"Well, I can't afford to stay here. I'll go someplace cheap, disappear for a while."

"Like where?"

"Honestly, I don't know. I'd love to leave the country, but I don't have time to get a visa. Besides, that's not a permanent solution. For some reason, North Dakota keeps coming to mind, although I hate cold weather."

"Go to El Paso."

"No way. People know me there. Family is there. I'm supposed to disappear, not go home."

"No, go to the Lower Valley. Anyone can disappear there."

Margo thought about it. She didn't really know anything about that part of El Paso. In fact, she rarely left the West Side. The Rio Grande flowed along the border from north to south, curving between two desert mountain ranges, one in the US and the other in Mexico. El Paso's shape resembled the letter Y, wrapping around the east and west sides of its mountain, with a long tail that stretched along the river as it continued its journey to the Gulf of Mexico.

It was no surprise she and Liliana hadn't met until they were both in Rhode Island. Margo grew up on the far northwest side of town where the river ran through New Mexico before it curved to become the US/Mexico border. Many of El Paso's white people lived on the west side of town. Liliana grew up in the far eastern part of the city along the river in the so-called Lower Valley, many miles and cultures away.

"I'm not sure it would be safe."

"Chica, El Paso is huge, almost seven hundred thousand people. Anyone can disappear there. And it's cheap."

That was true. Snuggled up against Ciudad Juarez, Mexico, the city's economy and prices operated somewhere between most US cities and its southern neighbor.

"I bet you can get a room there for a couple of hundred bucks a month. Probably a tenth of what you'd pay here."

"I don't know. I wouldn't even know how to find a place like that there."

"Like you know how to find a place in North Dakota? Besides, you can't beat the food."

"Great tacos. Can't think of a better reason to decide on where to live." Margo rolled her eyes, although the idea did have some appeal. Sunny days, a climate she liked, a sense that she hadn't actually lost everything in her past.

"Let me help you. Please," her friend begged.

"It's too dangerous."

"No. It's not." Liliana picked up her phone and began scrolling through it. "Write this down. Dame La Mano."

"Give me the hand?" Margo typed the words into her new phone. Something in her gut told her this was a mistake, but she needed to appease her friend.

"It's a women's crisis center. Ask for Carmen. We went to school together. Just tell her you need to find a room to rent where you can't be found. I think she'll be able to help."

"That's a great idea. Not necessarily El Paso, but I could probably use your strategy anywhere."

"Just go home."

"I can't. And besides, you can't know where I end up. Liliana, Andrei is a really bad guy. I have to vanish, but you have to be very careful as well. Please."

Liliana reached for Margo's hand across the table. "I understand. But if you need help, reach out to me. Can I at least get your new phone number?"

"No. I'm serious about this. Besides, it's a burner. I'll probably get a new one when I'm done with this plan."

"How will I know you're okay?"

"I don't know. Honestly, I just don't know right now."

"This is crazy."

The waiter set their food down, and Margo could tell from Liliana's jerky movements how angry she was. They ate in silence. Margo shoveled food into her mouth. She'd been here too long. It was time to move. But she couldn't leave Liliana like this.

"Lili, I'll be watching you on social media. All your channels. When it's safe, I'll reach out. I promise."

Liliana sighed. "Okay. But if you need me, let me know."

The seriousness in Liliana's eyes made Margo lie to her friend. "I promise, I'll reach out. This isn't forever."

"Worst-case scenario, we're a lot younger than he is, so he'll die first." Liliana smiled.

Margo squeezed her hand. That might be the next time she contacted her friend. She reached for her wallet.

"No way, this one's on me."

Margo nodded. "Thanks. I've got to get moving. Until next time."

She slipped out of the booth, trying to keep her tears in check. Liliana handed her the bags, tears brimming in her eyes. Margo hugged her friend, her own tears falling freely. How much had she cried in the past week? She squeezed Lili hard, then grabbed the bags and left.

Chapter 16

The bus left Atlanta at nine in the evening. Her first bus had departed from New York two days before. She headed south to find an inexpensive place to call home. Her body ached from the twenty-four-hour ride. Liliana's talk of El Paso being inexpensive had stuck in her mind, nagging at her. Margo figured the deep south would be the least expensive part of the country. She'd spent most of the day riding a bus around Atlanta. She hadn't been impressed. The traffic made getting around the city almost impossible, and she didn't like feeling stuck. Hopefully tomorrow she'd find her future home out the bus window.

The ticket from Atlanta to Dallas cost eighty-four dollars, more than she wanted to spend, but it would give her almost eight hundred miles worth of potential places to live. If she found her perfect place along the way, she'd get off and never look back.

From the night she'd fled the castle, she'd dragged her body from one place to another. Scrambling down a mountain, in a car, an airplane, now a bus. As much as she'd always loved traveling, she'd had enough. She wanted nothing more than to hunker down in some anonymous town and recover from the past weeks.

Green fields and pine forests alternated outside the window. The same fast-food chains and gas stations passed by exit after exit. When they left the freeway to drop off and pick up passengers, it all looked the same. Dirty streets, churches, green trees. The same oppressive heat. She hated all of it. Hated everything. Finally, night fell, pulling a curtain down on the interminable sameness.

The next afternoon, the bus pulled into the station in Dallas. Another eighteen hours, and still no closer to home. She wandered the streets of downtown. Grabbed a bagel and a hot coffee and found a park bench. The strong coffee was harsh and delicious, exactly what she needed.

Sated from breakfast, she roamed the area to get a feel for the place and decide if she could live here. Dallas itself was likely outside her budget, but something about having her feet in Texas made it easier to breathe.

She walked for hours, finding a touristy part of downtown, then the arts district with a huge park and glamorous building. Despite the heat, the city felt cold, unlived in. A few times, she spun around, feeling eyes on her back, but each time no one was there.

She wandered through the park and found a memorial. Dealey Plaza. Where President John F. Kennedy was shot. A chill went down her spine. Snipers. Suddenly, every person on the street seemed suspicious. A businessman's briefcase could hold a gun.

She needed to relax. No one had followed her. She'd studied the face of every person who'd gotten on her bus. But this wasn't the place. Something about the tall, mirrored buildings glinting in the harsh Texas sun made downtown seem like a funhouse she needed to escape. She turned toward the bus station, again.

She needed a home, some place to truly lay her burden down. The weeks of fear, the years of striving prior to that, it had worn her out. She wanted to lay her head some place familiar. Liliana was right, the way El Paso spread around the mountain and across the desert, she could disappear thirty or forty miles away from where she'd grown up but still breathe the same air and feel the same desert sun. She returned to the bus station and bought a ticket for El Paso. Maybe she'd been heading there all along.

***

A raging windstorm greeted Margo on her return to El Paso. The sky had turned the color of sand, half of which might have blown in from Arizona. She'd expected sunny skies and a warm greeting and instead faced grit and a downtown bus terminal.

She'd called Liliana's contact, Carmen, from the bus. There'd been some confusion at first. The organization Carmen worked for primarily served as a homeless shelter. Margo said she wasn't homeless but needed a place to live. She almost hung up the phone as her words carved away a part of her identity. She might own an apartment in New York, but she'd unmoored herself from any definition of home.

She thought about continuing, searching for the place that could become home, but the thought of spending one more mile on a bus glued her to the phone. She told Carmen she needed to find a room to rent, one where no one could find her. She'd have to build her own home, one decision at a time.

"I understand," Carmen said. "We take domestic violence very seriously here."

"It's not domestic violence. It's a work thing. A very unstable person." She couldn't attempt to explain the real situation and didn't need to.

Carmen spoke with the calm resolve of someone who had heard far too many stories from far too many women. She encouraged Margo to file a police report if she could, if she wasn't afraid. Her words ripped a hole in Margo that spewed images of young women in colored dresses. So many reasons existed to explain a woman's unwillingness or inability to ask for help.

One step at a time. Find a place to live, to hide, assess your life, and determine a way forward. She had to start over. Completely.

"I only need a single room. I have some money, but not a lot. I'd like to find a place as far from the West Side as possible." Far from her aunt and the possibility of recognition. Far from the one person who would take her in without question and give her a hug that tried to make all the bad in the world disappear. She should have taken advantage of that love when she had the chance. She'd waited far too long.

"Call me back in an hour," Carmen said.

After she'd trudged down the Greyhound steps for the last time, the wind pushed her through two blocks of downtown to the local bus terminal. She called Carmen, then typed the address and a name into her phone.

She found the route map and paid one last fare. Fifteen minutes. She stretched, trying to relieve each sore muscle and realign every joint that had suffered from the long journey.

She boarded the bus with a dozen other people, she the only blond among them. The trip took her past the familiar. Shops with pinatas hanging from the eaves, used car dealers, the county hospital. Bars and taco shops. The roaring wind blew trash and dirt, and the one-story buildings sported sun-faded signs.

The desert could be harsh, full of poverty in a sun-scorched landscape. But it held beauty, even on the windiest dirt-filled day. Unpretentious at its core, the city stretched for miles, digging into the desert sand, allying itself with the water in the river valley, and using the mountains to protect it from inclement weather. Built to survive, this strange country had beckoned people for generations, millennia, offering them its tough brand of love. One could survive here. Every thick-skinned, prickly cactus had a soft, watery core. The people were similar, both hard and soft. Conditioned for toughness and knowing they needed each other to survive. It was a good place to start over.

Margo got off the bus in front of one of El Paso's many high schools. This one had a beautiful brick façade that ran two blocks down a four-lane street rife with stoplights. It had probably come into existence at a time when horse-drawn carriages filled a street now jammed with vehicles.

She crossed that street, passed a convenience store specializing in Mexican confections, and turned into a hidden neighborhood of tiny stucco and adobe homes. The homes exuded personality. One had three large pickups in a yard protected by two mutts, a huge lab mix and a shepherd. Both dogs growled as she passed.

The next home, pink stucco, had red velvet curtains shading the patio and a matching red velvet grill cover. She passed a mint green home with flowering white rosebushes, a home built from rocks so dark they must have been volcanic, and a white adobe cottage with a red-tiled roof. Finally, she arrived at her destination. The front house, stucco the color of sandstone, had a wall niche that held a statue of the Virgin Mary. Iron ropes crossed the niche and caged the woman, perhaps to deter thieves.

Margo continued down the driveway to the second house on the lot. Between the two lay a cement patio with lawn chairs, a grill, and a vegetable garden along one wall. Clucking turned Margo's head to the back corner of the lot where a six-foot-tall wooden chicken coop held a number of red hens. The door to the second home squeaked open, and a tiny woman stepped into the yard.

Margo had always considered herself short at five-four, but this woman couldn't have reached five feet. Her heavily lined face matched the warm stucco of the home behind her, and Margo could see her scalp beneath the wisps of fine white hair. She wore what her grandmother would have described as a housecoat, baby blue with snaps down the front and large pockets. Her face remained unmade except for a cheery red lipstick. Hazel eyes lit the smile on her face. Margo loved her immediately.

"Emma?" the woman asked.

"Yes, I'm Emma." The unfamiliar name tasted sour on her tongue, but she'd have to get used to it. It seemed like half her class at school had been named Emma, making it a useful alias.

"I am Alá. Welcome." The woman gestured for her to enter the home. A small living area contained two chairs facing a wall-mounted TV. A chrome and Formica table had been pushed against the wall between the living area and a New York apartment sized kitchen. Alá led her down a hallway with doors leading to a bedroom and a bathroom. At the end of the hall, a door opened to a second bedroom. It held a double bed, a cheap dresser, and a plastic chair. A rag rug covered the linoleum, and a pink quilt covered the bed. A window over the bed let in light but looked out on a wooden fence. A strange combo of stark and homey, it looked exactly like a place where someone would hide.

"Thank you," Margo said. She wanted to crawl into the bed and forget the last few weeks, forget everything in her sorry life. That would come. First, she needed to shower off the grit from the windy day and the grime from too many hours on buses.

She took the small bottles of shampoo and conditioner she'd snagged from an Atlanta hotel and reveled in the warm water. It took many long minutes for the outside of her to become clean. Her insides might never feel that way again. Surely, exhaustion caused the emotion. She just needed to sleep. Perhaps when she woke, she'd be able to leave the past behind and turn her eyes to the future

---

Hours later, hunger pulled Margo from her bed. At the front of the house, Alá hovered over a large pot on the stove with steam curling above it.

"You will eat. Sit," Alá said.

Margo wasn't sure whether they were questions or commands, but she sat. Alá placed a bowl in front of her, and Margo dipped her head toward it. The steam warmed her face, and the aroma of chicken and chiles opened her sinuses.

Margo sat back while Alá dumped cubes of avocado into the soup and handed her a spoon.

"Caldo Tlalpeño. Very nourishing." Alá didn't speak much, but the soup said far more than words. It tasted like an ancient cure for the sick and wounded.

Margo let the warm, spicy broth trickle down her throat. She might not have had this particular soup before, but it reminded her of her grandmother's chicken soup and her caldillo, a concoction of beef and green chiles. The thought, or perhaps the spicy chipotles, brought tears to her eyes.

"Thank you, this is wonderful." She hoped the soup would cure her. She needed something to replace the fear and bitterness, the lost hope.

"You should meet my granddaughter and her husband. They live in the front house. They will be home from work soon."

"Thank you, I would like that." But as soon as she'd finished the soup, Margo went back to bed. She should have gone to the drugstore to purchase toiletries or the grocery store for food. She couldn't expect Alá to feed her, that wasn't part of their deal. She also wanted to meet the granddaughter and learn who shared the property. But the lure of the bed, of burying herself beneath the covers and sleeping to forget, overcame any sense of responsibility or desire. She just wanted the world to go away. She'd deal with her life tomorrow. Or maybe the day after that.

Chapter 17

The next morning, Margo stayed in her room, door locked, and listened to the old woman go through her day. Kitchen sounds reached her, the clang of a pan and the clatter of silverware. A radio played mariachi music. At ten o'clock, the radio stopped, and the screen door slammed.

Margo opened her door silently and slid to the front of the house in socked feet. She glimpsed Alá opening the door to the house on the front of the lot, one arm wrapped around a basket of laundry.

Margo ran back to her room, slipped on her shoes, and grabbed her bag. She'd already gone through her meager provisions and needed to restock. She peered out the front door looking for any sign of movement, then made a break for it. She jogged down the driveway, backpack slung over her shoulder.

Her ridiculous behavior grated on her. She knew what escape really meant, and yet she'd changed it into hiding from a woman who had helped her. Still, the desire not to speak with anyone outweighed any pull to be social. She needed to keep everything that had happened to herself, not just for safety, but for sanity. If she told someone, they'd ask what she was going to do next, and she had no answers. So, she slipped through the driveway, afraid to even look at the front house in case Alá saw her through a window.

She had no idea where to go. She needed to find a drugstore or grocery store to buy food and toiletries. She'd eaten so many snack bars and pretzels that she hoped to never taste them again.

She wandered toward one of the main streets in this part of El Paso. Sunshine warmed her skin, and a light breeze ruffled her hair. The elements spoke to her of freedom.

She turned left at the high school, away from downtown El Paso. After three blocks, she passed a small stand-alone restaurant with a big glass window. Bright orange booths and the enticing aroma of Mexican food lured her back and through the door. Suddenly starving, she claimed the booth farthest from the window.

Everything on the menu looked delicious. The two middle-aged Hispanic women in the kitchen ensured quality. In the end, Margo couldn't decide between pancakes or her favorite Mexican breakfast, chilaquiles, so she ordered them both. Her bill, with coffee, would total less than fifteen dollars, less than half the cost of a New York brunch.

When the waiter set the food on the table, she wanted to dive into it as much as eat it. The ceramic plate of chilaquiles held day-old tostada chips enrobed in a spicy red sauce topped with cheese. Two perfectly cooked over-easy eggs topped them. She attacked the plate like she hadn't eaten for weeks. Once finished, she asked for another cup of coffee, then started in on the fluffy buttermilk pancakes.

"Did you like them?" the waiter asked when he stopped by with the bill.

Margo looked down at her plates which held only a few scraps of pancakes and streaks of red sauce. "Delicious. Thank you. Is there a grocery store near here?"

He likely thought her a glutton, eating all that then asking where to buy food, but she couldn't have cared less through her sated haze. He gave her two options, a nearby Food King and a Super Walmart less than a mile away. Margo opted for the local market, where she picked up a mix of food and toiletries and shoved them into her backpack.

On the way back, she passed a sign for a library. She detoured a couple of blocks and found it. A banner out front offered citizenship classes and a teen hangout. She entered the rectangular building and found rows of books, an information desk, and a few desks sporting computers placed around the perimeter of the room.

She approached the information desk and asked the woman behind it if she could use a computer. Once seated, she immediately checked all of Liliana's social media accounts. Nothing out of the ordinary: fashion, a shot from a bar at night. Maybe Margo had overreacted. Perhaps the danger, now that she was an ocean and half a continent away, existed in her head and not in the space around her. But even here, so far away, she feared taking too deep a breath.

She tried searching for versions of Radmi Petska and found nothing. According to Google, no one in the world had that name. At least no one recorded on a computer. Had she been nothing more than the shadow of a memory? Perhaps she lived so deep undercover, not even her aliases existed. Margo hoped, wherever and whoever she was, that she was okay.

Next, she searched for Darpan. Unlike with Radmi, many Darpan Yadavs existed online, a musician, an actor, a CEO, someone looking for work. She found him, she thought, at a company called XL ComWorks. The company specialized in building communications networks. The website contained many high-tech stock photos, some fancy words, but relatively little real information. The about section only had the establishment year, a Mumbai address, and mentioned Darpan Yadav as the manager. The contact page contained a fillable form and nothing more.

Margo stared at the form a long while. She kept that tab open and continued to search the internet. She did not search for Tiranistan or Andrei Andropov. She had no idea if or how searches could be traced, but she would not reach back into the tiger's cage.

She stayed at the library for hours. She created a new email address under an alias. It surprised her that the librarian let her stay on the computer for so long. Looking around the space, Margo realized more employees than customers filled it.

She asked about getting a library card—it might be nice to check out some books. Unfortunately, the requirement of a photo ID made getting the card impossible. The possibility of a normal life faded. She had no identity.

She finally left the library in the early evening. It stayed open until seven, and some other day she'd probably stay that late. However, she still wanted to explore the area. She'd seen a recreation center, senior center, and huge park behind the library.

She wandered through the park, full of soccer teams and baseball prac-tice. Squeals and peals of laughter drew her to the far side where she found a play area. Beside it, a splash pad shot water straight up at intervals, and two mini water slides brought moisture to the desert air.

Although the sun touched the far horizon and the cool air of the coming night filtered into the desert heat, children ran through the spraying water as if finding relief from the hottest summer day. Margo sat on a nearby bench and watched the kids, from toddlers to middle schoolers, with nothing but pure joy on their faces.

One little boy wore jeans and a long-sleeved T-shirt, all completely soaked. He spun in a fountain, water swinging from his arms and hair. He screeched with laughter. A tiny girl wearing a pink sparkly bathing suit with a built-in tutu toddled like a drunken sailor, always reaching a spray hole just as the water disappeared. She slammed her bottom to the ground in frustration, and water shot to the sky between her dimpled legs. Astonished laughter quickly followed her cry of shock, and she stuck her hands into the stream, soaking herself.

For the first time since she'd left Tiranistan, Margo wanted her camera. She wanted to document the mundane joy of children in a park, just so people could know it existed when life became too hard to believe in innocent pleasure. The kids' beautiful faces, all dark olive skin, jet black hair, and obsidian eyes, popped against the aqua blue of the spray park. She might not be okay, but the world was.

Dark had fallen by the time she returned to the house. She hoped to somehow sneak in. Maybe she could wait in the dark of the yard for Alá to use the restroom, then she could rush to her room and only speak to her through a closed door.

If Margo spoke to her face-to-face and had to look into the woman's kind eyes, she might break down and tell her what transpired. But if she talked, she risked the very people helping her. That couldn't happen. Margo had to swallow her past and keep it inside.

She trod past the silent front house, intent on peeking in the window of the rear house. Instead, she walked into an ambush. Alá, as well as her granddaughter and her granddaughter's husband, sat at the table between the two houses sharing a meal.

"Emma," Alá said with happiness. "Please, come meet Karin."

Margo stepped toward the table, hoping the shock and guilt didn't show on her face. Only a few years older, Karin had pale skin, black hair, and Alá's eyes.

"I am so happy to finally meet you," Karin said with a smile that seemed about to explode into laughter. "I was starting to think Alá had made you up. This is my husband, Ramón."

Margo started to reach her hand toward the man.

"No, no. Too greasy." He dropped the piece of chicken he'd been holding onto his plate. "Please sit and have something to eat with us."

"Yes, please," Karin said. "I'll get you a plate."

Before Margo had a chance to protest, Karin had slipped into the front house.

"Sit," Alá said, pointing to the empty chair.

The heat of embarrassment surged up her cheeks, but she did as she was told. She didn't want to talk to people, didn't want to make friends. She wanted to wallow in how unfair the world had become. The emotions pinged through her, but in no time, Karin had set a plate of barbequed chicken, beans, rice, and salad in front of her.

She dug into it lustily. And keeping her mouth full kept her from answering too many questions.

"So, where are you from?" Karin asked.

"Denver," Margo said, immediately taking another bite of chicken. She'd vacillated between New York and El Paso when the lie came to her lips. It was safer, and she had no accent to give her away.

"How did you get to El Paso?" Karin asked.

Margo let silence fill the table before answering. "I just needed to get away."

"Karin, enough questions," Alá said.

Since she'd found out about Alá from the domestic violence center, women who needed to remain unknown had probably stayed with Alá before.

"Karin, you know better," Ramón said. "We are happy to have you here. You don't have to hide in your room all the time. You're welcome anywhere."

"Thanks." Margo took a good look at him. His curly hair and five-o'clock stubble framed a deeply tanned face. Striking green eyes met hers. She broke his gaze and moved her eyes back to Karin. "What do you do for a living?"

"I teach at the elementary school. Second grade." Karin smiled as if about to spill a secret. "Today the kids were terrible and exhausting, and I love them all."

"I saw the cutest kids at the splash park today," Margo said before she could stop herself.

"That park is full all the time," Karin said. "You should see it in the summer. They've got a huge pool there also. I used to go to the Zumba class there on Saturdays. Perhaps you could go with me."

"Maybe." Margo wanted to say she didn't have time, but she had nothing but time these days.

The longer they sat at the table, the more Margo wanted to leave. She really liked Karin, but she didn't want to make another friend she'd have to abandon. She had absolutely no idea what the future held, but she knew she wouldn't be living in the house with Alá forever. She waited for a bolt of lightning to strike and tell her what to do next.

Finally, she excused herself, claiming she needed to make a call. Not that she had a single person in the world to phone. But it allowed her to retreat to the small room, lock the door, and lie on the bed. And try to forget what her life had become.

The next morning, Margo slipped into the same habit, leaving as soon as Alá had gone to the front house. She walked with purpose to the restaurant and ordered the breakfast special: one pancake, one egg, and one slice of sausage for three dollars. She needed her money to last, but at these prices she could afford a hot breakfast in the morning. At least for now.

She stood at the library door at ten o'clock when a different librarian unlocked it for the day. She breathed a small sigh of relief. She planned on spending a lot of time here and didn't need anyone wondering where she came from or why she'd suddenly shown up.

Other customers quickly filled the library, mostly children with their mothers or grandmothers. They filed over to a corner of the main room where a sign announced the children's reading and crafts hour.

She hopped on the computer again. Like the day before, she checked Liliana's social media accounts first. A gasp escaped her when she saw the latest photo on Liliana's Instagram. The photo showed Kirk at O'Brien's, one of Liliana's favorite bars and a place Margo had taken Kirk one night.

She quickly clicked on the photo to read the caption.

Ran into this a-hole last night. Seems he's looking for my friend. Begging me for info. Told him to take a hike. #totaljerk

Margo stared at the screen, forcing her breath to slow. The other option, hyperventilating, would spin her into panic. What the hell was Kirk doing chasing Liliana down? Was he still working for Andrei? Would he hurt Liliana?

Nausea washed through her. She needed to know how much danger Liliana was in. How much did Kirk know? Had he worked for Andrei before that night in Italy? She couldn't imagine it. Kirk had built a career as a respected war journalist. He'd know how dangerous someone like Andrei could be—how a person like that could turn on you. But then, she'd never have imagined he'd drug her and let some thugs ruin her room and thus her career.

She couldn't risk calling Liliana. Could she? What if she purchased a different burner phone? But then it would have an El Paso number. Could she comment on her account? That seemed dangerous. One of the easiest things to do was monitor an open account. She created a new Instagram account but, in the end, fear overcame her desire to reach out.

She opened an incognito window and returned to the site she believed belonged to Darpan's company. Margo leaned toward the computer, her bottom lip caught in her teeth, wondering what to say. Was he okay? Alive? She couldn't ask that.

I'd like to speak with Darpan Yadav about a network that includes drone-based communications.

It didn't seem like enough and seemed like far too much all at once. She had to give a name, email address, and phone number. She smiled as she typed in the name. Baba Yaga. A statue of the ferocious woman from Slavic folklore had been stuck in the notch of a tree in the strange forest behind his tent. Darpan had told her the legend of the witch. The statue had been placed there so long ago the tree had grown around Baba Yaga's boney legs.

Margo created a new email, calling herself darpansghost. It was a bread-crumb trail of hints. She hoped he'd figure it out and no one else would. She used her burner phone from New York to sign up for the account. As soon as she left the library, she'd dump it and get a new one.

Children laughed as a librarian read to them. It made all these precautions seem ridiculous. But the photo of Kirk with Liliana proved she couldn't be too careful.

———

Margo returned home midafternoon after stopping to watch the children at the splash park. Again, her fingers had itched to hold her camera. She'd told herself she needed a new career, but the expressive children, crystal water, and El Paso's deep blue sky would have made for award-winning photos. But she couldn't do that anymore. Ever. It was the surest way to be found again. The determination to never experience the terror of that last night in Tiranistan far surpassed any desire to take pretty pictures.

As she walked down the driveway, Karin pulled in behind her. Margo quickened her step.

"Emma, hello. Good to see you again."

She'd almost made it to the front door. Almost. She turned and waved. "Hi, Karin. How are you?" She walked back to the car. No matter how badly she wanted to disappear into her room, she wouldn't be rude to someone as nice as Karin.

"I'm good. Just getting home from school." Karin pulled a box full of papers and folders from the back seat. "I was going to have a snack. Will you join me? I made some cookies last night."

"Oh, I better not. I've got some work to do."

"Please. I could really use the company. I promise I won't keep you long. I've got to go through the children's latest project tonight."

Margo followed Karin into her house, each step feeling like a mistake. They walked past a laundry room with a washer and dryer.

"If you ever want to do laundry, just let me know. Any day works except Tuesday, which is when Alá does hers."

"That would be fantastic." Margo hadn't figured out where to do laundry yet. She wondered if her dirty, wrinkled clothes contributed to Karin's offer. Thankfully, she'd bought new underwear at Walmart earlier that day.

"You can go get it now if you'd like, and I'll get our snack ready."

Margo jumped at the chance and soon returned with a full load. She joined Karin at the kitchen table after starting the machine.

Karin had set the table with cobalt blue glasses and salad plates with two oatmeal cookies each. Something in Margo's heart twinged with the effort. What a nice person.

"Sit, sit," Karin said. "I make the cookies with extra cinnamon, and the drink is limeade, my favorite."

"Oh, my god. These are great." The butter content in the cookies made them melt the second they hit Margo's tongue. The tart limeade perfectly contrasted with the sweet cookies. "This might be the perfect snack."

Karin giggled. "It's my favorite, but I have to hide the cookies from Ramón, or he'll eat them all. He thinks I only make twelve in a batch, but I actually make twenty."

"Good trick," Margo said.

Karin gave her a long look. "I won't keep you long since you said you had work to do. What do you do anyway?"

Margo sighed. "Actually, I need to find a job."

"I can help. What kind of job are you trying to find?"

"I don't really know. I thought about applying for a job at Walmart, but it doesn't look like interesting work."

"I don't mean to pry, and you don't have to tell me anything, but you seem smart, educated. Can you do whatever you were doing before you came here?"

"I was a photographer." Margo couldn't keep the words from spilling from her lips.

"Oh, like weddings and babies?"

Margo suppressed a groan. She didn't want to photograph weddings. Yes, lasting memories of the big day meant the world to the families, but to Margo, photographing lines of happy people day in and day out sounded like torture.

Photography combined light and emotion and magic. It would break her heart if that became mundane.

She wished she could explain this to Karin, whose kind eyes told her she'd understand. But the pain remained too close to the quick, and the need to hide prevailed. "I don't do that anymore, but I do need to find a job."

Karin rested her chin in her hands, elbows on the table. "Let me think. We always need substitute teachers at the school, but most people we get are working on their teaching certificate."

That actually sounded nice. Memories of working with the kids at the YWCA on summers off brought her a trace of joy akin to watching the kids in the spray park. But she'd need an ID to get a teaching certificate, probably to do anything at the school. "I'm not in a good position to get a formal job." Margo hated admitting the truth. The conversation needed to end before she said too much.

"A friend of mine does after school art classes at a local studio. I can ask her if they need help. I mean, I know it's totally different, but I don't think they'd need documentation to bring someone on. Do you speak Spanish?"

"Un poco." Just a little. Anyone who grew up in El Paso spoke a little Spanish, but here in the Lower Valley, she heard it more often than English. "And thanks about understanding about the documentation."

There. She'd said it. She was a nobody. How would she ever get her life back? Surely, Andrei would tire of searching for her soon. If he even cared. He might not even try to track her, but she didn't know and couldn't risk her safety or that of others. The photo of Kirk on Liliana's Instagram proved danger's close ties.

Karin reached her hand across the table. "I don't know what you've been through, but we're here to help."

"Thank you." The words came out garbled, her heart caught in her throat. "This is very kind of you, and delicious," she gestured at the now empty plate, "but I need to go."

Margo practically ran across the patio and through Alá's house, barely shoving out a hello as she passed the woman at the stove. She buried herself in her bed, pillow over her head, and cried for everything she'd lost and everything she still feared.

Chapter 18

The next morning at the library, Margo saw the first of her photos of Andrei. He wore a tux, and the shot looked candid as if he'd been caught at a gala event. The planes of his face looked like that of a lion, all blond hair, high cheekbones, and proud eyes. He looked like someone you should follow. She hated herself for the photo, for making him look respectable. Beyond that. Handsome, powerful, a leader.

The headline doubled her over as she tried to keep her breakfast in her gut. Andrei Andropov had been nominated for a Nobel Peace Prize. It couldn't be.

She scanned the article. In it, the reporter interviewed the university professor who'd nominated him. He had so many good things to say about Andrei, he must have been paid. In the last paragraph, the reporter mentioned that the Nobel committee did not reveal nominees, but the professor had come forward of his own volition.

The lack of verification from the Nobel committee hadn't kept the story from running. Margo searched Andrei's name and found the article running in other journals, including the AP and UPI. It would be everywhere. In addition to the photo in the tux, she found another she'd taken of him standing in front of the castle with his retinue of government officials. He knew how to look like a leader, and she'd made sure he could decorate his propaganda with pretty pictures.

Sick with how she'd contributed to Andrei's success, Margo switched to Liliana's social media accounts. Another photo of Kirk. Same bar. Different seat. Different clothes. She wanted to reach through the ether and shake Liliana, scream at her to stay away from him. He led to Andrei and smashed rooms, drugs, and bombs. She touched the scar fading from her temple. Stay away, Liliana.

But her fearless, bossy friend had another agenda. Margo read the caption.

This guy wants you to feel sorry for him because he screwed up and did something bad. He wants to say he's sorry because he hasn't been able to work since then. Sounds to me like he just feels bad for himself. Is he the a-hole? Vote in the comments.

Margo scrolled down. Two comments, one *yes*, one *he's hot*. She didn't recognize the handles. Didn't care. Liliana had to knock this off.

Margo needed to get a message to her. She didn't want to comment on the post. If Kirk was trying to lure her out on behalf of Andrei, commenting would give her away. She could try to send an email in incognito mode, but if Andrei had someone like Darpan tracking her, he might have access to Liliana's accounts.

The thought of Andrei using Darpan against her slid a knife into her gut. Surely, Darpan wouldn't do that. They'd had such a connection. But maybe, to him, it had just been sex. She'd thrown herself at him, after all. Just when she'd hoped to fall into a new, safer life, fear returned and kept her on edge.

She opened the incognito screen and checked the email she'd set up to send Darpan a message. She had one message.

From: info@xlcomworks.com

Subject: request

We cannot fulfill your request. Please do not contact us again.

She closed her eyes and sank into the blackness in the world. He was alive. Somewhere in the depths of her mind, she'd feared Andrei had killed him. That relief lasted mere seconds before the full force of the message hit her. Darpan wanted nothing to do with her. Far too smart to have missed that she wrote the message, he decided to cut her off. Those mornings in the tent, when she'd melted into him and he into her, when she'd believed sharing herself made her part of something bigger, something beautiful, they'd meant nothing to him. She closed the computer and left the library.

She had nothing to do. Nowhere to go. The hole in her heart threatened to swallow her into its darkness. Without thinking, she returned to Alá's and grabbed one of her old cameras.

Margo wandered along the main road, camera in hand but no destination in mind. She had to get her life back. She wasn't going to hide forever, and she wasn't going to endanger her friends.

A squealing sound caught her attention, and she turned to see a blue sedan executing a quick U-turn from the other direction. She darted down a side street out of pure reflex. She'd entered a small mobile home park. Without taking time to think, she ran around the side of the first mobile home.

She heard a car turn onto the street. Margo edged around the back of the mobile home and watched the blue car pass slowly by. They'd found her. Terror pulsed through her, beating in time to her heart.

The car engine turned off. Margo heard a door open, then slam shut. She flattened herself against the mobile home baking in the midday sun.

"Margo," a woman yelled. "Margo."

She recognized the voice. Aunt Joyce. What the hell was her aunt doing down here, so many miles from home?

"Margo! Where are you? Please come out."

Shit. What was she supposed to do now? Her entire body trembled from the fear memory of escaping Tiranistan. She couldn't expose her aunt to that.

"Margo. I just want to talk. Please come out. I won't leave until I find you."

Footsteps approached. "Please, Margo. I won't hurt you."

That slayed her. Her aunt thought she was afraid of her. She stepped out from behind the trailer. "Aunt Joyce."

"Oh, Margo. I knew it was you." The woman who ran to her had changed. Joyce now looked a lot like her grandmother. Her hair, more salt than pepper, bounced at her chin with each stride. Once-fine lines around her eyes had deepened, but the blue irises radiated concern. Margo should have visited more often. She hadn't realized how quickly the years could pass. This was the only family she had left.

Her aunt wrapped her in a hug, then pulled back and took her by the shoulders, her gaze swept the length of hers. "What are you doing here? Why didn't you call?"

"It's really good to see you." How much she meant those words surprised Margo. "I've got some things to work out, but I'll be in touch with you when the time is right."

"No." Aunt Joyce tightened her grip on Margo's shoulders.

"No?" What was her aunt thinking? She hadn't asked a yes or no question.

"The last time I talked to you, you were in Italy and needed forty thousand dollars. Now, you're wandering around El Paso's lower valley and trying to hide from me. What's going on?"

"It's nothing." It wasn't nothing, but she didn't know how to explain it or how to make her aunt understand the danger. "Someone is trying to find me. I think. He's very dangerous, and I was warned not to be around friends or family. I'm okay here, but for your own safety, you need to leave and forget you ever saw me." Her words sounded ridiculous, like her life had become some overwrought movie.

"Are you listening to yourself? There is no way I'm leaving until you tell me what's going on. Let's go get a coffee and you can explain." Her aunt slipped her grip off Margo's shoulders and took her hands. "I want to help you."

"It's too dangerous."

"I don't care. You're the only family I've got."

The comment hit Margo in the gut. Of course, that went both ways.

Her aunt tugged her toward the car. Margo followed and slid into the passenger seat. She couldn't believe she'd gotten her aunt involved. It made her want to throw up. It made her want to run. It made her want to ask for help, but she couldn't risk it.

"What are you doing in this part of town?" Margo asked.

"The local branch of the YWCA is literally on the other side of the wall from the mobile home park."

"You're kidding. I didn't even know you had one down here." Great. She'd driven across most of the country and the place she picked to hide was just blocks from the YWCA. She sucked at this.

"Can I take you to lunch?" her aunt asked. "I know of a great local place."

"Sure." The dejection in Margo's voice wasn't fair to her aunt. Margo had to figure a way out of this without hurting her further. One lunch. Then maybe she'd pack her things and leave town again. Although, she'd run out of money soon. There had to be a way out of this mess.

Joyce called the office and told them she'd be out the rest of the day and asked the person on the other end of the line to reschedule her meetings. That further worried Margo. Was Andrei tracking her aunt? What if he noticed something different?

Her aunt drove to the outskirts of the city. They passed the Ysleta Mission. Margo remembered visiting El Paso's three missions. They'd been here since the sixteen hundreds. So many people had passed through El Paso del Norte. The pass of the north. It made her life seem short, just a grain of sand in a vast desert. What if Andrei didn't care that she'd left, had given up on her? She didn't want to waste what little time she had left, yet she refused to endanger anyone else.

If only she knew of a way to show the world the real Andrei, not the regal man her photos portrayed. She needed to expose his dangerous side.

"Here we are," Joyce said, pulling into a walled-off courtyard with a sparkling white adobe building at one end. Wooden picnic tables and chairs adorned the open area near the arched doorway, with Lupita's painted above it in large letters.

They went inside and found a table in a back corner. Margo buried herself in the menu, commenting on each item and hoping to avoid an interrogation. The second the waiter took their order and turned away, her aunt started in on her.

"Tell me what the hell is going on, and be honest."

Margo had rarely heard anger in her aunt's voice. Not even those many times her mother had screwed something up, like forgetting to pick Margo up from school or dance practice. Or that time her mother had met someone at the country club pool when Margo was five. Rather than take Margo the eight blocks home, she called Joyce to come pick up her daughter so she could leave with the guy.

But all that happened years ago. "I'm sorry you're angry with me. I know you want facts, but believe me when I say you're better off, safer, not knowing."

"I am exasperated with you." Her aunt took a long drink of water. "And with me. I thought you were okay. You seemed to love photography, and I was so proud of you for going off and living your own life in New York, even though I missed you terribly."

"I'm not your burden."

"Margo McAllister! You have never been a burden to me. Just the opposite. I always wanted more from you than you were able to give."

Her aunt's eyes filled with tears, another thing Margo had rarely seen from the practical woman. She had no idea how to react.

"I loved you so much. From the moment you were born, I wished you were mine. I hated my sister for how lost and broken she was after your dad died and for how she took that out on you. Mom thought it would be better for you to live with them, even though I told her I'd take you. And now, you're in trouble and I want to help, and you won't let me in."

Margo's eyes filled with tears, her heart in tatters. How was she supposed to respond to this? Perhaps it would have been better growing up with her aunt, but she'd never know. That time had passed long ago. It was unfair, bringing this up now.

"You never told me."

"It seemed unfair, with your mom right there. And my mom, Grandmom, she always thought your mother would pull through. She hoped Sophie would become a good mom." Joyce sighed heavily.

"You disagreed?" Margo had known her mother wouldn't change fairly early, but she still felt the echo of hope in her veins from those earliest years.

"Each man she was with took a little more confidence away. I wish you'd known her when she was young. She was so beautiful and full of life. She got her first local modeling gig at fourteen. Even then, she was determined to leave El Paso and make it big. And she did."

"Yeah. I've seen the fashion spreads and makeup commercials. She was the ultimate wholesome girl-next-door type."

"And then she met your dad, and they fell madly in love with each other. Your father was already a famous photographer, but when he fell for your mother, he fell hard. He just couldn't do the one thing she wanted him to do." Her aunt shook her head, seemingly lost in the memory.

"What?" Margo had heard parts of the story before. Everyone always told her how in love with her mother her father had been. Even her mother told her that, on those sad days when one of the losers she dated broke up with her. She'd hold Margo close, sobbing about how wonderful her father was, how much he had loved her. Then she'd go to bed for days, and the sun didn't come out again until she had another guy's interest. Margo was never enough.

"He couldn't stop going to battle zones. Your mom asked me to come to New York to try to talk some sense into him. She knew she was pregnant and thought I could help her convince him to stay home."

"You went to New York?" Had Margo ever known her aunt at all? Who was this woman?

"Of course. I used to go several times a year. My baby sister had this glamorous life in the big city, and I worked for a nonprofit in El Paso, Texas. Visiting her kept me sane."

"So, I take it you didn't convince my dad to stay home."

"No. I'm sorry, Margo, but that's not who he was. He loved his job and thought he was making a difference in the world. I understand that. That's why I work for the YWCA, to make a difference." Silent tears fell down her aunt's face. "I ended up taking his side, and I don't think your mom ever forgave me."

"And then he died."

"And then he died. And your mom was inconsolable. And you weren't even born yet." Joyce looked up at her, her clear blue eyes the same color as Margo's own. "I owe you so much. Please, let me help you."

Damn, her aunt was good. Margo's defenses had completely fallen. She'd been trapped in the past and had forgotten Joyce's desire to deal with the present. "You don't owe me anything, and I've got to get myself out of this mess. It's complicated."

"Does this have anything to do with how you got the money to repay me the forty thousand?" Joyce crossed her arms and settled into the chair. The interrogation stage of lunch had begun.

"I know you want me to explain everything, but I'm telling you it's not smart. I need to deal with this myself." This lunch was a mistake. She needed to stay off the main road. If Joyce had seen her, others could too.

"What are you living on? You wouldn't even let me pay the whole hotel bill."

"I've got a little savings." Every day a little less. She couldn't talk about Andrei, but she could be honest about this. "Actually, I need to find a job."

"Let me help. Please." Her aunt rested her chin on her hand, apparently deep in thought. "I know, you can help at the YWCA where I found you. I assume that's close to where you live?"

"I shouldn't work where people might know me. And by the way, I go by Emma now."

"Okay, Emma. No one on staff there knows who you are. It's been a decade since you volunteered at the Y anyway, and you always worked on the west side of town. We've got a job training program for women who want to get back into the workforce. You could take photos of them for their resumes and the online job boards. You wouldn't be on staff, so there'd be no paper trail, and I could pay you, if you really want something to do. I'll give you money no matter what."

Tears formed in Margo's eyes, and she willed them to stay put. Her aunt proved again and again that she'd do anything for her, and yet Margo had always tossed her aside with everything else in this god-forsaken town. Now, she needed help. Realistically, no one would hire her without paperwork. She could try to build a business photographing weddings and portraits, but she didn't want to, at least not yet. Not until the sand quit shifting beneath her feet.

Margo looked at the camera bag in the chair beside her. She'd grabbed it out of habit, but at the moment she hated everything photography had caused in her life. But a camera was only a tool. She had caused the problems that upended her life. The time had come for different decisions.

"That would be amazingly helpful. I'll find a way to repay you."

"Can we stop with the repayment bullshit already? You are my only living blood relative. Did you know you are in my will? You inherit everything of mine when I die. I would love to have a closer relationship with you, but whether or not that ever happens, you are one of the people in this world I care about most. How else can I help?"

The tears fell. Tears of guilt and lost chances. "Why are you always so nice to me when I treat you like shit?"

"Because I love you and you had a really crappy childhood. I carry so much guilt about that. I was right there, and I let it happen." Joyce sobbed. "I'm sorry."

"I'm the one who's sorry. I wasn't your problem."

"You are my family. You aren't a problem or a burden. You are someone I love so much more than you'll ever know."

Margo couldn't hold in the pain and regret a second longer. She stood and pulled her aunt from the chair and wrapped her in a hug. "I'm so sorry. I'm sorry for not being nicer to you, for not knowing how you felt about me, for not saying thank you enough." She buried her face in the taller woman's shoulder and cried away years of hurt. Margo had looked to her mother for love. Joyce had been there all along, and Margo had ignored her.

Her aunt held her, kissed the top of her head. "Can we start over? Today. I know I can't take the place of your mother, but I want to be your family, the person you turn to. I want to help you get out of the mess you're in."

Margo gave her one more squeeze, then sat back down. She used her napkin to wipe her eyes. Once her breathing had returned to normal, Margo smiled at her aunt. "You are persistent. Please, just give me a little more time before we talk about what happened."

Joyce waited a breath, then sighed, apparently resigned to Margo's request. "Okay. But you must let me help you however I can. Do you need a car?"

Margo laughed. This woman would not quit, in the very best possible way. A layer of the dread that had weighed on Margo for weeks floated away. Maybe things would get better. She had no idea how yet, but she had someone on her side, begging to go into battle with her.

"I do not need a car, but thanks for asking. And a job sounds wonderful."

"Great. Does noon to five work, Monday through Friday? If not, just let me know when you'd like to work."

"That's perfect. Thank you." Margo reached across the table for her aunt's hand. "I mean it."

Joyce smiled, pure joy on her face. Then her eyes clouded over. "You're not homeless, are you? Do you need a place to live?"

"I have a place to live, thanks." Her small room in the back house would do for now. Her grandfather had always told her to play the hand she was dealt. Alá's pedestrian house in a forgotten neighborhood felt safe, and Margo had never needed glamour.

Something released in Margo. The fear inched back a bit, perhaps because of the inconspicuous little house or finally having someone on her side. A surprising desire for revenge took its place. She'd been mad at herself for drinking out of Kirk's flask, for taking the job with Andrei. But they'd deceived her, and for the first time, she wanted to expose them.

She'd never hungered for revenge before. Only she had. The burning emotion reignited as she remembered her mother's last boyfriend. The one who drove her mother off the mountain.

Her desire for revenge hadn't been for that act. In some ways, that had been her mother's destination all along. Her longing for retribution came from one afternoon when he sat alone in her grandparents' den, waiting for her mother. Margo had gone in to get the camera she'd left on her grandfather's desk, not to talk to her mother's latest drunk cowboy. This one's hat and boots looked stiff and shiny with newness. Margo bet he'd never ridden a horse.

"I hope you're good at taking pictures," he'd said. "Because you sure don't have your mom's looks."

Stunned, she grabbed the camera and fled. "Asshole." The word slipped out as she left the room.

"Hey, you can't talk to me like that." Alcohol already coated his voice even though it was midafternoon.

She'd walked outside into the hot desert sun, burning at his insult. She wanted to slash his tires, kick him in the nuts, turn him in to the police. Anything to get back at him for that comment. Anyone with eyes knew she wasn't as beautiful as her mom, but he didn't need to say it out loud.

That rage came back now, a lit wick from years earlier. Only now it reached toward Kirk. And Andrei. She'd been wronged.

Margo looked at her aunt. Perhaps there was a way to get back at them after all. Fury felt a lot better than playing the victim. She didn't have any ideas yet, but she'd start searching.

"Hey," Joyce said, interrupting Margo's thoughts. "Do you want to stay in our condo in Cloudcroft? You've been there before. No one uses it when we're not up there."

Margo had visited the homey two-bedroom condo in the nearby New Mexico mountains. Pine forests covered the mountain range and provided respite from the hot El Paso summers. Nestled deep in the trees, the condo would keep her far from prying eyes. In a forest. Margo started to shake, some weird physical manifestation of PTSD taking control of her body.

"Honey, are you okay?"

Margo grabbed the table with both hands to stop the shaking. "I'm fine. Thanks for the offer, but I think I'll stay here." No forests. Here in the wide open desert, she had a chance to see them coming.

Chapter 19

Margo sat in front of the library computer the next day filled with hope. After speaking with her aunt, the thought that trouble would keep following her indefinitely seemed, if not faded, then at least a step further away. She finally had something to occupy her days beyond worry. She would help women develop life skills. Margo tried not to think about the irony. If she'd had better life skills, she wouldn't be hiding out in east El Paso.

Still, it gave her something to do. She wished she could start now, not in four hours. But until then, she'd visit the library. She also needed to find a way to thank Joyce. Especially after the way they had left things. Margo had her aunt drop her off at the YWCA near Alá's house so she wouldn't know where she lived. She also wouldn't give Joyce her phone number. Even after she explained it was a burner phone and she'd throw it away soon, the hurt on Joyce's face left guilt that had yet to fade.

Things would get better. Margo just needed a little more time to put the past behind her and be absolutely certain Andrei would leave her alone.

The second she logged on to Instagram her hope faded. Liliana had posted photos of her ransacked apartment.

Came home to this! You can't scare me. Took NYPD 4 hours to show up. Now I got to clean this shit up.

She'd posted four photos, two of her bedroom, drawers open and mattress askew. One of the kitchen, cabinet doors and drawers ajar. And one of the living area where the green couch had beige stuffing billowing out of slashed cushions.

Margo's heart slammed into her chest wall again and again. They could have hurt Liliana. This intimidation tactic might not have scared her friend, but it terrified Margo. Liliana had to leave, but she probably wouldn't. Margo had to warn her.

She pulled her phone from her pocket. Would it endanger Liliana to reach out? Nothing could be more dangerous than her friend staying in her apartment.

You have to get out of NY. RISD friend.

She wished for brilliant words, but they hadn't come. Hopefully by mentioning their college, Liliana would realize who sent the text.

Already gone.

Margo heaved a sigh of relief. She didn't care, didn't want to know where her friend had fled. She was gone, and hopefully safe.

Her second shock came when she scrolled through Instagram. Kirk had tagged her on a beautiful photo of a dhow sailing across the placid Indian Ocean at sunset. She knew the photo, remembered the scene. It had been one of the best weeks of her life. A beautiful location, a gorgeous guy. For a week she pretended she had a normal life and an ordinary, if extraordinarily hot, boyfriend. How things had unraveled since then.

She read the caption. *I'm sorry. I'm so sorry.*

The words hit her gut, making her want to rage and cry at the same time. He took everything! Her prize, her career, her safety. He'd almost taken her life, and he'd left her with this half-existence of hiding and fear. Sorry didn't cut it. Not even close.

She closed the window on the screen. Hatred filled her. A question formed in her belly, then rang through her heart and mind. Why? Why would anyone do that? For a prize?

She stood, wanting to get away from the photo no longer on the screen, wanting to escape the thoughts it had caused. But she had nowhere to go.

She sat again, opening a news page this time. "Andrei Andropov amassing troops on the border." He smiled back at her, the way he had when she took the photo. He held the black and silver drone in front of him. That fucking death machine.

The article quoted him. He called the sovereign country next to Tiranistan an occupied territory, a homeland. Her gut lurched. The article mentioned his drone army capable of blowing up cities, bridges, nuclear facilities.

She'd seen the blast. It had destroyed a swimming pool and cut her face, but not a city. She wondered about the importance of the lie, or if it was one.

"Oh, my god." Margo's memory from her last night at the castle came flooding back. She still had the photo drive she'd hidden. She'd moved it from her shoe to an inside pocket of her backpack after meeting with Liliana.

She ripped open the pack. The tiny disk glinted at her. How had she forgotten it in her travels? The disk carried staged photos of Andrei, and more candid ones as well. All the drone photos hid inside a device the size of a postage stamp. Perhaps one of them held a key, some type of technology that would be useful to the right people, like the US military.

She slipped the drive into the camera she carried with her and thumbed through the photos. The drone photos practically popped off the screen, sending a chill of memory down her spine. She had kept shooting as the drone attacked her, the menacing device closing in until it filled the screen. Photos of the bomb dropping sent nausea through her gut. She had skimmed over these photos when picking ones for Andrei to use. Partly, she didn't want to be reminded of the bomb, but also, he only wanted photos of himself. He'd been smart enough to stand far from where he deployed the bomb and was absent from these shots.

She hadn't realized she'd gotten pictures of the bomb dropping from beneath the drone. Another showed it halfway to the water. She even had a photo of water, tile, and grout spraying out after the bomb's detonation. Her finger must have pressed the shutter one last time before she turned and hit the ground. Probably before a piece of shrapnel had cut her temple. She was right to be afraid, and it was time to show the world Andrei's depravity. She also had all the photos she'd shown him so he could pick his favorites. They included several with the missiles and other weaponry Andrei had brought in as a decorative backdrop. Perhaps this show of power could be used against him.

For the first time, she wished she'd spent more time photographing wars. If she had, she'd have the connections needed to get the photos to the right people. A military expert could identify the weapons and hopefully learn something about Andrei's military capability. Of course, the one person she knew with military connections, Kirk, was the last person she wanted to contact.

Margo left the library and took the back streets to Alá's. She'd been afraid to walk on the main roads since Joyce had found her. An old strip shopping center she passed had a donut shop, a liquor store, and a place called Fantasie Hair Salon.

Margo entered the salon. A woman about her age with a huge mane of curly hair sat behind the counter.

"I'd like to get my hair cut and colored. Do I need to make an appointment?"

"I can take you right now if you have time."

Time was one thing Margo had plenty of. She didn't need to be at the YWCA for hours. She sat in the chair and took her long hair out of its ponytail. Blond locks tumbled down her shoulders and reminded her of the dark nights and bright party dresses of Tiranistan. That woman needed to disappear. "Cut it all off, above my shoulders. And I want it to be brown."

The stylist lifted Margo's hair and let it settle around her face, dripping gold down her chest. "No."

"What do you mean, no?"

"Your hair is naturally blond. It is beautiful. I don't know anyone who wouldn't kill for this hair. I'll trim it for you."

Margo stared into the mirror. The woman's caramel eyes stared back at her, defying her to argue.

"It needs to be short, and I'd like it to be as dark as yours." Margo studied the woman's medium brown curls highlighted with blond. "But I don't need the highlights."

"You can't do that to this beautiful hair. I won't do it." The woman crossed her arms.

Margo wanted to scream. She hadn't wanted any of this, but she needed to feel safe, and blending in would help. She tried again. "Have you ever needed to escape, to become someone different so things in your past wouldn't hurt you?" She saw a flash of pain in the other woman's eyes. "I need that."

The stylist closed her eyes for a few seconds, then nodded. "Fine." She pulled Margo's hair back into a ponytail. "Are you sure?"

Margo nodded, no longer able to speak. She had always had long blond hair, just like her mother. Her identity coursed through each strand. But she needed to be someone else now.

The sound of the scissors slicing through her hair made her want to scream again, to somehow get her old life back. Then, suddenly, the tension around her shoulders eased. She shook the blond strands now floating a couple of inches below her ears. She felt ten pounds lighter. Any remaining princess dreams lay in strands around her feet. A new vibrancy flowed through her. She was Margo McAllister, and she could be anything or anyone she wanted.

The stylist dyed her hair a light brown she said would complement Margo's skin tone. Then she shampooed her, gave her a final trim, and blew out the hair until soft waves fell neatly around her chin.

By the time the hairdresser had finished, Margo looked less like a girl and more like a smart, chic woman. The darker hair brought out the blue in her eyes. The woman staring back at her from the mirror had a different future than the blond she'd left behind.

As she walked toward the YWCA for her first assignment, Margo toyed with the idea of how to get a message to Kirk. She didn't trust him, but he had better military connections than anyone she knew. According to Liliana, he felt bad about what he'd done, and he'd apologized to her in the photo.

He might be lying. He'd already proven himself to be a liar. But if he truly had regrets and no longer worked for Andrei, he might get the photos into the right hands faster than anyone.

She wouldn't reach out to him directly in case he did still work for Andrei. The chance of that was likely fifty-fifty.

She needed to find someone with integrity, someone who knew her, to be an intermediary. Only one person fit the bill, Dave Hirschhorn with *World Geography Magazine*. Yes, he had introduced her to Andrei, but surely, they didn't have more than a social connection. Dave's magazine was one of the most respected in the world. Kirk had sold photos to the journal. She hated having to contact Dave after their last interaction, and he might not take her call. But if Andrei's bragging about his missiles and drones meant something important could be gleaned from her photos, she had to try.

She needed an untraceable way to get the photos showing weapons to Dave. The easiest thing would be to load them into cloud storage and have Dave pull them from there, but online, the photos could be found and traced back to the computer she used to load them. She hadn't found a solution by the time she pulled open the door to the YWCA.

"You'll be helping with our job training and empowerment program," said Mrs. Montoya who ran the program. "Today we've got resume workshop classes. The first class is for adults. The second class happens after the high school lets out and will be all teenagers. Have you ever put together a resume?"

Margo nodded at Mrs. Montoya. The woman's artistically highlighted and shadowed face and frosted, spiky hair belonged on someone about to visit a nightclub, not a middle-aged woman showing up for an ordinary workday.

"Great. Did you go to college? Are you good with words?" Mrs. Montoya's rapid-fire, staccato voice portrayed someone used to giving orders. Her foot tapped, waiting for Margo's response.

"Um, yes. I graduated from college. I'm okay with words, better with this." She gently lifted the camera case in her lap. She'd decided to bring it at the last minute. The photos she'd taken of the children when she worked summers at the Y had been some of her best. Everything else in her life had changed, but the heft of the device in her lap brought the security of a comfy blanket.

"Ah, yes. They told me you'd take photos of the women. That will be helpful. The working moms need photos the mosts, but I also hoped you'd take professional photos of our high school kids."

"Of course." She couldn't imagine saying no to this woman. Besides, Margo had picked up an official YWCA envelope with her name on it and one thousand dollars in cash, hundreds, when she'd walked in. The receptionist also handed her a zip-top tote with two pairs of jeans and two colorful print blouses, probably appropriate attire for her new job.

"So," Mrs. Montoya said, jerking Margo back to the present. "You will take their pictures. I think tomorrow is best. I will bring in professional clothes for them to wear."

Margo looked at the small, stout woman in front of her, almost drowning in a flowing navy dress covered in scarlet and turquoise flowers. A white fringed jacket and silver sandals completed the outfit. This was going to be interesting. "I'll bring the camera again tomorrow. Today I'd love to get to know each of them a little. It will help me take better photos."

"That's it, then. I'll help each of them with their resumes today, and you can interview them."

Just then, the door to the classroom opened, and a young woman entered. Mrs. Montoya looked at her and sighed. "Well, there's your first one. Go introduce yourself to Daniela."

Margo approached the young woman and introduced herself. Daniela, or Dani, as she preferred to be called, had thick dark hair that fell midway down her back, as long as Margo's had been a few hours ago. One bleached blond lock framed the left side of her face. She looked like a teenager, and her curled lip and the glint in her obsidian eyes told Margo she probably found her share of trouble.

"Tell me a little about yourself and why you're here in the job training program."

A perfectly manicured brow arched. "Because I need a job. My mami told me I had to start paying rent. And I should give my abuela some money for taking care of my daughter when I get a job."

"You have a kid? How old are you?" Margo wished she could take back the astonishment in her voice, but the woman looked like a child herself.

"I'm almost twenty, and I want to work for the post office."

"Why?" Again, Margo had sounded incredulous.

"You get to be around people all day, and you help them stay connected to their loved ones. Think about all the letters and packages that pass through a post office every day on their way to a person somewhere else in the world. Besides, they pay well and have health care and a pension. Mrs. Montoya taught me about that."

Dani made the post office sound almost romantic. In fact, a post office might be exactly what Margo needed. She could mail a disk of photos to Dave by overnight mail and pay in cash. No one would even ask for her ID.

Chapter 20

The next morning, Margo woke early. She knew Dave made it into the office before eight, and she wanted to catch him first thing. She snuck out of the house at five-thirty to make up for the two hour time difference and heard Alá gently snoring as she left.

She made her way to the park near the library, her burner phone tucked into her hand. A man walked his dog on the far side of the park. Margo sat on an empty bench, the only other person in the park, and called.

"Dave Hirschorn." His gruff voice rang through the quiet air.

"Dave. It's Margo McAllister." Silence. "Please take a minute to listen to me." She waited until he acquiesced. "Go on."

"The last time I saw you, in Italy, you introduced me to Andrei Andropov. I accepted his offer to take his portrait, seeing as all my other options had fallen through." Margo couldn't help the dig at Dave reneging on the job opportunity.

"It turns out," she continued, "that Andrei admitted to drugging me that night and having his goons wreck my hotel room." She debated whether to tell him about Kirk's role that night, but the story already almost defied belief. The less ludicrous it sounded, the better.

"Andrei has some odd connection with my father because of photos he took of the prior dictator's demise. That's why he wanted me there."

"The assassination?"

"Yes. Anyway, I had to flee Tiranistan, and I still believe my life is in danger. However, some of the photos I took might be useful to the US military, especially now that Andropov is waging war on his neighbors. I'd like to send the images to you and have you get them to Kirk Jones. He has contacts in the military and can get them into the right hands."

Dave waited so long to answer, Margo feared he'd hung up. Finally, he responded. "This story is incredulous."

Margo sighed, exasperated, but also wondering if perhaps Hirschhorn was involved. "Please, Dave. I need your help. I want to send you the photos via overnight mail. All you need to do is call Kirk. I'm sure he'll come pick them up. I wouldn't call you if I weren't desperate. Andrei's aggression could destabilize Europe. Surely, you don't want that."

Another long pause. "Fine. Send them to me here at the magazine."

"Thank you. They'll be there in the morning." She pressed end on the call. What a jerk.

She jumped off the bench and headed toward Walmart to buy a second disk. She'd send one to Dave but keep a copy. Just in case.

She hadn't even made it out of the park when her phone rang. Dave. Surely, he wouldn't refuse this one favor. "Hello?"

"I just called Kirk to corroborate your story. His answering service picked up and said he was on assignment. I asked where and for whom out of habit. They said he was on his way to El Paso, and I could reach him tomorrow. Wait to send the photos until I've talked to him."

Margo ended the call. Panic surged through her. How had Kirk found her?

She threw the phone onto the sidewalk then slammed it with her heel. The haunting message made her attempt to kill its source. She threw the phone to the ground again and again, until she'd broken its carapace and its guts spilled out. Then she picked up every small piece and threw them in the nearest trash can.

She looked around, hoping no one had seen her deranged behavior. The man with the dog had left, and she stood alone in the cool morning.

How much time did she have until Kirk found her?

She continued to Walmart. Now she needed a new phone as well as an extra disk. She had to store the photos some place safe, although with the vise tightening, no place seemed safe.

She dropped over two hundred dollars to purchase a new phone, several disks, and a converter that would allow her to store the photos on a thumb drive.

She mailed copies of the photos to Liliana in New York and to her aunt. She kept the remaining disk.

Her stomach rumbled as she finished the work. Hungry, she found a Mexican restaurant tucked into a back street and opened the door.

Heat and spice emanated from the kitchen of the old adobe building, making her mouth water and pushing the tense fear that followed her out into the desert sky. A few simple wooden tables lined the walls, set atop a scuffed but clean linoleum floor. She stepped through a portal to a place of safety. Kirk, Andrei, and any other evil that chased her couldn't exist in this space.

A grandmotherly woman took her order of migas—a mix of scrambled eggs, tortillas, fresh onions, and jalapeños. Locals swarmed in and out of the restaurant, picking up pre-made bocadillos, sandwiches on thick Mexican rolls that Margo hadn't tried since she was a child.

She thought about Kirk on his way to El Paso, perhaps already here. Worst-case scenario, he still worked for Andrei, and they had located her. This put Alá and Karin in danger. Margo needed to leave, but how would she escape and where would she go?

Perhaps she would take a bus north to New Mexico or Colorado. If she kept riding, she might make it all the way to North Dakota. She could head south, to Mexico. Getting across the border would be easy, but unless she stopped by Alá's and got her passport, she would never get back. No one ever asked for ID going into Mexico. But without a passport, she wouldn't be allowed to return. She'd stand out in Mexico, even with her darker hair, and without papers she couldn't work. She didn't even speak much Spanish.

Perhaps she should take her chances in California or the Pacific Northwest, but those places were expensive. Anywhere, she'd run into the problem of needing papers to get a job. Papers left records. Maybe she could find something off the books. But how? She didn't know anyone, didn't know where to start.

She wanted to stay in the restaurant forever, drinking scalding coffee and eating spicy food. But as much as she tried to keep the thought away, she needed to check in on the outside world. Email and social media accounts begged her for attention. Perhaps there was a message from Liliana or Kirk that would at least signal what to avoid.

As always, she refused to get a phone with data, so she needed to return to the library. Should she go to a different branch? Taking the bus would expose her to more people, but what if they'd found her because she repeatedly used the same library computer?

She left the restaurant and went to the bus stop. She'd seen a poster of the various library branch locations. The closest one lay due north up one of the busier streets. She stayed in the shadow of the bus stop until hers arrived.

Fewer people seemed to notice her with her new hair. Why had she worn the princess look for so long? Maybe she'd always wanted saving. But her version of her father's dream hadn't saved her, nor had princes in dark castles and canvas tents. It was time to step up and save herself.

The bus made halting progress down an endlessly busy street. The houses and businesses of east El Paso crowded the desert until the road dead-ended at the airport. After that, the vast expanse of army bases, airfields, and missile ranges capped the city's northern growth.

She left the bus just short of the airport and strolled into the library, trying to appear natural. At the same time, she scoured every face for danger.

She didn't talk to the librarian but scanned the building for computers. Once she found them, she sat at one that gave her a partial view of the library entrance. She logged in and checked Kirk's social media account first. Nothing new. The last entry contained the photo of the boat and his plea for forgiveness. Bastard.

Next, she looked at Liliana's accounts, searching for something, any explanation or signal. The first photo in her Instagram account showed the top of Liliana's head nestled into a tall airline seat. The image also caught Kirk, eyebrows raised and with his trademark smirk, in the seat directly behind her.

No! Not Liliana. Why had Margo ever dragged her into this? Margo might be able to save herself, but could she save Liliana too?

Margo's eyes dropped to the caption. "Well, it looks like this a-hole has become my own personal bodyguard. Unfortunately, he's growing on me. I'll be taking a few weeks off social media for a tropical vacation. See you in the future."

Tropical vacation? But Dave said Kirk was on his way to El Paso. Margo didn't know who to believe. But beliefs were irrelevant. She had to get to Lili before Kirk, or worse, Andrei, got his tentacles too far into her.

Liliana had encouraged Margo to disappear in El Paso. She'd told her about its size and diversity. Liliana had family here, lots of family, spread generations deep and wide with siblings, aunts, and cousins. Liliana wasn't headed to the tropics. She was coming home and bringing danger with her.

Margo had to get a message to Lili or her family. The time had come to ask her aunt for another favor. If her aunt called Liliana's family from a YWCA landline, surely that wouldn't be noticeable. It had to be worth the risk.

The YWCA wouldn't open for another hour. She went to the nearest post office, deciding to force Dave's hand. The service area wouldn't open for another fifteen minutes, but she found everything she needed in the lobby: an overnight mail envelope, a machine that took cash in exchange for postage, and a slot for overnight mail. If he couldn't get the photos to Kirk, perhaps he knew another photographer with military connections. Yes, he'd been a jerk and hadn't believed her story. But when presented with facts, surely he'd make the right decision.

She had one more stop before the YWCA. She would go to the library near Alá's one last time. There, she'd hide the second disk. Some of the books there looked like they hadn't been opened in years. Originally, she'd figured she'd slip the disk into a dusty book and hope no one would open it. It wouldn't have to be forever, perhaps just a week. It was an insurance policy.

The visit to the post office changed her plan. Someone had left a roll of tape on one of the counters, and she'd snagged it. She'd tape the disk to the underside of her favorite desk.

Now that she stayed off the main roads, she approached the library from the back. She'd run in, get Liliana's mom's phone number to relay to her aunt, then tape the disk to the table. It would take just a few minutes, then she'd be gone.

She peeked around the side of the building, almost expecting to see Kirk waiting for her. Instead, on a bench, sat one of Andrei's goons. The man stared toward the main road. He'd picked her up at the airport when she'd first flown to Tiranistan, and she now believed he had helped trash her hotel room in Italy.

Margo jerked back from the edge of the building, her heart thumping so hard she feared he'd hear it. She turned and tiptoed down the sidewalk, then ran, slipping down one side street and then another until her heaving breath made her stop. It was all falling apart. They'd found her.

Part of her wanted to get on the nearest bus and flee, perhaps even disappear into Mexico. But other people remained in danger. Unlike Andrei, who wanted to destroy his neighbors, she'd find a way to save hers.

She'd get a message to Liliana's family and somehow convince them she needed to escape Kirk. She'd stay far from Alá's. She'd tell her aunt she needed to leave town for a few weeks. These steps were non-negotiable. She'd worry about herself later.

By the time her breath had calmed, she'd made it to the YWCA. She was pretty sure Andrei's guy had found the library because of her emails and online searches. She didn't understand the technical details, but it was the only thing that made sense. She'd never done anything like that from the YWCA, so unless there was some kind of tracker on her, they shouldn't know about it.

Nonetheless, she approached the building carefully. She checked each car in the parking lot for someone lurking inside. She peered behind the building, and while she couldn't see over the wall to the mobile home park next door, she watched the top of the wall for any sign of movement. Nothing. It looked safe. One quick visit, then she'd leave this place as well.

She saw Mrs. Montoya drive into the parking lot, then followed her inside the building, staying out of sight until the woman reached her office. Margo knocked on the door frame.

"Well, good morning, Emma," Mrs. Montoya said. "You're here early. We don't have a session until this afternoon."

"I know, but I need a favor. I met the YWCA director here before I started, Joyce Morehead. I was hoping you would call her and leave a message for me."

Mrs. Montoya's puzzled expression seemed to demand more information. "When I met her, she asked me for information about a friend of mine. I think she and her family used to come to the Y. I can talk to Mrs. Morehead if you'd like." Margo let the silence hang in the room.

"Sure. Why not?" Mrs. Montoya finally said. She picked up the receiver and dialed a few numbers. "Yes, this is Pilar Montoya. May I speak with Joyce?"

A confused look passed over Mrs. Montoya's face. "She hasn't been to the office in a day and a half, and you don't know where she is? Doesn't she usually call in when she's gone?" Silence. "I'd call the police to do a home check. I've worked with her for years, and that's never happened. Yes. File a missing person's report if they'll let you."

Mrs. Montoya hung up the phone, a troubled gaze creasing her forehead. "She's not in the office and no one knows where she is. That's extremely unusual."

A wave of nausea passed through Margo, threatening to bring the morning's breakfast with it. They'd gotten her aunt. *Please let her be okay*, she silently prayed to any god who might be listening. The absolute worst thing had happened.

The time for hiding, whether behind a camera or in an El Paso neighborhood, had come to an end. She looked at the flamboyant Pilar Montoya with her nightclub hair and heavy makeup. Desperate times called for desperate honesty.

"Mrs. Montoya, I'm Joyce's niece, Margo McAllister. She's in trouble, trouble I caused, and I need your help."

Mrs. Montoya looked at her for a long moment, her heavily lashed eyes opening and closing. "You're her sister's daughter."

It wasn't a question, and Margo didn't answer.

"What do you need from me?"

"I need you to contact the family of a friend of mine, Liliana Escobedo. She's traveling with a man, Kirk Jones, who is very dangerous. Well, I'm not sure he's dangerous, but he will bring people here who might kill Liliana and her family. The man in charge, he's happy to kill as many people as he needs to remake his warped version of the world."

"Do you think this man has Joyce?" The woman's voice remained calm, but worry deepened the lines around her eyes and mouth.

Margo didn't want to give voice to her worst nightmare. "Yes. He's after me. I'm going to fix this."

"We need to go to the police." Mrs. Montoya's voice was firm.

"This is way bigger than the police. This man has bombs, terrible weapons. All he wants is me."

The woman gave her an incredulous look. "Well then, I'm certainly not letting you go to him. Joyce would never allow that."

"I'm sorry, ma'am, but you don't understand. This guy is demented. But I think I can convince him to let Joyce go." She had no idea if Andrei would let Joyce go, but she had to try. She'd gotten Joyce and Liliana into this, and she'd get them out if it was the last thing she did.

"Honey, listen to me." Mrs. Montoya's voice had taken on the same schoolteacher's tone she used with the young women in the class. "The person you're describing doesn't sound like someone who leaves loose ends. Take it from someone who knows about this sort of thing, you need reinforcements."

Margo stared at the woman in front of her. Her sunset orange top had a rhinestone applique pattern. Margo had watched her walk in the building and had seen the snug white jeans and six-inch gold sandals. She was the last person who would know about crime. Convincing Mrs. Montoya would take precious time she didn't have. Margo sighed. "Mrs. Montoya . . ."

"Stop." The older woman held up her hand to emphasize her words. "First, please call me Pilar. Second, you've been gone from El Paso for a long time. Most of us in this part of town have family in Juarez, and a drug war has been raging there for over a decade. I was born in Juarez. I've lost family to that war. Truly evil people don't negotiate, and you're a fool if you think they do."

What the hell? A godfather speech from a middle-aged woman working at the YWCA was the last thing she'd expected. "Pilar. I appreciate your experience, but this isn't some drug lord I'm talking about. This guy is a dictator. He controls armies and has a fleet of drones with bombs."

Pilar raised one finely drawn eyebrow. "I promise you, he would cower in front of some of the men I've known in Juarez, and they certainly have their own armies. Nonetheless, you are not equipped to deal with such a man."

"But I have dealt with him. And I escaped."

"And fled to El Paso and hid under an assumed name. And got your aunt trapped in this mess."

The verbal daggers hit their mark, but Margo would not cry. She needed to get out of here. She glanced at Pilar, who had pulled a dark blue business card out of her desk drawer and dialed a number from the phone at her desk. The card triggered a memory of Andrei handing her his black metal business card in Italy. She remembered the email address embossed on it. She'd only used it once, when she'd reached out to him to accept his offer. But she could use it again and offer him whatever it would take for him to leave her people alone.

She thought back to the selfish girl she'd been that night, so caught up in her own dreams she'd left everyone else behind. Andrei terrified her, but taking responsibility for her own actions tied her to the world in a new way. She was a part of something, not someone completely alone. Caring about loved ones was a choice, not an option, and not an obligation.

"I've got this." Margo stood.

"Sit," Pilar barked, still holding the phone to her ear.

Startled, Margo sat.

"Sergeant Castro, please," Pilar said into the phone. "His big sister. Please patch me through to him. I need to talk to him immediately."

Pilar had morphed again, this time into a drill sergeant. Involving the police seemed dangerous, although nothing about Andrei existed outside a world of danger.

"Jaime. I need you to come down to my office right away. There's someone you must talk to."

When she hung up, Margo tried half-heartedly to talk her out of involving the police. Pilar wouldn't listen and wouldn't let her leave. Margo was pretty sure she'd have tackled her had she run for the door.

Finally, Sergeant Castro entered the room, escorted by one of the receptionists. It shocked Margo that he looked nothing like his sister. He had to be fifteen years younger than Pilar, and his muscles clearly strained his conservative police uniform.

"Margo, this is my little brother, Jaime Castro. He works for the El Paso Police Department. You need to tell us the whole story." Pilar turned her attention to Jaime, pointing at the seat beside Margo. "Sit. Joyce Morehead is missing. This is her niece, Margo, and she's afraid someone she knows has Joyce."

Margo recounted the entire tale, starting in Italy and ending in El Paso. "This morning, I saw one of Andrei's thugs outside the library. I'm sure he was waiting for me."

"Do you think President Andropov is here?" Jaime asked.

"No. I'm sure he's not. After all, he's just attacked two of Tiranistan's neighbors. But he has some weird obsession with me, and I'm sure he hates the fact that I escaped. I know how to contact him, and I want to ask him to trade me for Joyce."

Pilar rolled her eyes at her brother. "Please talk to her. She is not reasonable."

Sergeant Castro took a deep breath and turned to Margo. "Given what you know about this guy, do you really think that's going to work?"

Margo didn't want to contemplate that. She wanted to act. No more sitting around. No more hiding. The time for desperate measures had arrived. "It's the only tool I have."

He ran a hand through thick salt and pepper hair. "If you've only got one tool, let's make sure you get everything you can out of it. I'll pull a team together to go over the details. Do you want to come down to the station with me?"

"No." It sounded like a trap. Once she'd given up her freedom, she'd lose control of the timeline and the outcome. Just like she had in Tiranistan.

"Margo, let us help you," Jaime said.

"Help by going to check on my aunt. You need to see if she's okay. They haven't heard from her in two days, and that's not like her."

"I asked the main branch to call in a check," Pilar said.

"Okay, we'll follow up on that. Contact whoever made the call and get any information they gave her. I'll put a call in to dispatch," Jaime said.

"I need to use the restroom." Margo jumped out of her seat and exited the office before they responded. A whirlwind of panic raged inside her. She looked out the glass doors of the entrance, but danger lurked there. She turned into the ladies' room and paced back and forth in front of the sinks. Where had they taken Joyce? How many people did Andrei have in El Paso? She'd seen the guy at the library. If he was the only one, that meant no one was with Joyce. She didn't want to think about what that meant. Better to imagine her aunt tied up than no longer needing a guard at all.

But Andrei wouldn't kill Joyce. Not when he could use her as leverage against Margo. How had she gotten into this mess? What was it about her, or her father, that taunted him so? Why build a shrine to a dead man's photos, entrap his daughter, and break laws to lure her back when she escaped?

She had to think forward instead of dwelling on the past. If she emailed him, he would message her back. The certainty of that anchored her and made her fingers itch with the desire to type. She needed a computer but couldn't return to the library with Andrei's thug waiting outside. She wouldn't go back to Alá's and endanger those wonderful people. Logging in from here seemed stupid. These women had enough trouble without bringing in evil from the other side of the world. She remembered Pilar's talk about the drug war. Yes, they had already born a heavy burden.

Finally, a plan occurred to her. She'd work with the policeman, but on her terms. When Margo opened the bathroom door, Pilar leaned against the opposite wall, arms crossed. Margo sensed a toughness in her that the colorful clothes and makeup tried to hide.

"You don't trust me," Margo said.

"I don't know you. But no, I don't trust many people. But I do trust Joyce, and she is what is important to me. Therefore, I can't have you screw up."

"I have an idea." Margo headed toward Pilar's office.

"Seargent Castro, I want to work with you but on my terms."

"Call me Jaime. What are your terms?"

"I have Andrei Andropov's private email. I am certain he will get back to me if I reach out to him. I don't want to put anyone in danger who isn't prepared to deal with it. But I can send the message from any device." She stared at the phone in his palm.

"We've got computers that can't be traced at headquarters. Why don't you use one of those."

"Because I don't want him to know I'm working with the police, and while you say your computers can't be traced, he's got people who can probably trace anything. I believe that would endanger Joyce." She wouldn't expose Darpan to this police officer, but she didn't doubt his abilities.

"Well, he's going to know the police are involved as soon as we pick up his guy casing the library."

"No. You can't do that! Andrei, he's, he's not well. We need to see what he wants first, before he knows we're on to him. Please. I know this guy. If he feels he's losing control, he'll burn everything to the ground. So far in his war, he's bombed a school and a hospital and he's threatening to bomb a nuclear power plant. He doesn't care about anything except returning his country to greatness. Let's find out what he wants first. Then we can make a plan."

"I understand how badly you want to be involved, but we need to let the professionals handle this." Jaime sat forward in his chair.

Margo had retaken the seat near him. She wanted to run for the door to ensure she stayed out of his grasp, but she needed him to find Joyce. "No offense, but my aunt's life may be on the line. I'm the only one here who knows this guy. If you want to help, let me use your phone. That's the only way I'll keep you involved."

Margo looked from Jaime to Pilar as the air hummed with tension. Jaime crossed his arms, securing his phone next to well-cut pecs. Pilar's eyes distilled to hard black points as she watched her brother. Margo let the silence stretch.

Pilar broke first. "Jaime, if you don't give her your phone, I'll give her mine." She picked up the oversized, rhinestone-encrusted phone on her desk.

"That's not how this works," Jaime said.

"It is today." Pilar passed her phone across the desk, and Margo reached for it.

"Wait." Jaime's booming voice stopped both women. "Here. You have to share all your information with me so we can plan an appropriate response." He handed Margo the phone.

"Thank you." She took the device.

"Can I drive you someplace else to use it? We don't want the geo-coordinates of the YWCA showing up anywhere."

"That makes sense." Margo rose, then turned to Pilar. "Thank you. I hope I get the chance to know you better." Her fingers itched to photograph this woman in the harsh desert sun just to see if she could capture all her facets. She helped other women for a living, dressed like a circus, and had a core of pure steel.

She followed Jaime to his car and breathed a sigh of relief at seeing a black sedan instead of a marked police car. He opened the door for her, then took the driver's seat. Within minutes, he'd pulled into a parking lot near one of the international bridges to Mexico.

"Why here?" Margo asked.

"The phone companies tend to get confused about which country you're in when you're close to the border. Figured it wouldn't hurt."

"Smart." She activated his phone, then handed it to him to unlock. As soon as he returned it, she navigated to her old email address. She scanned through the unopened emails, surprised at the number of them from Kirk, a majority with "sorry" in the title. Asshole.

She decided she needed to trust Jaime. "My best friend, who's from El Paso, may be coming here with someone who works for Andrei Andropov. I told you about this guy. He's the one who drugged me in Italy. I'm not clear about the whole story, but I'm worried she's in danger. That's why I went to Pilar's. I wanted her to call the family and warn them."

"I'm happy to do that, and we can send a patrol car by the house to check on them."

"Thank you." Margo turned back to the phone.

"What the hell have you done with my aunt?" She typed. Hitting send made her want to throw up. She felt Andrei's evil tentacles reach for her through the airwaves.

She glanced at Jaime. "Now we wait."

"So, this all started because of some photo award?" Jaime asked.

Margo thought about the question, considered the girl from the night of the party who seemed so different from the woman she was today. "I had my priorities in the wrong place back then. It left me vulnerable to attack by someone like Andrei." She straightened her spine. "Make no mistake, I was wronged by this guy, but I understand what's important now. These people whom I've put in danger, they mean so much more to me than any award ever could."

"You remind me of another young woman I know. Be careful about sacrificing your safety for bravery. These people you love, they love you too. I'm pretty confident you'd ruin their worlds if you allowed this guy to capture you again."

She looked at him, all kind eyes and big muscles. He'd be easy to photograph. His insides matched his exterior. A rare trait. "I'll be careful. And I appreciate your help."

She glanced down at the phone in her hands. A new message had arrived. "Margo. I've been waiting for you. I want to call you."

"No way." She showed Jaime the email before she sent it. He nodded.

This time they waited ten minutes for a response. "You always disobey me. If you want your aunt to survive, you will follow my instructions. Confirm."

"I need to know what they are first."

"Someone will email you the arrangements."

They waited again, longer this time. She wanted to ask Jaime questions, learn about his job, his youth in El Paso, his big sister, anything to pass the time. But she kept her mouth shut, shackled by fear and worried about everyone she'd endangered since returning to the US.

Eventually, she received an email from a different address, instructing her to go to the boardroom at the Paso del Norte hotel at two o'clock that afternoon. Alone.

Chapter 21

Jaime burst into action. He told her he'd post undercover officers at the hotel. They'd also monitor the boardroom. He initially received pushback from his call to the fancy downtown hotel, but after a few minutes on the line with the hotel manager, they'd reached an agreement. They'd have a camera and recording device in the room.

Once he finished the call, he let Margo know the hotel had been instructed to set up the room for a visual conference call. He invited her down to police headquarters to wait. "I can't think of a safer place for you to be."

She considered her options, but none existed. At least none that didn't put herself or others at risk. "Fine. Thank you. But would you also send someone to check on the house where I've been staying? There's a wonderful older woman there and her granddaughter. I wouldn't want anything to happen to them because of my actions."

"Certainly." He took the address and made the call. Then they drove downtown.

She sat in his spare office, vacillating between fear and boredom. She couldn't imagine how the meeting would go. Andrei would never give up her aunt unless he could have her back, and she couldn't imagine stepping on a plane and returning to his lair. But she would, for Joyce, she just couldn't put the pieces together in a way that would ensure Joyce's safety.

Jaime dashed in and out of the office in a flurry of activity. He let her know the officers he'd sent hadn't noticed anything unusual at Alá's house. They'd driven by Liliana's mother's home, where everything seemed fine, but no one had reached her yet.

At noon, he came in with two turkey sandwiches and bags of chips. Starving, Margo thanked him then greedily took a bite.

"Sorry, I should have asked you if you were hungry earlier," Jaime said, a grin on his face.

"It's really good," Margo said, as soon as she could speak. They ate in silence for a while. Full, Margo put the rest of her sandwich aside. "So, tell me something about yourself. Are you married with kids?"

"No. No wife, no children."

"Really?" That surprised her. While too old for her, he was a good-looking guy. "I thought everyone in El Paso married early and had children."

"Not everyone." He almost seemed a little sad. "What about you?"

Margo chuckled. "I've had no luck with men. Zero. Although, I've always been pretty focused on my career." That had been a good decision once. Her mind ran to Darpan. Perhaps someday, when all this was over, she'd make a different choice.

It seemed to take forever, but finally, time moved forward, and they left for the hotel. It was only a few blocks from police headquarters, but Jaime drove her to a side door where she would enter through the bar instead of the main entrance. He mentioned that undercover police officers were posted at the hotel. She'd be safe, even though they hadn't found the goon who'd waited for her outside the library.

Margo slipped out of the car and trotted up a set of stairs. She opened a wooden door that led to a large bar. She stepped onto the hunter green carpet and gazed at the pink marble walls that soared toward a high ceiling decorated with a Tiffany dome. A large, perfectly round bar sat below it and mimicked the dome's shape.

Two men sat at the bar, and several people half hidden by high-back chairs occupied sitting areas scattered about the room. Margo crossed the bar and made her way to the front desk.

"Would you direct me to the boardroom?"

She followed the directions up a marble staircase to the second floor. She trod down a hallway and passed a ballroom with a Rotary Club sign outside. A line of people cued near a registration table. A little further down, the hall emptied save for a tall man in slacks and a polo shirt. He looked young for a Rotarian, and perhaps he was a police officer. Or perhaps one of Andrei's men. He gave her a friendly nod.

She found the boardroom on her right and stood before the door for a minute, afraid to grab the handle. Perhaps it would burn her or sear her skin with poison. But that was just the fear talking, and this was a time for bravery. She opened the door to a wood-paneled room. The windows on the far side would have provided a spectacular view of downtown, but blinds had been pulled, making the room dark and foreboding.

A giant TV monitor rested at one end of a solid mahogany table. At the other end, a bottle of water, a notepad, and a pen waited for her. No one else was there.

She sat in her assigned seat, a tremor of fear running through her body even though she would face an image of Andrei, not his actual body. She understood the power of images. She pulled out her phone to look at the time. Three minutes until two. The phone shook in her hand, and she hid both hands beneath the table so no one could see. As she did so, she hit the record button on her phone. The police had told her they would record the meeting, but Margo knew how quickly things might go wrong.

At two on the dot, a hotel employee came in and turned on the TV with a remote, then left the room. Margo wished he'd left the remote on the table, giving her the power to end the meeting. No such luck.

Almost immediately, the screen flashed green, and then there he was. Andrei sat in a chair facing her. Unlike her, he had no table to hide behind. If anything, his chair reminded her of the captain's chair in the starship *Enterprise*. What, was taking over his neighbors not enough? Did he have his eyes on the entire universe?

Of course, right now, his eyes focused on her. The bulk of him seemed ready to pounce through the screen and grab her, pull her back into whatever twisted nightmare he inhabited.

"Margo McAllister. We meet again, as I knew we would."

Margo said nothing. This was his show. Let him run it.

"What have you done with your hair? That is a terrible mistake. You should be proud of being blond and blue eyed. Like me."

Fuck. On top of everything else, he was an Aryan supremacist? He actually could get worse. Still, she kept her mouth closed.

"It wouldn't have stopped me from finding you. My men were on your tail. Not to mention that of your loved ones."

That did it. "Where is my aunt?"

"We are," he paused, "taking care of her."

Margo wanted to rush the screen, break it, or reach through it and rip him apart. Joyce didn't deserve any of this. Regret washed through her, carrying away the anger.

"I want her back. Safe." She hoped she sounded firm.

"And if I give you that, what do I get in return?" His sinister voice spread through the room.

"I will destroy the photos I have of your missiles and drones," she said. "There are people who might be very interested in your technology."

He laughed the way a person laughs when they've caught something in a trap, a mix of glee and anticipation. "That is your offer? I would pay you to release those photos. I want the world to know how powerful Tiranistan is. My people dribble your pictures out in pieces searching for an audience. Your story would provide context. The world would love it. Perhaps I will kill your aunt unless you do this."

It had never occurred to her that had been his goal. He didn't want her, just good photos. The slight relief quickly fell away. She had only one bargaining chip left.

"What will it take to guarantee my aunt's safety?"

"I think you know, Margo. Do you not want to say it?"

She closed her eyes. "Me."

Silence. He made no sound. The boardroom's thick walls and windows dampened any noise that might have come through. Her only option: open her eyes and accept her fate. She looked into his cold face.

"I think you have the wrong impression of what I want," he said. "I can have anyone I want in my bed. And with what you have done to yourself, you are far less appealing to me. What you fail to understand is that you are part of a legacy, part of my legacy."

Why did this guy always speak in riddles? If it got Aunt Joyce back, she'd give him whatever he wanted. An idea hit her. "Does it have to do with that creepy room you made with my dad's photos?"

"I don't know that creepy is the right word. Historic is probably more appropriate. Your father didn't just document the end of an era, he damaged my country's reputation in the world and caused decades of strife at home."

"He took photos." Just three words.

Yes, her father's photos showed a gruesome moment in the country's past. But they were merely images. Her father hadn't executed a dictator. Just like her images couldn't make Andrei dignified. Or sane.

"I have hated your father for many decades. When he splashed my father's death across the world, he tried to steal my future."

"Your father? You told me you were an orphan." She'd felt sorry for him. Worse, she'd felt some kinship to him.

"I was, after that." A long moment passed where Andrei's focus moved away from her. She almost saw the thoughts crossing his face. "There is a woman who gave birth to me, but she is a prostitute. That is not a mother."

Margo kept herself from rolling her eyes at him. Poor little dictator boy. "Look, I don't know what you want from me, but I can't help you with your family problems. Believe me, I've had plenty of those myself. I need you to release my aunt."

Andrei visibly reacted, morphing from human to a pillar of steel. "You still don't understand. Our bond is greater than any individual. Tiranistan is a country where old beliefs hold sway. I have clawed my way to the top of the military as a poor orphan boy, but I will soon reveal my true lineage. I will remind my people that we once had a prosperous, respected country, and we can again as we return to our greatness by returning to a monarchy. My people believe in the tales of our forefathers, and together, you and I are the subjects of the next chapter in this story. The father destroyed the father, and with it, his country's power. Now the son has risen, and he will use the daughter to tell a new tale, to bring on a new age of greatness."

The zeal in his eyes flashed through the monitor. He had fully bought into his crazed story of destiny. Did her images play a role in this? Did they show him he could be the man/god he wanted to be, the king a monarchy required? She wished she'd never picked up a camera.

"You will return to Tiranistan. In the Grand Plaza, in the exact location where they beheaded my father, you will kneel before me. Banners depicting my greatness will be hung from the walls. The very photos you took. You will pledge your allegiance to atone for the sins of your father. Then, I will send you into battle."

War. She'd die like her father did. But why would anyone care? She pictured herself on her knees before him, in front of a crowd. She looked into his eyes, trying to see through to the core of him. When she'd photographed him, his ego showed through. Now, another light brightened his eyes. In pursuing his destiny, he'd stepped beyond the edge of reason.

She'd once chased a destiny that her work and talent would bring to fruition. She understood how those dreams could cloud your vision. Like Andrei, she'd focused so tightly on her goal that she'd thrown others aside. He couldn't speak of his mother without hate in his voice. He had cast her aside. She'd spent plenty of time dwelling on the shortcomings of her own mother and had cast aside the woman who deserved that role. Margo understood the heart of a dictator.

But that had changed. Andrei, in part, had shown her the lonely destination of that path. And she had escaped. Returned to friends and family.

And before she'd escaped, she had opened her heart, for the first time, to something more rewarding than her own vision. A pang of longing for Darpan pierced her. She hoped he had escaped as well.

To escape only to return yourself to captivity to protect those you loved. She couldn't help the tears that filled her eyes as her heart grew to encompass all the loss the man in front of her would require. But she would not let her loved ones fall. She was no longer the woman behind the camera. She'd grown into a woman brave enough to face Andrei without a shield. She'd bare her chest to his sword, as long as those she loved remained safe.

"Whatever you want from me to finish your tale, you can have it. But only if I know my aunt is safe first."

"I cannot trust you to keep your word. You turn yourself in to my men and then we will release your aunt."

"No." She might be desperate, but nothing would make her believe his lies. She looked at her phone. "You have two hours for my aunt to make it somewhere safe. Tell her to contact her work, or better, to go there. Once that happens, I'll do whatever you want."

"You do not get to dictate what happens." He spat the words at her.

Margo stood.

"Ah, Margo. Always wanting to leave the party early. If you only knew how little power you actually have. Sit, or your aunt dies."

Margo paused but didn't sit. She didn't know how to move beyond the impasse.

"Have Margo return to the hotel boardroom in two hours." A voice spoke from the shadows behind Andrei. "We'll prove her aunt's release and take her into custody."

She strained her eyes toward the darkness behind Andrei. Then he walked into the light. Darpan. She slumped into the chair, her legs too weak to hold her. Utter defeat. She had believed in love. And it had ripped her heart out. She stared at the table but only saw a pool of black. Kirk stole her career, Andrei stole her safety, Darpan stole her heart. She might as well give up now and hand over the shell of a person she'd become. She'd deliver to Andrei flesh, bones, and a gaping hole of nothing.

"It seems you have surprised your lover." The hateful words spilled from Andrei's mouth. "Your idea is sound, Darpan. Margo, you are free to go, but return in two hours if you value your aunt's life. And Margo, please remember that we will find you, whether you return or not. You are the missing piece of my story. The prince must always slay the dragon before becoming king."

She stood, unwilling to face the screen, and left the room. Andrei might see a dragon, but Darpan had removed her claws and extinguished her fire.

Chapter 22

Margo descended the hotel's marble staircase. She walked straight to the bar, completely numb. "A double tequila, please."

The bartender nodded. She hated tequila. Although, not nearly as much as she hated herself. She threw the drink into the back of her throat, hopefully avoiding her tastebuds. It almost made her gag anyway. Fuck life.

Joyce. Saving her aunt remained the one worthwhile feat she had left to achieve. With any luck, she'd survive as well, thanks to Jaime's helpers. Although Andrei would never stop. She'd have to disappear again, for real this time.

She scanned the bar and didn't see anyone who looked like a police officer. Quickly, she paid for her drink and made for the door. The glass doors of the hotel slid open as she approached.

Margo stepped into the harsh desert sun. Inside her skin, bleakness prevailed, yet above her a cheery lemon sun decorated a cornflower blue sky. For others, life would go on, even if she gave up and returned to a dark fairytale or hid like a terrified mouse.

In front of her, the marquee of an old theater known for hosting great musicians gleamed. To her left, a modern art museum flanked the older building. Between the two lay a larger stepped plaza where she'd drawn chalk art at an annual festival. The past she'd hated now glowed like diamonds compared to her dark future.

A handful of people gathered halfway up the plaza. Perhaps someone had chalk. She had two hours to kill. Why not look at something pretty?

As she approached, angry words crossed the air. Instead of artists, she saw two burly men. And Kirk. And Liliana. For the second time in ten minutes, her world dropped away.

Margo yelled without thinking, no words, just a roar. How had three enemies surrounded her best friend? They would not take Liliana to the evil castle or the haunted wood. Margo sprang forward. She couldn't match their bulk, didn't have their muscles, but she had blinding fury on her side. She'd rip the goons to shreds and pull Kirk's fetid heart through his chest.

"Wait!" Margo heard a voice behind her, then strong arms wrapped around her. Her feet lifted off the ground as a man pulled her into his broad chest.

Another man ran by, shouting. "Stop. El Paso Police."

Margo watched in slow motion shock. The burly men turned toward the voice. Liliana jerked her arm away from the one who'd grabbed her and placed a sharp-toed kick in his groin. He bent, a savage grunt of air escaping. Kirk pulled Liliana one direction as the two goons sprinted away, one hunched in obvious pain.

Margo wriggled and kicked at her captor. "Put me down!" she screamed. Her feet touched the decorative pavers, and she dashed toward Liliana. "Don't touch her," she screamed again, slamming her fists into the arm Kirk used to hold Liliana tight.

"It's okay. I'm okay." Liliana wrapped her in a hug the second Kirk let her go. "Cálmate. Calm down. Everything is fine."

A sob escaped Margo. She'd put so many people in danger. *Joyce*. Margo kept her fierce grip on Liliana as she tried to thread the steel back through her spine. She wouldn't break now. She had to hold it together for two more hours.

She finally pulled away from her friend, the desperation pushed down for now. Liliana appeared unphased by everything that had just happened. "Why are you here?" Margo asked. "They almost got you."

"I'm fine. Did you see me kick that guy in the nuts? That felt good."

"Margo!" A shout came from the direction of the hotel. Jaime had pulled his black cruiser onto the curb.

"Sergeant, I'm in pursuit," the man who'd held Margo said. Then he sprinted by, going after the goons and the police officer following them.

"This is Sergeant Castro," Margo said to Liliana. "He can keep us safe for now."

They headed toward the vehicle, but Margo stopped when she saw Kirk following. "What the hell do you think you're doing? Shouldn't you have run off with Andrei's other goons?"

Hurt shot through his eyes, then he glanced at Liliana.

"He's with me. You need to hear his story," Liliana said.

"You can't trust him!" Outrage trembled through her voice. Liliana had more street smarts than anyone Margo knew. She couldn't believe Kirk's charm had worked on her.

"You need to hear what he's been through. Besides, we're going with a police officer, right? If he's not legit, they can put him in jail." Liliana's voice remained flat, but Kirk's eyebrows rose at the threat.

Damn, Margo loved this woman. Liliana might have been able to beat even Andrei at his game. But he'd named Margo the dragon. They needed to get back to the police station so she could update Jaime on her conversation with the dictator.

———

Back in Jaime's office, Margo fumed at Kirk across a small table. Liliana's eyes darted back and forth between them while Jaime took notes at his desk.

"I'm so sorry." Kirk ran his fingers over his mussed hair. "I feel like this is all my fault. I'm such a fucking twit."

The proper amount of shame shone through his eyes, but sorry wouldn't cut it. "You gave me drugs. You ruined my life. You stole my prize. My aunt might die because of you. I—you have no idea what I went through, what I barely escaped. And now, if I'm lucky, I'll trade my life to save Joyce's. All because of you." Pure hate singed her bones.

Tears formed in Kirk's eyes and fell silently down his cheeks. Fucking bastard looked even more handsome when he cried.

"I shouldn't have done it. He promised me you wouldn't get hurt."

"How long have you been working for Mr. Andropov?" Jaime asked.

"Just that one night. He paid me five thousand dollars in cash, and I haven't heard from him since."

"Why on earth should anyone believe you?" Margo barely kept herself from screaming the words. "My life is in danger. My aunt is missing. Other people are in danger."

Margo turned to Liliana. "I told you how horrible Andropov is. He has Joyce. He could go after you and your family to hurt me. Why did you trust this guy?" She nodded toward Kirk.

"I saw him out at a bar one night. I knew what he'd done to you, and I just flipped." Liliana looked away from Margo and started picking at her nail polish. "I chewed him out. He shouldn't have gotten away with what he did. He shouldn't have won that prize. That was yours."

"I had no idea about the hotel bill until she told me," Kirk said. "That made me feel even worse. I'm a complete fraud. I haven't taken a photograph since that night. I won the prize, but I knew it wasn't mine. I'm so ashamed." Tears trailed his face.

"He kept pestering me, and eventually I felt sorry for him." Liliana sighed heavily after the admission.

Margo turned on Kirk. "Do you think I care if you're ashamed? You ruined my life. You're still ruining it. I'm terrified about what they're doing to my aunt."

"You're right. I'm a complete loser, just like my dad always said. I'll do anything to make it up to you. Anything."

"Are you still in contact with Andrei Andropov?" Jaime asked.

"No, not since that night."

"I need you to give us any information you have on him." Jaime's pen hovered above a notepad.

"I don't have anything. I met him at the party that night. He told me I should win the prize, but he'd heard Margo would get it. He said some of the decision-makers had decided to give it to her because of her dad. He's a hero in our industry, one who gave his life in pursuit of photography. They felt bad she'd had to grow up without him."

Margo wanted to throw up. She'd worked so hard, had strived to be as good as her dad. Did people really think she'd gotten a leg up because of him? She'd never even met him. "That's disgusting. It's not true." Tears of shock filled her eyes.

"You're right. It was a convenient excuse for me to do something inexcusable. He gave me an envelope with fifty-one-hundred-dollar bills, and a vial of what he said was Rohypnol."

"You jackass." Margo couldn't keep the anger from her voice.

"He promised he wouldn't hurt you. He even said I could stay with you to make sure you were safe."

Margo crossed her arms in front of her chest, trying to hold in her rage. She had more important things to deal with than Kirk, but she wanted to destroy him the way he'd so easily destroyed her.

Kirk turned away from her glare and looked at the cop. "I put it in her champagne. He said to take her outside and some of his people would be waiting. We pretty much had to drag Margo to the hotel, the drug hit her so hard. They even had a key to her room."

"And you thought all this was okay?" Jaime asked. "You didn't think about getting help from the hotel staff before you took a drugged woman up to a hotel room with a bunch of people you didn't know?"

"I keep telling you. Andropov told me she wouldn't be hurt. He said he would get the committee to re-evaluate the prize, that it should be based on quality photography, not nepotism. I wanted to believe him." Kirk looked at Margo. "I'm so sorry. My photos weren't as good as yours. They never have been, and I've hated that from the moment I first saw your work."

"But we were together." Margo felt the past shift beneath her as a former truth turned to dust.

"Yeah, well that was just sex."

"I'm going to fucking kill you." Liliana's voice entered the fray like a viper. "I actually felt sorry for you."

"I'm telling you, I screwed up, but I didn't leave her alone with those guys. And you know I've been trying to help ever since." Kirk's pleading eyes stared at Liliana.

The whole mess disgusted Margo. She checked her phone for the time. Just over an hour to go. "He can't tell us anything helpful. Why did you bring him here and how did you get to the plaza?" she asked Liliana.

"I bought into his sob story. He said he wanted to make things up to you. I know you told me to be careful, but he followed me around every day, saying he felt guilty and wanted to help. When they ransacked my apartment, I called him and yelled at him. I thought he had something to do with it. Instead, he insisted I leave town. He showed up with tickets to El Paso. I'd told him I wanted to go home. I guess by then I trusted him."

"That probably wasn't a good move," Jaime said.

"Yeah. I know that now. We were downtown because I needed to get out of my mom's house. Cousins and aunts have been dropping by all day to see me. I got tired of trying to explain the gringo boy and why I still lived in New York and why I didn't have kids yet. I thought I'd show him downtown, but then those goons found us."

"Those two guys were part of the team from Italy," Kirk said. "I recognized them. Unfortunately, they recognized me too. They seemed shocked to see me."

"What exactly happened out there?" Jaime asked.

Before Kirk could respond, a uniformed officer walked in. "Sergeant, we still haven't apprehended the two men, but we've got several units on the ground searching."

More bad news. They'd have time to get word back to Andrei, or to get to Joyce. She turned on Kirk. "You. You caused this. You started all of it. If you hadn't drugged me at the party, none of this would have happened." She hated

Kirk with every cell in her body, but in the back of her mind, she knew Andrei would have found her another way if this plan hadn't worked.

Whatever fantasy turned nightmare held him in its grip, he believed it. And needed his people to believe it to legitimize him so he could become all powerful. Kirk had been a pawn in a much larger game.

"Why didn't you tell me the whole story?" Liliana glowered at Kirk.

"It's all my fault, and I'd give anything to have made different decisions." He turned to Margo. "I'll do anything to make it up to you. I'll give you the prize money. Everything I haven't spent yet. If I could trade places with you and take on this asshole, I would. Please. Let me make amends."

"If I survive whatever goes down next, I'll take the fucking money. And you need to make some phone calls to people in our industry to tell them what you did. You cratered my reputation."

"All of this because you were jealous?" Liliana piped in, coiled anger in her voice. "What the hell is wrong with you?"

Kirk dropped his head into his hand. "I'm a total dick."

"There are laws against drugging people without their knowledge," Jaime said.

"Yeah. Although that was in Italy. No jurisdiction here," Kirk said.

"Man, you really are an asshole," Jaime said, shaking his head. "You aren't allowed to leave here until I give you permission. Do I need to lock you up?"

"No, sir."

"Okay, let's move on," Jaime said. "We've got about an hour before the next meeting. Margo, are you sure you want to do this?"

"I have to. Hopefully, Andrei will keep his word and we'll hear from Joyce before then."

"That's the best case scenario," Jaime said. "We'll keep his guys from getting to you at the hotel. Although, I'd appreciate it if you'd wait for our help instead of slipping out the hotel door opposite of where we expected you."

"Sorry about that. It was a lot to deal with. The guy with Andrei, well, I thought he was against Andrei. It shocked me to see him behind the scenes assisting him."

"I guess you can't trust anyone," Liliana said, sneering at Kirk.

Liliana rarely showed that kind of hurt anger. Margo wondered what drove it. No, she didn't wonder. Kirk made it easy to get close to him. Margo had, although she'd proven to be a spectacularly bad judge of character, at least when it came to the guys she slept with.

"Hey, Jaime, can I use your phone again?" Margo asked. "I want to check and see if I have any messages. Like, from Joyce."

Jaime handed her the device. She checked social media, checked the new email address she'd given Joyce, then scrolled through the various emails she'd created since she'd been on the run.

There it was. Her only new email came from Darpan at the address she'd set up specifically for him. She hadn't even realized she'd looked that one up. She glanced around the room. No one looked at her. She'd check it first, then tell them. The date stamp carried today's date. Her finger hovered over the bold black type. Pain and betrayal welled in her, finally giving her the power to click the message.

"Joyce is safe. The drone etching contains maps of Tiranistan's war-related communications assets. Please get to US military. I'm sorry."

Margo broke. She couldn't tell the difference between lies and truth anymore, had no idea who wanted to help or hurt her. The phone slipped from her fingers.

Liliana appeared and wrapped her arms securely around her, tethering her to reality. "Margo, it's okay. I promise you this is going to be okay."

"This says Joyce is safe." Jaime had grabbed the phone. Do you think he's telling the truth?"

That was the question. Margo had no idea. Which Darpan should she believe? The one she'd loved and trusted in Tiranistan? The one behind Andrei in the video? Neither? Neither was probably the better place to start.

"I don't know," she answered. "Probably not. But there's no reason not to deal with the second half of his email. Kirk, I need a favor." How she hated muttering those words. But he owed her, and if he delivered . . .well, it didn't count for much, but it was a start.

"What do you need?" he asked.

She pulled a slim storage device from her pocket. "According to Andrei's communications expert, the etchings on the drone show the war-time communications assets of Tiranistan. Of course, he might be lying, and Andrei himself said he wanted people to see his capabilities. But we should let the experts decide. There are lots of drone photos here. Get them into the appropriate hands at the US military."

"I can do that." He looked at Jaime. "Do you guys have a computer that takes this size disk?"

"Yeah. Let me take you to our IT department."

After they'd left, Liliana pulled a chair to Margo's side and wrapped an arm around her. "Are you okay?"

The question had no easy answer. No, obviously, but for so many reasons. Joyce. Darpan. Andrei. Herself. "I've screwed up so many times with this one. I really have horrible taste in men. Kirk is a total and complete asshole. Andrei—I thought that was a job. Instead, it was a nightmare. And Darpan broke my heart." She looked at her friend and saw compassion. "I thought I could see the world differently with him. My life came into focus, and I realized how much I'd missed by chasing my father's dreams. And then he betrayed me."

Liliana grabbed a few tissues from a nearby table and handed them to Margo. "You've never been in love before."

"Yeah. I'm just one solid tragedy after another." She blotted at the tears that wouldn't quit falling.

"Hey, we're all just trying to make our way through the world the best way we can. Honestly, I hate to admit it because you warned me about him, and you used to date him, but I started to crush on Kirk a little. That man is just too attractive. But don't worry. I'm over it."

"Where are the honest, uncomplicated guys?"

"That Jaime's not too bad."

"He's like twenty years older than us." Margo shook her head. "You are always on the make." The easy conversation tilted the world back to normal. Margo could breathe again, and more importantly, she could make plans.

They only had ten minutes until the meeting, and Jaime still hadn't returned. Margo paced his office and had decided to give him sixty more seconds before she went on her own.

Just then, Jaime rounded the door. "We caught Andrei's goons. They haven't given us any information yet, but it's a start."

"You mean information like where my aunt is and whether they're Andrei's only two guys in El Paso?"

"Yes. Exactly."

"Well, we can't wait any longer. I've got to get back to the hotel." Margo started for the door.

"I'm coming too," Liliana said.

"No. You're not. Please stay here. Keep an eye on Kirk and please let me know if anyone hears from Aunt Joyce. Andrei wants me to go alone, and I don't want to risk Joyce's safety by having anyone else there." She didn't want to risk Liliana's safety either and didn't have time to argue with her friend.

Jaime drove her back to the hotel. "We've got three times as many people at the hotel this time," Jaime said. "As soon as you're done, exit the boardroom and you'll be escorted to my vehicle."

"Got it." Margo left the car. In the hotel, she trudged up the marble staircase once again. Her stomach roiled as she approached the boardroom door. Fear didn't take over like the first time, at least not fear for herself. She'd been through so many emotions today, she just wanted it to end, as long as Joyce survived.

She sat alone at the table facing the blank monitor. The black matte screen mirrored Andrei's soul. It mirrored the part of her that used to believe love was possible. She should have known better.

The hotel clerk entered the room and turned on the monitor, just like before. This time, the device didn't spark to life with a bright green screen. He rummaged around the back of the monitor, plugged things in, pulled them out again, made adjustments. Each time he tried for a signal, nothing came through.

"Could they have changed the time?" he asked. "They aren't online."

"Please keep trying." What else could she say? Andrei was her lifeline to Joyce. And her death sentence. It didn't matter if the police managed to get her out today. She'd seen Andrei's crazed eyes and his belief in his self-made legend. No matter how far she ran, he'd follow. She could live with that. She couldn't live with Joyce's blood on her hands.

The clerk continued to work on the machine, but after ten more minutes, he gave up. "I'm sorry. The signal's just not there."

She hated those words. They meant the end. Whether Andrei had found out about his guys being caught, whether he'd realized she wasn't alone, or whether he'd finally figured out the way to destroy her wasn't to recapture her but to make her responsible for the torture or death of her one remaining relative, it didn't matter. Andrei's great game had ended, and she'd lost.

She laid her head on the cool wood of the table, wishing she could melt into it and cease to exist. An ache as vast as the desert and the seas and the mountains filled her. Maybe she did have the time wrong. Maybe she could convince the clerk to come back on the hour or half hour and try again. Maybe the world hadn't stopped spinning.

Margo had no idea how much time had passed when a knock came at the door. She didn't lift her head. Didn't speak.

"Margo?" Jaime's voice. The door opened and footsteps approached. "What happened?"

"He didn't show." She didn't bother to lift her head. Perhaps she would stay in this room until she turned to bones. She could haunt the hotel with tales of sadness and evil.

"It's okay. We'll eventually get some information out of his guys."

Andrei's guys would never break. Their punishment back home for squealing would overshadow anything the cops might do to them here.

"Come on, let's get back to the station," Jaime said.

"I'm going to stay here."

"Here? In this room?"

"No. Not forever. I guess I'll get a guest room. I'll talk to the front desk. I want to be here if he tries to contact me."

"But we're waiting to hear from Joyce. My sister has set up a whole phone ladder."

"You can reach me here if there's any word." There wouldn't be. She feared saying it out loud. That might make it true. But she still believed it.

"I don't think it's safe for you to be here," Jaime said.

Some spark lit deep inside her and managed to flare through the pool of sadness and regret. "Fuck safe. The only person's safety I care about is Joyce's. If there is any chance my being here gets me in front of Andrei a little faster, then I'm not leaving."

"I can't protect you as well here as I can at headquarters."

Her head finally came off the table. She made sure her voice registered disgust instead of despair. "I don't want your protection. I didn't ask for it, and I don't want it. I know this guy. My last, best chance is to talk to him again."

Jaime ran his hand through his thick hair, pulling at it. "What is it with women your age? You never listen."

Curious. She wondered who else antagonized him like this. In the end, it didn't matter. She'd made up her mind. "I'm going to get a room."

"I can take you into custody."

"That would be a fucking terrible idea." She brushed past him and headed for the stairs.

He followed and stood beside her as she checked in. She voluntarily showed him the room number. He rode with her in the elevator, along with some other guy he'd signaled to as they crossed the lobby.

"We're going to keep eyes on you," he said as she opened the door.

"Thanks." She faced him. His kind eyes had filled with worry. She didn't care. She had crossed some invisible river where her emotions had become numb. The only thing that mattered, she didn't control. She'd explained to the woman at the front desk how something had gone wrong with the technology in the boardroom. She asked that they call her room the minute they heard from anyone that the meeting was back on. Jaime assured her he'd reach out if he heard anything about Joyce. She closed the door.

She pulled down the window's blackout shades, then turned off the TV and all the lights. She lay on top of the bed in the black room and tried to feel something. Tears leaked slowly from her eyes, dampening her hair and then the pillow.

Margo hadn't realized she'd fallen asleep until she woke. She had no desire to move and hoped she could lie still forever in the black room. As a photographer, she'd used color as a tool. White represented all colors all at once, as opposed to black, no color at all. Black meant nothing, complete emptiness. Like her.

The edges of the blackout curtains gradually lightened, and she knew morning had arrived. Still, she didn't move. Only to use the restroom, and even then, she kept the lights out.

She must have fallen asleep again because the ringing phone jerked her awake. A red light flashed on the phone, and she caught a glare around the blackout shades as she reached for the handset. The desert sun always finds a way inside.

"Hello." Her voice sounded rusty.

"It's Jaime. Joyce is back. She's at the station."

Oh, my god. Margo bolted out of bed. She struggled to get the receiver back in its cradle then dashed for the door. The light in the hallway hurt her dark-accustomed eyes. A man stood near the elevators. She turned the other way and jogged toward the stairs. She caught a glimpse of herself in a lobby mirror. She hadn't showered, hadn't changed her clothes, in more than a while. Whatever.

She sprinted several blocks to the police station. Asked for Sergeant Castro.

A panting man ran up beside her. "I'll take her to Jaime's office," he said to the officer behind the desk. He looked at Margo. "Man, you're fast."

Margo tried to pull herself together as the undercover policeman led her to Jaime's office. Surely this was a trick. She couldn't trust good news.

"Sweetheart," Joyce said, embracing her in a hug. "You're all right. I've been so worried."

Joyce squeezed her so hard Margo found it difficult to breathe, but she loved it. She buried herself in her aunt, a little life coming back to her with each breath. "I can't believe you're here. I thought they got you." Margo still wanted to doubt her good fortune, even with her aunt's arms wrapped around her.

"No, I was fine. Some guy named Darpan reached out to me. He said he was a friend of yours from Tiranistan. He told me you were in grave danger and that Andropov would try to kidnap me to lure you back there. He said to leave town and not tell anyone, so I did."

Darpan warned her? It didn't make sense. She shook her head, battling the confusion. She wouldn't think about Darpan. "Where did you go?"

"I've had a little cabin for a few years now. I lease it from the national forest in the Chiricahua Mountains in southern Arizona. I like to go hiking and birdwatching there. Not many people know about it. It's just a personal getaway. It's got an outhouse, no cell phone service, and is miles from any place else. I love it."

"I just can't believe you're safe. I thought . . ." She wouldn't tell her aunt what she'd thought. The utter depravity of Andrei and what he might have done to her would always be one of Margo's darkest fears.

"I'm fine, really. You, however, don't look so great."

Margo attempted a smile. "I'm actually a lot better now, knowing you're safe." The blackness in her brightened, just the tiniest bit. Joyce was safe. She'd had nothing to do with it. Instead, Darpan's warning and Joyce's quick action had saved the day. And it had been saved.

And somehow, she'd survived. She'd survived only to return to hiding, but at least that left open the prospect for a tomorrow.

Chapter 23

Margo looked out the glass wall of the penthouse apartment. La Jolla cove lay less than a quarter of a mile away, and the Pacific Ocean glistened in the afternoon sun. She loved the view after the morning fog burned off and the air seemed to sparkle in the sunshine. Grass and golden sand ran toward a long pier that stretched into blue water.

She'd heard sea lions swam in the cove, playing in the kelp beds below the surface. She hadn't been outside much and longed to walk down to the beach. Someday.

She heard movement in the kitchen behind her, the opening of the refrigerator door, followed by the popping release of a can of soda. A drawer slid open.

"Can I get you anything?" Joyce asked.

"No, but I'd love it if you'd come sit with me."

Joyce joined her on the sofa that faced the sea. "How are you doing?"

"Fine, thanks. Thank you for coming here with me. Thank you for paying for all this." Margo waved her hand around the condo.

"Margo, you can stop thanking me. This is the eighth day in a row. I'm happy to be here. I love spending time with you."

"But your job, your friends, they're all back in El Paso. Every day I feel guilty about that." And every night the fear they'd be caught lanced her gut.

"My job and my friends will both be there when I go back. I just took a leave of absence. Besides, I had months of vacation built up. This is something I've needed to do for a long time."

"Yeah, but we can't even really leave the condo." Not that she had anywhere to go.

"Not yet. But our view is gorgeous, and the workout room is spectacular. We should go to the pool. It should be safe since you need a keycard, and there is a doorman in the lobby twenty-four-seven. That'd be something different."

Margo glanced at her aunt and shook her head. Joyce always put a positive spin on everything, but she couldn't be happy locked up in a condo. Margo wasn't.

"Seriously. Why be glum? We get food delivery from the best restaurants and markets in La Jolla. For me, this is a dream come true."

Despite her aunt's cheerful tone, she had to be bored. Joyce had already read six novels and gave Margo a summary of each one after she finished. Fortunately, the local bookstore had a delivery service. But they didn't do anything. Andrei might not know where to find them, but he'd hit the pause button on their lives.

Joyce set a hand on Margo's thigh. "We might not know when we're going back, but we will go back. Andropov has a noose around his neck, and he's determined to hang himself. Just yesterday, NATO said they'd bomb Tiranistan if he kept threatening nuclear power plants in other countries. I think his days are numbered."

"I hope you're right." Margo tried to throw a little optimism into her voice, but the words came out defeated.

"When our little vacation is over, I've got a home and job waiting for me. Have you thought about what you want to do?"

Margo had waited days for this question. Her aunt had danced around Margo's future several times before. It relieved her to have the subject out in the open.

"There's only one thing I'm good at, and I don't think I can face taking photos again."

"Why not? You're so talented. And you don't want this guy to get the best of you. If you quit taking photos, he wins."

"I don't know that photography is enough anymore. I keep thinking about good and evil and the stories we tell ourselves and each other. I wish I could amplify the stories we don't hear." The stories of village women invited to dress up and attend parties. The stories of orphans. The stories of people losing their homes due to climate change or war. "If I could, I'd get a camera into the hands of every child, every person without the means to pay others to tell their story for them."

"That sounds interesting. How would you do it?"

"I'm not sure yet. The easiest way for most people to access a camera is via a cell phone. Even most digital cameras now have Wi-Fi capabilities. I wish there was a place where photography and communications could interact. Almost a hotline for photos." The world needed a place of discovery, discovery of beauty but also of horrors. Photos as both art and evidence.

"I would never have chosen to go through any of this if I'd had the option," Margo said. But I learned from my experience. I was one thing before, an artist. But I was hardly a human. I threw away relationships, searched only for glory. I don't want to be that person anymore. I want to be as complicated as the world. I also want to do more than document the world's beauty. I want to help resolve its tragedies. Photos can do that." Margo ripped the words from her chest and flung them into the room. The longing to make a difference, to be more than she'd been before had consumed her thoughts these last days. She'd made mistakes, she'd fought, now she wanted to illuminate the dark.

"That's powerful. How can we make it happen?"

We. The word brought tears to Margo's eyes. Her aunt's investment in Margo's safety, and now in her dreams, stunned her. She needed to learn to show up for people like that.

"I, we, will need partners. I met an interesting woman from Nikon in Italy. I'm thinking about reaching out to her with my idea. Even if it's just to get another opinion, I think it will help me clarify what's possible."

"That sounds like a good plan."

They discussed Margo's idea until their conversation petered out. As the sun began its descent outside their window, Joyce asked Margo if she wanted to check the news.

Except for once a day, they pretended the outside world didn't exist. It helped with the nightmares, or at least Margo told herself that. Andrei had escalated his war, not just bombing Tiranistan's next-door neighbors, but threatening waterways, transportation networks, and energy and financial centers scattered across Europe and western Asia.

The consternation of world leaders, rapidly deployed on social media, had yet to result in action against her nemesis. She assumed Kirk got the photos into the right hands. He said he did. If so, it hadn't made a difference.

That's why she refused to watch the news all day or doom scroll deep into the night. Each evening, they'd turn on the TV and check in. If they needed more detail, they'd search the web, but most of the time they didn't. When Andrei bombed a school, Margo didn't want to know how many children he'd killed. When he destroyed a dam, she didn't want to delve into the downstream horrors. She had enough to feel guilty about. Fortunately, she'd learned that the family she'd lived with in El Paso and Liliana's family were safe. Evidently, the police had captured the only two people Andrei sent to El Paso. As for the war and its aftermath, that was on him.

At five o'clock, Joyce picked up the remote and tuned it to a channel with a repeating news update every thirty minutes. Breaking news from Tiranistan. Margo wondered what atrocity Andrei had delivered today.

"In a coordinated effort, NATO countries have carried out a bombing campaign on strategic targets in Tiranistan."

Margo leaned forward afraid her ears had deceived her.

"An allied group of northern European nations, with support from the United States and Canada, bombed Tiranistan this morning. Military leaders confirmed that over a dozen strategic targets were destroyed. Experts believe Tiranistan's ability to carry out attacks on neighboring countries has been severely diminished."

Margo barely breathed as images of explosions filled the screen. More death, but, perhaps, the beginning of the end if Europe and North America had entered the war. The program cut to a still of Andrei's castle. Margo jerked as if slapped, as a mix of fear and hate flowed through her. She thought she caught the scent of pine needles.

The noose had tightened around her in that castle until she'd taken her one chance at escape. Did Andrei have that same feeling now? Had the bombs that fell today mirrored the positions etched onto the drone? She'd never know, but she hoped she'd played some small role in this escalation.

Within seconds, the news program had moved on to flooding in the Northeast. The abrupt change left Margo behind, half a world away.

"Do you want me to find more information on another channel?" Joyce asked.

"No, it's fine." It wasn't, but she wanted the details and didn't want them in equal measure. It didn't really matter anyway. She'd remain stuck in a luxury condo with a beautiful view, unable to move on with her life.

"You know, we're not going to be here forever."

At the comment, Margo turned her gaze to her aunt who had seemingly read her mind. "We clearly can't stay here forever. I mean, I don't know what this place is costing you, but it can't be cheap. But there's no telling how many weeks or months until we'll be free to return our lives." Years? As long as Andrei remained in power, Margo wouldn't be safe. And neither would Joyce.

The next morning, Joyce waited for Margo in the kitchen. Margo reached for the coffee Joyce handed her.

"Sit," Joyce said. "There's been a development."

Margo sank into one of the chic resin chairs that surrounded the glass-topped table. She worked to keep her mind blank. So many things might have gone wrong.

Joyce picked up the remote and turned on the TV. A reporter filled the screen. Behind her, crowds chanted in a large square. Margo heard shouting and singing. People waved the gold and black flag of Tiranistan.

"This is Donna Barbieri reporting from Dustia Square, Tiranistan. NATO bombings unleashed a revolution last night. The people of Trianistan, many of whom have told me they were tired of the fighting and never wanted to be in a war with Europe, rose up against the government.

"We were here last night, as people gathered in the plaza behind me. President Andrei Andropov tried to address the crowd from the balcony." The camera zoomed in on an ornate balcony overlooking the plaza.

"The people threw rocks and Molotov cocktails at him. When he retreated, they stormed the building." The reporter's voice chilled Margo.

"That's what happened to his father," she said, glancing at Joyce. Photos in a secret room flashed through her head. A crowd on a dark night lit with torches. Had history repeated itself? Talk about the stuff of legend.

"We have confirmation this morning that President Andropov was killed from a self-inflicted gunshot wound."

The reporter continued, but Margo stopped listening. The great Andrei Andropov. He could talk of courage and valor and strength, but he had been made of different stuff. "He was a coward."

"I don't care what he was. He's gone. He's not a threat anymore. You're free."

Feelings cascaded through Margo, but freedom seemed absent. No urge to leave the building and walk through the streets possessed her. More than anything, she wanted to crawl back under the covers and sleep. She could ignore history's relapse, ignore the future. Margo took a long sip of coffee. "I'm relieved." She wasn't. She should have been dancing and applauding. Instead, she wanted blackness.

"Honey, do you want to talk to a psychiatrist? You've been through a lot."

"No. Thanks. I don't know what's wrong with me."

"A chapter of your life has closed. A very emotional chapter. I think you're struggling with what's next."

Margo tried to focus on the future, but instead, she pictured murky kelp forests and a dead man. "I'm fine," she said anyway. Perhaps she just needed a little time.

"Margo, I'm going to reach out to Darpan now that Andrei is dead."

"What?" She turned to her aunt. "What are you talking about?"

"He saved me. He told me to leave El Paso. He let me know when it was safe to return. He's been checking up on us. Would you like to talk to him?"

"No. You don't know everything that went on there. You shouldn't talk to him." The pain of his betrayal stung.

Joyce looked at her and sighed. She made no promises.

They went about their morning as if nothing had changed. Margo caught Joyce eyeing her, probably wondering why they hadn't headed out to breakfast or the beach. Margo sat on the sofa looking at the ocean, numb.

"What's wrong?" Joyce sat on the sofa beside her and wiped a tear from her cheek.

"I don't know. I feel stuck between wondering if I'm really safe and not knowing what to do next."

"Action. You need to act. Remember how you told me about wanting to talk to that lady at Nikon. Have you reached out to her?"

"No."

"Email her right now. Start the conversation." Joyce jumped off the couch and returned with Margo's laptop.

Margo started the email. She explained what had happened in Italy since Sonja had likely heard the rumors. She mentioned working for Andrei, the eventual escape. As she wrote each word, the story became real. She thought about telling the story in photos. A picture of her beautiful dress in Italy. Kirk and his flask of absinthe. The flight into Tiranistan. She'd taken photos from the window. A picture taken by Radmi. The pool before its destruction. Of course, most of the photos she'd taken in Tiranistan remained there. Andrei had stolen them when he'd taken her equipment. But she owned the experience.

Word by word and image by remembered image, the story she documented became real. She spent an hour writing, setting her history into stone, into a fable she would look back on but no longer had to live.

The narrative had everything except Darpan. She'd never taken a photo of him. She hadn't figured out that part of the story yet. Was he good or evil? Or something in between? The easy path lay in not writing the words and ignoring the mental images.

Finally, she saved what had started as an email into a document. Then she wrote a shorter email to Sonja, asking her for the chance to talk.

"Should we go out to lunch?" she asked Joyce when she'd finally put her computer away.

"Definitely. There's a place near the beach I want to try."

They walked outside into sunshine and a light breeze that smelled of adventure.

"We've got the condo rented for another two weeks," Joyce said. They'd found a table under the covered patio of an Italian bistro. "Let's stay. We can have a proper vacation with sea kayaking, dinners out, and visits to museums. We can get our nails done and have a spa day. Please?"

"Of course. That sounds fantastic." It did. After all, she had no immediate plans. More than anything, she wanted to get to know her aunt better and find a way to become part of her life. She couldn't undo her past behavior, but she sure as hell would do better moving forward.

"After lunch, let's go to the Apple Store and get new phones. We deserve it. And this radio silence has been hard on me. I mean, I've loved the time reading novels, but we really need to mix it up a little." Joyce smiled like she'd just landed in Disneyland.

Hiding had been hard on her aunt, and it thrilled Margo she could return to a normal life. Margo could too, but first, she'd turn the story she'd written into an article. She'd done so much wrong, made so many bad decisions. But she'd been brave, and most of all, she'd found a cast of everyday superheroes. This was a story worth sharing, not a fairytale with a magical prince who saved the day, but one with a few kickass women who made a difference. And a few good men. Definitely Jaime Castro. Kirk, Darpan, they both helped and hindered. But the women. They were heroes.

Chapter 24

Margo stretched out on the sand, digging her shoulders a little deeper into the towel at her back to mold the perfect indentation for lounging. They had two more days in paradise, and she planned on taking advantage of them.

She closed her eyes to better hear the crashing waves. The sun and light breeze coming off the ocean caressed her skin. A seagull cawed.

As much as she loved it here, now that she could take advantage of the beach and the beautiful weather, she looked forward to returning to El Paso. She doubted the city would be her forever home, but it gave her options, including a place to live with someone who cared about her.

She'd asked Joyce if she could take professional photos of all the YWCA patrons who needed them for their job search. Whether they wanted to work at the post office, a daycare center, or a corporate office, the photos might help. Not long ago, Margo thought of portraits as beneath her, now she saw them as an important piece of someone's story. Could her depiction of these women convince an employer to hire them? Life had taught many of these women about responsibility, organization, and loyalty far earlier than most learned those lessons. Far earlier than Margo had.

She would continue her conversation with Sonja Brava from Nikon. The woman had seemed legitimately excited about a platform where people would tell important stories in images. Not the curated, first world lifestyle images constantly displayed by would-be influencers on existing commercial platforms. Instead, Margo wanted to create a place for the stories rarely told. Cameras should be in the hands of those most often silenced. It would take time and expertise she didn't have to bring the idea to fruition, but even if it took a lifetime, it seemed like a worthwhile project.

She continued to work on her narrative, which she'd polished into a bright nugget of truth. As with most fables, it had become a warning, not just of the evil king but of the dangers of seeking fame. She loved the contrast with her new goal. In the future, she would amplify others' stories instead of focusing on her own brilliance.

She expected a major magazine to buy the piece. It was the perfect fairytale turned cautionary, with the unexpected twist of the princess and her friends having to save themselves.

If only she had the photos to complete the story. Maybe someday she'd fly back to Tiranistan, just to recreate the photo she'd captured from the wing of the plane. Perhaps she could pay someone to walk back into the haunted forest and photograph its oddities. She wouldn't return there.

Margo heard a soft grunt and whump of sand shifting as someone took a seat near her. Some of these tourists didn't understand personal space. She rose to her elbows and peered at the person.

Darpan.

Fear plunged through her, and she skittered away. Was he here to kill her, to finish the job now that Andrei was gone?

His original relaxed posture had his arms draped over knees, bare feet in the sand. But his grin turned pained as she reacted to him. "I am so sorry. I didn't mean to scare you."

"How the fuck did you find me? What do you want from me?"

"I just wanted to see you. Joyce told me you'd be down here."

"What have you done with her?" Why had Joyce believed his lies?

"Nothing. Nothing at all. We just chat. We have been since, well, since I first contacted her. I thought you knew."

"I hate you." The venom of his betrayal coursed through her veins and came out in her voice. She grabbed the cotton dress she'd used as a coverup and threw it on. Her bikini exposed too much when he sat there in linen pants and a pale Hawaiian shirt. Once, baring herself to him had seemed the most natural thing in the world.

Her words changed his features again. A new sadness shone through his eyes. He briefly lifted his hand to his forehead then ran it back through thick hair. "I'm so sorry. That is the last thing I ever wanted."

"You betrayed me. You were there with him while he hunted me. He hunted my friends and family."

"I had to stay close to him to protect you. And to do my job." The last words came out in a whisper.

"Oh, yes. Darpan, the great communications expert. Andrei paid you to help him invade his neighbors. How many people died because of that?"

"I think you know that wasn't my real job. And, frankly, I think a lot fewer people died because of my activities."

"What, exactly, are you saying?" Even if he told her he was a spy, would it matter? She'd trusted him. First, he'd ignored her, and then he'd shown up with the enemy. She didn't need this kind of complication in her life.

"My primary job was with a country other than Tiranistan. I can't say much about it, but I thwarted Andrei's plans as best I could." He raked his hand through his hair again. "I didn't expect you to show up."

His gaze burned into her. Her mind flew to the first day at the bridge. To the widow's walk at night on the top of the castle. To his tent.

"You changed everything." His raspy voice scoured her like sand.

"When I tried to reach you, you told me to go away. When I was most afraid, you showed up beside him." The raw emotion fueled her anger.

"I was never on his side. Everything I did, I did to protect you."

"Including the etchings on the drone?" She'd catch him in his beautiful lies if it was her final act.

"No. I did that to bring him down. And you helped. You saved many lives by helping bring an early end to the war."

She stood and shoved her book and phone into her backpack. She grabbed her towel and shook the sand from it. A rogue breeze, or perhaps her overzealous shake, flung sand at Darpan.

He rubbed the grains from his face. Shook it out of his hair and off his shirt.

"Sorry." She hadn't meant to appear petty.

"Please don't leave."

She looked around, not wanting to stay, but wanting an expanded explanation. This part of her tale she'd been unable to write. Maybe she needed his version to make hers real.

"Fine. Let's go sit on that bench over there." She pointed to an orange concrete bench fronting the boardwalk. Kids ran wild in the playground behind it, attended by chatting grownups. She couldn't imagine a safer place.

They sat awkwardly at opposite ends of the bench. She didn't want a conversation. She would have preferred to splay him open and see his true intentions. She needed a way to divine the truth from the lies. She didn't trust her ears and had trusted her gut one time too many.

"I'm sorry I wasn't more truthful with you from the beginning," he said. "My job required lies. I quit, by the way."

"Why?" Why should she care?

"You taught me there was more to life."

The saccharin words would have fit a romance novel. She would swoon and then they'd walk away arm-in-arm into the sunset. Only it was eleven o'clock in the morning. "I will never forget how you walked out of the shadows from behind Andrei, as if you were the man pulling all the strings. You played the wizard. I guess that explains the tent." She'd meant to be mean, but his face didn't show the hit.

"Do you think you'll always hate me?" He spoke the words without anger.

"I don't know." Petty. Truthful. She wanted to steer the conversation to firmer ground. Whether driven by anger, curiosity, or some other emotion she wouldn't admit, she didn't want him to leave yet. "Do you know what happened to Radmi?"

"No, I don't."

"Was she a spy too?" Of course she was. But she'd taken action to physically save Margo. Would Darpan have done the same if he hadn't already been sent away?

"Yes."

"Is she still alive?"

"I don't know."

"How can you not know? I want to know if her saving me got her killed."

"We didn't work for the same people. By the time I returned, she was gone."

Margo's eyes filled with tears. Gone could mean anything.

"I didn't know her well, but she seemed smart. She would have been able to get out."

Margo could tell he just wanted her to feel better. She'd probably never know what happened to Radmi. She decided to press him. "Could you find out? You're good at this. You found me."

He paused for a long time before answering. She heard the wail of a child from the playground.

"Perhaps. But it might compromise her. I won't do that."

"Fair." What else was there to say? She could leave him now, just get up and go and never look back. Something held her in place. "What are you going to do now?"

"I don't know. I'm good at communications systems. They are always in demand and there are plenty of legitimate jobs out there. I really do have my own company. What about you? What do you have planned?"

She wondered what a man of secrets would think about a woman bent on sharing everything. "I'm going to tell the story of what happened to me. It's a cautionary tale for women who are looking for someone or something outside themselves to make them happy."

"You mean, like, fame?"

He remembered their conversation. A part of her longed for that world of innocence and hope even though it let her down. "Yes. Or princes in castles. Or wizards in tents. You can never be sure where the danger lies. Don't worry. You're not in it."

"Ouch."

"There's a lot left out, actually. I wanted it to be a tale with both images and words. Unfortunately, Andrei stole my cameras and equipment before I escaped, so I lost a lot of my work."

"I have them. I recovered them for you."

"Really?" Her heart seemed to stop beating. If she used real images to look into the past, she could tell the story and move forward. She hoped he wouldn't require a price greater than she could pay.

"Andropov had them with him in the capital. He had an unnatural fascination with you."

"Were you there when he died?" She wondered if the answer would tell her more about Andrei or Darpan.

"No. I disappeared the day before. People in the know expected the revolt. The citizens never asked to invade their neighbors. They didn't want a war. Not the majority of them."

"Was the last dictator really his father?" This question interested her most. How much of Andrei's backstory consisted of lies?

"Rumors persisted about that. Some people thought Andropov started those rumors himself. We know his mother was a prostitute and turned him over to an orphanage when he was young. The prior dictator often had children from the orphanage visit the capital or his estate. He also had a reputation as a philanderer. It's possible, but we'd need DNA evidence to know for sure."

"What will happen to the country now?"

"Several men from his cabinet are vying for power, but none are likely to consolidate it the way Andropov did. The country will likely be unstable for years and will not pose much of a threat to its neighbors. That is a good thing."

The conversation stalled. Dark semi-circles underlined the eyes she'd wanted to photograph. Stubble that could have been fashionable or might have resulted from flying halfway around the world made his jawline sharper. She dropped her eyes to the long-fingered hands atop linen pants. An ache filled her. The best connection she'd ever had cut her the deepest. She wanted to sit beside him and learn more about his journey and wanted to push him away in equal measure. Love, loss, longing.

"I wish things had worked out differently for us," she said. It was the most she could offer.

"I can't give up. You inhabit all my dreams. But I will not push you. I am here for you if you need me. If you want me. And I am so sorry you thought for even a moment that I supported Andropov, or that I would ever hurt you or anyone in your orbit."

She stood. She would not bend, and she would not cry. Not yet. "I need to get going. How can I get my gear back?"

"I have it with me. In my rental car."

They walked toward one of the large public parking lots. If this were some other day, some other time, she'd take his hand. It seemed so natural, hanging there beside hers.

"Where are you staying?" she asked.

"Just down the road a ways. Your aunt, she wants to meet me. I can tell her no if that's easier on you."

Margo shook her head. Joyce saw Darpan as a savior. After all they'd been through, why didn't Joyce sense his danger? "That seems a little naïve of her."

"I've asked her about you," Darpan continued. "I wanted to know how you were doing."

"I'm fine. I've got a lot going on." How much had Joyce told him? "I've talked to Nikon about camera distribution and a platform to help people tell the stories we need to hear from around the globe. Stories from people like the ones in Tiranistan. If people have a place where they can be heard, perhaps we can help before things, or people, escalate."

"That's a fantastic idea. What are you going to use for the platform?"

"I don't know yet. That's the hardest part." She didn't even know where to start.

Darpan stopped walking. "Margo, let me help. This is what I do."

She stopped also but didn't turn to face him. It would be too easy to get drawn back in. She needed a clean break. Like she'd had when she left Joyce and rarely spoke to her again for years. That had been a mistake. But how did one tell the good from the bad? How did a person decide if another should be a part of their lives or blocked forever? She'd proven particularly bad at this.

"I can help you design the platform and deploy it. I'll do exactly as much as you're comfortable with. Please."

She turned. The breeze ruffled his hair. The same breeze cooled her skin. A photographer shouldn't see things in black and white, not when every color in the spectrum existed. Could she choose neither to ignore him nor to embrace him, but carve a path in the middle? At least until she knew his heart?

"We'd have to work together, and I don't know if I can trust you." She'd start with this one truth.

"Perhaps we moved too fast before. If we work together, I can spend every day proving to you that I'm someone you can trust."

"We should live in different places," she said. Attraction and opportunity had combined those first days to create a desire she didn't want to control. Even now, a physical attraction stretched between them.

"I don't know where I'm going to live. I haven't really gotten that far in my planning."

"Me either. El Paso to start, but I don't know where I'll end up."

He smiled, his face lighting up with hope. "So, it's a deal? You'll let me help?"

"Yeah. I guess so." She offered her hand.

He awkwardly shook it. Maybe she should have hugged him, but not yet. She had time.

They arrived at his car. Sure enough, the trunk held all her gear. She sank to her heels and checked every bag, every disk, every device. Everything was in place. She'd recovered a piece of her life. The journey to Tiranistan had been a battle hard fought and harder won, but she'd survived to tell the story.

"Thank you so much." This time she hugged him. He hadn't needed to save her equipment. In fact, it had probably slowed him down, may have endangered him. But somehow, he realized the importance of leaving no part of her in that country. Her work was hers again.

"I really appreciate this." She let her arms drop and stepped away. "We can talk more tomorrow about the project."

"Yes, partner." His voice seemed lighter. He even looked like he weighed less. They'd both carried the burden of Tiranistan and its dictator.

"Partner. I think I like that."

"Should we take a selfie to seal the deal?" he asked.

"A photograph? I thought you were against that." All those times she'd wanted to photograph him, and he'd said no. Perhaps he wanted to show her he'd changed.

"This is a new era. I want to build a different life, one with you in it." His dark eyes looked into hers, peering deep into her soul.

"Let's take it one shot at a time." She slipped her phone out of her backpack and held it up, catching them both in the frame. A row of palms stood behind them and the blue ocean sparkled beyond. The world seemed full of possibilities. She snapped the photo and captured the moment that would start the next phase of her story.

THE END

I hope you enjoyed this novel. If so, I'd appreciate an honest review on Amazon, Goodreads, or your favorite review site. It doesn't have to be long or complicated. Just a simple statement that you liked the book and what you found interesting about it—or for that matter, why you didn't like the book.

Additional novels by Kathryn Dodson

Tequila Midnight: When a hard-drinking woman is hired to find a tycoon's daughter, she'll need more than tequila to survive the night.

The Podcast Chronicles: She never expected to be a hero, but when a greedy developer threatens her town, can an ordinary mom rally the community to save her mountain home?

Sign up for updates at www.KathrynDodson.com.

About the Author

Kathryn Dodson grew up writing and riding horses in far West Texas. She graduated from SMU in English/Creative Writing and went on to get an MBA from Thunderbird and a PhD from Clemson.

She has worked on both sides of the US/Mexico border and has held jobs with governments, chambers of commerce, and other businesses. Now she spends her days writing about interesting women in fascinating places.

Join Kathryn for updates and extras at www.KathrynDodson.com.

NOVELS
Tequila Midnight
The Podcast Chronicles
Portrait of Deception

Acknowledgements

I'd like to start by thanking every reader who found this novel. You give my words meaning.

Portrait of Deception is my third novel, and I am grateful to the many people who subscribe to my newsletter. Their comments, electronic bouquets, and photos brighten my days and inspire my words.

I was fortunate to have much help along the way with this novel. Special thanks go to my critique partners Claudia Armann and Sydney Clark. I'd also like to thank the early readers of this novel: Libby Estrin, Kathry Urbanic, and Lisa Golden. Their input made the novel better.

Laurie and Rhett Dodson and Diane and Jody Lawrence deserve much thanks for supporting my writing.

Tom—it's been almost thirty years of adventure and love—you are my person in this world.

Jack, you are my world, my photographer, my biggest fan—and I am yours. Thank you.